*Hidden among the masked revelers
of an underground Regency gentlemen's club
where decadence, daring and debauchery
abound, the four owners of Vitium et Virtus
are about to meet their match!*

Welcome to...

The Society of Wicked Gentlemen

Read

A Convenient Bride for the Soldier
by Christine Merrill
September 2017

An Innocent Maid for the Duke
by Ann Lethbridge
October 2017

A Pregnant Courtesan for the Rake
by Diane Gaston
November 2017

And look for the concluding story
from Sophia James
A Secret Consequence for the Viscount
December 2017

Author Note

I've always considered myself very lucky to be among my fellow Harlequin Historical authors. These ladies have been a fount of information, support and, on the rare times we can gather together, sheer fun. So, I was thrilled to be invited to write a book for The Society of Wicked Gentlemen series. It was every bit as enjoyable as I thought it would be. We made a most efficient team, quick to answer each other's questions and to collaborate on our stories. Readers, enjoy The Society of Wicked Gentlemen! We loved telling their stories!

DIANE GASTON

A Pregnant Courtesan for the Rake

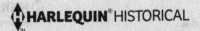
HARLEQUIN®HISTORICAL

Recycling programs
for this product may
not exist in your area.

ISBN-13: 978-0-373-29953-9

A Pregnant Courtesan for the Rake

Copyright © 2017 by Harlequin Books S.A.

Special thanks and acknowledgment are given to Diane Gaston for her contribution to The Society of Wicked Gentleman series.

All rights reserved. Except for use in any review, the reproduction or utilization of this work in whole or in part in any form by any electronic, mechanical or other means, now known or hereinafter invented, including xerography, photocopying and recording, or in any information storage or retrieval system, is forbidden without the written permission of the publisher, Harlequin Enterprises Limited, 225 Duncan Mill Road, Don Mills, Ontario M3B 3K9, Canada.

This is a work of fiction. Names, characters, places and incidents are either the product of the author's imagination or are used fictitiously, and any resemblance to actual persons, living or dead, business establishments, events or locales is entirely coincidental.

This edition published by arrangement with Harlequin Books S.A.

For questions and comments about the quality of this book, please contact us at CustomerService@Harlequin.com.

® and TM are trademarks of Harlequin Enterprises Limited or its corporate affiliates. Trademarks indicated with ® are registered in the United States Patent and Trademark Office, the Canadian Intellectual Property Office and in other countries.

Printed in U.S.A.

HARLEQUIN®
www.Harlequin.com

Diane Gaston's dream job had always been to write romance novels. One day she dared to pursue that dream and has never looked back. Her books have won romance's highest honors: the RITA® Award, the National Readers' Choice Award, the Holt Medallion, the Golden Quill and the Golden Heart® Award. She lives in Virginia with her husband and three very ordinary house cats. Diane loves to hear from readers and friends. Visit her website at dianegaston.com.

Books by Diane Gaston

Harlequin Historical

The Society of Wicked Gentlemen

A Pregnant Courtesan for the Rake

The Scandalous Summerfields

Bound by Duty
Bound by One Scandalous Night
Bound by a Scandalous Secret
Bound by Their Secret Passion

The Masquerade Club

A Reputation for Notoriety
A Marriage of Notoriety
A Lady of Notoriety

Three Soldiers

Gallant Officer, Forbidden Lady
Chivalrous Captain, Rebel Mistress
Valiant Soldier, Beautiful Enemy

Linked by Character

The Diamonds of Welbourne Manor
"Justine and the Noble Viscount"
A Not So Respectable Gentleman?

Visit the Author Profile page
at Harlequin.com for more titles.

To Christine, Ann and Sophia,
my fellow Society of Wicked Gentlemen authors.
It has been a pleasure!

Prologue

Paris—1816

'He is dead?'

Cecilia Lockhart stood in the doorway of the shabby Paris room where her husband insisted she should be grateful to lodge. Sounds of babies crying, a man and woman quarrelling, and an old woman wailing could be heard from behind closed doors. The scent of cooking meat, urine and sweat filled her nostrils.

A captain of the 52nd Regiment of Foot stood stiffly in the hallway, unable—or unwilling—to look her in the eye.

'Killed,' he said. 'By a Frenchman. In a duel.' His tone was disapproving. Why not? Duelling was forbidden in the regiment. 'He apparently had a great deal to drink.'

Of course he had. What day did Duncan not have a great deal to drink?

'What happened?' she asked. 'Did he cheat at cards? Insult the French army?' Why did she bother to ask? Cecilia did not care about the reason.

The captain stiffened. 'The Frenchman apparently found Lieutenant Lockhart in bed with his wife.'

Oh.

Why that detail should have stung, she did not know. It was merely one more humiliation.

Another slap in the face.

She almost laughed at her little joke, but this stern, disapproving captain would never have understood.

'What happens next?' she asked.

'We'll bury him,' the captain replied. 'You may return home. Do you have enough money to make the trip?' He asked the question without sympathy, perhaps worried he would have to take up a collection among his fellow officers on her behalf.

'I need nothing.' Not from these men anyway. 'Do what you must, and thank you for informing me.'

He nodded and turned away. She closed the door and leaned her forehead against it. The baby cried. The old lady whined. The couple cursed each other. And the captain's receding footsteps sounded on the wooden stairs.

But for Cecilia it was as if the sun had burst through a sky of dark clouds.

She was free. Her husband was gone, never to return.

Never to slam his fist into her flesh ever again, nor throw her against the wall. No more bruises to hide. No more pain.

She had little money, no friends—Duncan had seen to that—and no one in England who would welcome her home. In a moment she might panic at being alone in this foreign country, among people who, a few short months ago, would have considered her the enemy. But for now she felt as light as air.

Free.

Chapter One

Paris—August 1818

Oliver Gregory strolled along the River Seine as the first fingers of dawn painted the water in swirls of violet. The buildings of Paris, tinged a soft pink at this time of day, were even more beautiful than in the brightness of a noonday sun. London at dawn would seem a dark maze of streets and shops.

And Calcutta... Calcutta, the city of Oliver's birth, defied description, except in words whispered in memory—Hindi words.

Oliver struggled to remember those steaming, fragrant, exotic days of his childhood and the smiling woman swathed in brightly coloured silks holding him in her arms and calling him her *pyaare bete*, her sweet boy.

In the quiet of dawn he could bring it all back. He feared forgetting even more than the depths of depression that followed. Lately his decadent lifestyle provided no ease from the blue devils.

He'd crafted his life to distract him from the sadness of loss. What better setting than a gentlemen's club devoted to pleasures of the flesh? Oliver was one of the owners of Vitium et Virtus—Vice and Virtue—the exclusive gentlemen's club he and his three friends started when they were mere students at Oxford. Vitium et Virtus specialised in decadent pleasure, whether it be beautiful women, the finest brandy or a high-stakes game of cards.

To think he'd just left a Parisian club that made Vitium et Virtus look tame. This club featured sexual gratification through pain, whether self-inflicted or inflicted by another. Vitium et Virtus included some fantasy games with one of their tall, beautiful, dark-haired women playing dominatrix, but this French club went way beyond, so far Oliver nearly intervened to stop it. He knew some people found pleasure in pain, but these Parisians flirted with death. He had no intention of bringing those ideas to their club.

His mind flashed with an image of a nearly naked man swallowing a snake. And another man running over hot coals.

Memories from India again.

A cry jerked him back to the present near-dawn morning. In the distance a swarm of street urchins accosted a woman, pulling at her clothes, their demands shrill in the early morning air. He'd seen street urchins in Calcutta rush a man and leave him with nothing, not even the clothes on his back. The dark rookeries of London posed similar dangers.

Oliver sprinted to her aid. '*Arrêtez! Arrêtez!* Stop! Stop!'

The woman lifted her arms. 'No! No!'

The children scattered.

When he reached her, she placed her hands on her hips. 'Look what you've done!'

'You are English?' He was surprised.

She merely gestured in the direction the children had disappeared. 'They've run away.'

'They were attacking you.' At least that was what he'd thought.

She gave him an exasperated look. 'They were not attacking me. I was giving them money so they might eat today!'

'Giving them money?' He turned to where he'd last seen them and back to her. 'Is that wise?'

Her eyes flashed. 'Wiser than having them starve or be forced to steal.'

He could not argue with that. 'Forgive me. I thought— Can you call them back?'

'No, they will be too frightened now. They are gone.'

He shook his head. 'I am sorry.'

She frowned. 'Another time—tomorrow—I will be back.'

She turned to walk away.

'Wait.' He strode to her side. 'What is an Englishwoman doing on the banks of the Seine at dawn?'

Now mischief sparkled in those dark eyes. 'Why, I was giving coins to street children until you chased them away.'

She was lovely! Those beautiful eyes were fringed with dark lashes, and her brows, delicately arched. An elegant nose and full, luscious lips adorned her oval face. Her bonnet covered her hair, but as the sky grew lighter, Oliver saw her dress was dark blue and her hair a rich brown.

'What is an Englishman doing on the banks of the Seine at dawn?' she asked, mocking his tone.

Oliver smiled. 'Attempting to rescue damsels in distress.'

She laughed. 'You must keep searching, then. I assure you I am not in distress.'

'But I am at your service.' Oliver bowed.

She kept walking, and he kept pace with her.

She finally spoke again. 'Enjoying the delights of Paris now that the war is over?' Her tone was a mockery of polite conversation, but at least she'd not dismissed him.

'Actually a bit of business.' Although his business was pleasure. 'And you?'

'Moi?' She fluttered her lashes. 'I live here.'

He was pretty astute at perceiving the character of a person, a skill he'd honed so he'd know right away the degree to which a person might accept him as an equal or as a lesser being. She was guarding her own privacy, not giving him any information at all.

He pretended to peruse her. 'I would surmise there is quite a story about why an English lady such as yourself lives in Paris.'

She looked suspicious. 'Why do you say I am a lady?'

His mouth widened into a smile. 'It is not difficult. The way you carry yourself. The way you speak.'

She shrugged at that. 'Well, I am not telling you anything.'

And he would not press her. He understood the need to keep one's privacy, but he also did not wish to say goodbye to her. The sky had lightened, turning the water blue and the stone path to beige. He suspected she would soon leave this path and be gone.

'I have a proposal,' he said impulsively. 'Eat breakfast with me.'

She laughed derisively. 'Why would I do that? I do not know you.'

'Allow me to introduce myself, then. I am Oliver Gregory. My father is the Marquess of Amberford.' He never explained further. People who did not already know his father usually assumed he was a younger son. 'Now you know me.'

She laughed again, this time with more humour. 'I know your name. Or at least the name you deign to give me.'

'I assure you it is my name.'

Her brows rose and she nodded with exaggerated scepticism.

He spread his palms. 'I am telling you the truth.'

She cocked her head. 'It does not matter.'

'So,' he tried again. 'Will you have breakfast with me? I promise to be amusing. We can sit in the open at a café if that will ease your discomfort.'

Her expression sobered and she stared at him for several seconds, as if deciding how to respond. 'At a café?' she repeated.

'Wherever you wish. You choose where you would like to eat.' He'd dined at Le Procope, a café that had been in existence for two hundred years. Would she choose some place as grand? He was suddenly very eager to find out.

'Very well,' she finally said. 'But you must also give me some coins for the children. They will be even more hungry tomorrow.'

He reached into a pocket and pulled out a leather purse. He loosened its strings and poured out several coins. Then he extended his hand. 'Here.'

She scooped up the coins and slipped them into her reticule. 'I know of a place we can breakfast.'

She walked him past La Fontaine du Palmier, the monument to Napoleon's battles in Egypt, in the Place du Châtelet, to a small café just opening its doors. They sat at a table out of doors. With the sun came warmer temperatures and a blue sky dotted with white puffy clouds. A perfect day.

'The pastries are lovely here,' she said.

'Pastries.' He rolled his eyes. 'Everywhere in Paris I've been served pastries and I do not possess a sweet tooth.'

'Some bread and cheese, then?'

'*Ah, oui. C'est bon.*' He smiled. 'With coffee.'

The waiter arrived and greeted her warmly. Obviously she was known to him. She gave him their order, selecting a pastry and chocolate for herself, bread, cheese, and coffee for him.

He watched her as she settled herself in her chair. She removed her gloves and rearranged the colourful Kashmir shawl she wore that reminded him of India. She wore a dark blue walking dress and looked as if she'd just spent an afternoon promenading in Hyde Park. Was it only the children who caused her to be on the banks of the Seine at dawn?

'Tell me what your business has been that brought you to Paris,' she asked with some evident interest.

Oddly enough, he did not want to tell her of the business that brought him to Paris lest she disapprove. He'd come to explore the decadence of Parisian gentlemen's clubs to see what they might include at Vitium et Virtus. This trip had not been as productive as the previous one when he'd found a satisfyingly buxom, Titian-haired French songstress eager to come to London to work in their club. He usually did not care if a lady disapproved of his activities. For the ladies who did disapprove of him, the gentlemen's club was the least of their objections.

'Exploring opportunities,' he responded vaguely.

'Opportunities?' Her eyes, lovely as they were, showed little interest.

He challenged her. 'You are making polite conversation with me.'

Her eyes sparkled. 'Yes. I am. But tell me what opportunities anyway.'

Those eyes distracted him. In the sunlight they appeared the colour of fine brandy and just as liquid. A man could lose himself in those eyes.

He glanced away. 'Business, you know, but nothing came to fruition.'

The waiter brought a pot of coffee, a pitcher of cream

and a sugar dish, placing it in front of him. He placed a chocolate pot in front of the lady, produced two cups and poured for them.

When he left, Oliver added only some cream. He took a sip of the coffee and nodded to her. 'This is excellent.'

Her captivating eyes appeared to concur. 'It always is here.' She sipped her chocolate and made an appreciative sound.

He faced her, fingering the handle of his cup. 'The topic of business is always a boring one. Perhaps there is something else you would like to ask me?'

Her eyes flickered in surprise, then fixed on him with a challenge of her own. 'Do you mean why you do not look like an Englishman?'

He was not certain if she was asking or not.

Who was he attempting to fool? Women always wanted to know why his skin was so dark, why his hair was so dark. She simply was more direct than most and much quicker.

'See. You are wondering why the son of a marquess looks like something spawned on a foreign shore.'

'Am I?' Her brows rose. 'Or is this what you desire to tell me?'

He paused, unsure of his own motivation. He did want to tell her, though, he decided. 'My father is the Marquess, but my mother was from India.'

He waited. Usually the women with whom he spent the most time found his looks exotic and appealing but, then, such women were typically interested only in sharing the pleasures of the night with him.

Ladies of the *ton* with marriageable daughters steered them away from him, however. Even though they knew he was wealthy. Even though some of those same ladies did not mind sharing his bed.

She took another sip of chocolate. 'That does explain it. Were you born in India?'

'I was. I left when I was ten.' He would not tell her everything about his birth and those first ten years of his life. He never talked about it, although many who knew his father knew some of it. His partners in Vitium et Virtus knew nearly all and they'd accepted him as an equal since their days at school.

'You must remember it then.' She sounded truly interested now.

'I do.' He'd been remembering it that morning when she appeared.

'Tell me,' she said, licking off the chocolate from her lips and nearly driving India from his mind.

'I remember the sounds and the smells and all the bright colours,' he began.

He told her about the man charming the snake and others sleeping on a bed of nails or walking over hot coals. He told her of the music and the singing and dancing, of statues and paintings of gods. He talked of fragrant gardens and cool houses with pillows.

He did not tell her about his mother. Or about how his father shared his time between his Indian house and his English one on the other side of the garden.

'I cannot imagine it,' she said, her face alight with animation. 'I would love to see such a place some day.'

His insides clenched in a familiar pain. He would never return there, never see those sights again.

He made himself smile. 'Is Paris not enough for you?'

Her expressive face turned sad before she composed it again. 'Paris...has not been unkind.'

How much was hidden in that statement?

The waiter brought a flaky confection filled with

whipped cream and jam for her and, for him, a selection of cheeses and a loaf of bread still warm from the oven.

She nibbled on her pastry. 'There is much beauty here in Paris. I gather some of the buildings, statues and art were almost lost during the Revolution. We can credit Napoleon for preserving them.'

'If we must,' he said, smiling wryly.

He was gratified she smiled in return.

'I have seen very little of the city,' he went on. His hosts had taken him to places where pleasure was more valued than architecture. 'And now I have only today left.'

She lowered her pastry from her lips. 'You have only today?'

'I leave tomorrow.' Somehow that information did not seem to disappoint her. 'Tell me what sights I must see before I leave.'

Again her face animated. 'Notre Dame, for certain. It is the most impressive and beautiful church one could ever see. The Louvre, as well. It is a beautiful building filled with beautiful art that once graced the houses of the aristocracy before the Revolution. And I suppose one should see the Palais-Royal. It is now filled with shops and restaurants.'

She went on to describe these sights in more detail as they finished their meal and drank the last of the coffee and chocolate. He paid the waiter and reluctantly stood. He could have remained all day in her presence, even though she'd told him nothing about herself. She wrapped her shawl around her, despite it being warm enough now to go without.

'Thank you for breakfast,' she said. 'I did enjoy it.'

'As did I,' he added.

'I suppose I must say *adieu*.' She did not look happy about it, though.

'I suppose...'

They left their table, but stood together on the pavement. The city had come alive while they'd eaten. The streets were full of carriages, horses and wagons. The pavement was abustle with workmen, servant girls, children and a few finely dressed gentlemen.

He held her elbow and guided her away from the fray.

Then he took her hand. 'Do not say *adieu*. Stay with me. Show me the sights you have so wonderfully described.'

Cecilia glanced into his face. He had a memorable one—as handsome as any woman could wish. That was not what captivated her, however. Duncan had been handsome. After Duncan she'd learned not to be seduced by a handsome face.

His complexion was darker than one would expect from an Englishman. Knowing he was half-caste explained that. His hair was as dark as the night, worn longer than fashionable as if he did not trouble himself to visit the barber overmuch. His eyes were unexpected, though. They were hazel, the kind of eyes that changed colour from green to brown with the hue of his coat. When he fixed his gaze upon her she had the feeling he could see inside her, directly to her thoughts.

Perhaps that was why he asked her no questions about herself. He asked nothing of her, but shared about himself. What other man of her acquaintance would tell of his life before age ten? Duncan certainly had not.

What harm could there be in spending the day with him? She had no other obligations for today and he was leaving tomorrow. She liked his foreign looks and she relished the sound of his English accent, so familiar, so reminiscent of home. He was an easy companion, agreeable, unhurried and undemanding.

With those enthralling eyes.

Her hands started to shake and her knees grew weak, not from his allure, but from her decision. 'I will show you Paris.'

He smiled and her knees grew weaker.

'We should start at Notre Dame,' she said quickly lest he notice he affected her. The famous cathedral was close by, its spire and towers visible from where they stood.

As they neared Notre Dame, she said, 'Before we go inside, we must walk around the cathedral, because it looks very different from each side. You would hardly know it is one structure.'

They first faced the western façade, looking up at its symmetrical towers and carved stone. From where they stood they could see only the tip of the spire.

Slowly, they walked around to the north side. 'See the rose window? How big it is? You will be astounded when we see it from the inside with the sun illuminating it.' They continued walking. 'You can see now how the cathedral is in the shape of a cross. All cathedrals are in the shape of a cross.'

He smiled at her. 'You are quite knowledgeable about this.'

'I suppose I am.' She felt suddenly self-conscious.

She often had days free and the cathedral had become one of her favourite places. Sometimes she wandered for hours inside it, especially when she needed to feel peaceful.

They continued what was a fairly long walk around the building. The Seine was behind them, not too far from where he'd chased away the poor street children, busy now with boats and barges transporting people and goods up and down the river.

'Flying buttresses,' he pointed out, then smiled. 'See? You are not the only one who is knowledgeable.'

Humour. It was as welcome as the clear summer air. She so rarely experienced the levity of humour. She could not help but return his smile.

They concluded their walk around the cathedral, talking of its architecture, and finally went inside. As they entered the church, the bell tolled the hour, its sound echoing against the stone walls.

Cecilia loved the inside of Notre Dame, loved the colours the rose windows cast upon the interior. Oliver Gregory seemed interested in everything she drew his attention to. Was he pretending? If so, he was very good at it.

Others filed into pews and soon a priest and his attendants appeared at the huge altar. They had come at the time of the Catholic Mass.

'Do you mind if we stay?' she asked. There were so many English people who would abhor attending a Catholic Mass.

'Not at all,' he said.

They chose a pew in the back, but with a good view of the altar.

She liked the ritual, a little like her church at home, but different as well. Watching and listening to the Latin service drove other thoughts from her mind and calmed her. It made her forget the strange way she made her living and how lonely she was.

When the service was over he clasped her hand. 'I am glad we stayed.'

They walked around the cathedral some more, marvelling at the windows, peering at the statues until they had seen enough.

As they came towards the long aisle to the door, she stopped him. 'My name is Cecilia.'

Surely it would not hurt to tell him her given name.

She had never told anyone in Paris her real name, not since the day the captain came to tell her Duncan was killed, but she wanted this man to know. For one day she wanted to be herself, as she might have been had she never fallen under Duncan's spell.

This lovely man beside her did not act as if she'd said anything unusual by giving her name so abruptly.

'If I am to call you Cecilia,' he said in a matter-of-fact tone, 'you must call me Oliver.'

'Oliver,' she whispered.

'Cecilia.' He smiled.

It was not the done thing for a gentleman and a lady to call each other by their given names, not unless they grew up together from childhood. She'd known him only a few hours, but still it seemed natural that they should do so.

'We should go to the Louvre next,' she said.

The Louvre was another place Cecilia visited when she needed to remind herself that there was incredible beauty in the world. She loved the Renaissance art, especially the portrait called *La Gioconda*. She tried to imagine any other man of her acquaintance walking through the museum without any sign of boredom.

Was this man—Oliver—really what he seemed? Or was he pretending, hiding his true nature? Every day she pretended to be someone she was not. Every day she hid her real self. Today, though, she would be her real self, even if he were not.

When they again stepped outside, they could hear the bell of Notre Dame strike four o'clock, reminding her of when Oliver had last eaten.

'There are restaurants at the Palais-Royal, if you are hungry.' She was accustomed to going without food.

When she'd followed the drum with Duncan, she'd been allotted half his food rations, but when he could, he ate her portion as well as his own. She'd quickly learned not to complain.

'Do you wish to eat?' he asked.

Throughout the day, he'd checked on her wishes before stating his own, she noticed. Another technique of seduction? Or did he truly wish to fulfil her desires?

'I know it is country hours, but I am quite famished,' she admitted.

'Then we must eat.' He offered her his arm and they leisurely walked to the Palais-Royal, once the home of the Duc d'Orléans and, earlier, Cardinal Richelieu. The *palais* was not far from where she earned her money.

No. Cecilia Lockhart, who strolled by the side of this English gentleman, earned no money.

That was the job of Madame Coquette.

Chapter Two

~⟡~

The restaurant Oliver chose was the Beauvilliers, with its tables covered in white linen, shining silverware and sparkling crystal. He had dined there once already during his visit.

'This restaurant is very expensive,' Cecilia warned him as they were led to a table in a private corner.

'Do not concern yourself,' he told her. 'I can afford it.'

He was used to ladies' eyes kindling with greed when realising he was wealthy, but Cecilia merely nodded sceptically.

He laughed. 'I assure you, Cecilia. Order whatever you desire.'

After they were seated he said, 'There is something to be said about *liberté, égalité, fraternité*. I have yet to have any Paris high servant or shopkeeper regard me with disdain.'

She looked surprised. 'That happens to you—being regarded with disdain?'

'Because of how I look. Like a foreigner.' In England, members of the *ton* and their servants often peered down their noses at him. It happened often enough in London shops as well.

'I do not think you look all that remarkable,' she said.

He laughed. 'Thank you...I think.'

They perused the printed menu with its numerous choices for each course, deciding to begin with an onion soup followed by a platter of oysters and sausages. For the main course they chose beefsteak, then an entrée of duck. They could have ordered additional courses of fish and roast poultry or veal, but Cecilia said she would burst from that much food. Each course was accompanied by a different wine.

'This meal reminds me of dinner parties at home,' she said over the soup.

This was the most information about herself that she'd divulged yet. This was an aristocratic meal, so it was likely she came from an aristocratic family.

'Home meaning England?' he ventured.

Her expression sobered. He surmised she debated how much to disclose.

'Surrey,' she replied.

He smiled inwardly. It was as if she'd bared her soul to him.

'We were practically neighbours, then,' he said. 'My father's estate is in Kent.'

They went on to taste the oysters and sausage and sip the wine before she spoke again. 'I am not welcome back in Surrey. My family disowned me when I ran away to Gretna Green to marry.'

This was a great deal to divulge and it made him sad for her. He knew how it felt to lose someone.

He was also disappointed to hear her mention a marriage.

Oliver usually did not care much about the details of a woman's life, not the least of which was whether or not she was married. The woman's apparent character and disposition of the moment were enough to satisfy him, but his reaction to this woman was different. He was intrigued by Cecilia. Maybe because she kept information about herself so close to her chest, he wanted to know all about her. Mostly he wanted to know what experience had put that sadness in her eyes. Had it been that Gretna Green elopement? Being disowned by her family?

He would continue to tread carefully, though.

'They disowned you,' he repeated as neutrally as he could.

'My parents declared my husband to be unsuitable.'

He certainly knew that feeling. Most noble parents felt Oliver was unsuitable.

'My husband thought they would come around if we were married. He thought my father would relent and turn over my dowry—but my father never did.' She finished her glass of wine. 'My husband had no fortune, no name to speak of, but he was dashing in his regimentals.' Her voice turned sarcastic.

'He was in the army?' he guessed.

She nodded. 'That is how I came to be in Paris. His regiment was ordered to Brussels and I came with him. After the battle at Waterloo, his regiment marched into France and, ultimately, Paris.'

Oliver had honoured his father's wishes and had not purchased a commission. He regretted that decision to this day. He should have been fighting along with his friend Frederick.

She nodded as the waiter filled her wineglass again. 'The battle was a horrific thing!'

'You witnessed the battle?' He was shocked.

Oliver had been there, too. At Waterloo. Unable to enlist, he'd gone to Brussels to be a part of it all, like so many others. Brussels had been filled with the British aristocracy and British tourists at the time. On the day of the battle he and other spectators rode to the site where the troops were amassed. Never had he felt so helpless as he watched the carnage unfold. Cecilia would have witnessed horrors no woman should ever see.

She took a long sip of her wine, and her voice turned to a mere rasp. 'So many men killed.'

Oliver had done what he could to pull wounded men off the field, but it had never felt like enough. After he'd returned to London from Brussels, it had taken him a long time to again lose himself in the pleasures of Vitium et Virtus. In fact, he'd never quite managed to free himself of Waterloo. A part of him always remembered the sights, the sounds. The agony.

'I saw the battle, too,' he told her.

Her eyes turned wary. 'Oh? You were in the army?'

'I was not.' He pushed the food around on his plate. 'My friend Frederick was, though.'

'Did he live?' she asked.

'Yes.' He lifted his glass to his lips. 'Thank God.'

They had barely touched the oysters and sausage, but the waiter removed those dishes and brought the beefsteak, smothered in sauce. Another bottle of wine was opened and new glasses poured.

'And your husband?' he asked. 'What happened to him?'

She shrank back as if his question had been an attack. 'In the battle, do you mean?'

'Yes.' He had meant in the battle, but suddenly realised he wanted to know so much more.

'He came through without a scratch.' She sounded disdaining.

Oliver cut a piece of his beefsteak and brought it to his mouth.

She tapped the stem of her wineglass with her fingernail, making the crystal ring. 'My husband died here in Paris. In a duel.'

'A duel?'

'Two years ago.' She did not say more about the duel. 'Since I was no longer welcome at home, I stayed in Paris.' She drank her wine.

Oliver knew she was not the only British expatriate to find living in Paris more affordable than London.

She turned her attention to her food, apparently consumed by her own thoughts, but it seemed that she was pulling away from him. Perhaps she'd regretted confiding this much to him. He would not press her for more, no matter how he yearned to know.

Finally, she spoke again. 'But what of you, Oliver?' Her tone was defensive. 'I have said all there is to say about me.'

He doubted that. 'There is little to say about me.'

She smiled, but he still felt she'd gone back into hiding. 'Surely you do not expect me to believe that.'

'It is true. I'm a simple man with simple tastes.' He lifted his wineglass, filled with fine, expensive wine, in an ironic salute.

'Come now, Lord Oliver.' She wagged a finger at him.

He frowned. 'I am not Lord Oliver.'

Her brow furrowed. 'But you said your father was a marquess.'

'He is, but I have no honorific.' He was admitting himself to be a bastard.

Understanding dawned on her features. Understanding. Not distaste.

He went on. 'My father was not married to my Indian mother, as you have no doubt surmised.' He was a bastard son—his father's only son. 'But he brought me with him to England when he assumed the title.'

His mother had been an Indian *bibi*, a mistress. A prostitute. The love of his father's life, his father had often said. But his father left her behind when he unexpectedly inherited the title, something his British wife had insisted upon. His wife had also promised to raise Oliver as if he were her own son—a promise she broke as soon as she could.

'Did you ever see your mother again?' she asked.

'No.' He poured himself more wine. 'She died.'

Oliver's mother died shortly after he left India. She died before the ship Oliver sailed on even reached England. His stepmother told him she'd lost her life giving birth to another of his father's bastards. So he'd believed he'd lost a mother and a brother or sister.

It wasn't until he was a young man that his father told him that story was not true. His father had to show him the letter he'd received from India for Oliver to believe him. His mother had died, but from a fever—or perhaps from a broken heart.

Cecilia's face filled with sympathy. 'I am so sorry! How very sad for you.'

He took a gulp of wine. 'It was long ago.'

She had not commented on him being a bastard. She'd hardly blinked at that information. He was not sure why he'd even told her. He never spoke about that. Or about his mother.

He had the illusion that they were old friends who knew each other well and could trust each other. As he knew and trusted Frederick, Jacob…and Nicholas, wherever Nicholas might be. Not dead. He'd never believe Nicholas was dead. The fourth founding member of the gentlemen's club had simply disappeared from Vitium et Virtus one night six years ago, leaving only a pool of blood in the alley and his signet ring.

'I still miss my family.' Her voice turned low. 'Even

though—' She stopped abruptly and stabbed at her meat. 'Never mind. It is foolish to wish for what one can never have.'

'I could not agree more.' He lifted his glass as if in a toast.

He turned the conversation to something less emotional for them both—the sights they had seen that day, their favourites and least liked.

Pretty soon the dessert was served, profiteroles and *éclairs* and finally coffee and liqueur.

When they left the restaurant, the shops were still open. To walk off the sumptuous dinner they strolled under the galleries and through the gardens. The Palais-Royal was filled with people and the shops were busy.

Oliver was accustomed to giving gifts to ladies whose company he enjoyed and all the ladies he knew received his gifts eagerly. He wanted something to commemorate this day, this companionship that had been unlike any other he'd experienced.

When they came upon a jewellery shop, he stopped. 'Let us go in.'

She accepted the idea impassively and he was surprised. Most ladies would surmise they were about to receive a gift.

They gazed at necklaces and bracelets with diamonds, emeralds, rubies and garnets, but he could not discern any special interest on her part.

'Beautiful, are they not?' he tried, hoping she would give him a clue as to what she might like.

'Oh, yes,' she agreed dutifully. 'Quite beautiful.'

He pointed out several other pieces, but she showed less interest than she had gazing at the paintings in the Louvre or at the stained-glass windows of Notre Dame.

Finally, he faced her. 'Do you not realise, Cecilia, that

I wish to buy you a gift? I am trying to discover what you would like.'

'A gift?' Her voice turned wary. 'Whatever for?'

'To commemorate our day together.' So she might remember him as he would remember her.

She stepped back. 'And what will you desire in return?'

He was startled. 'In return? Why, nothing. It is a gift.'

Her eyes narrowed as if she did not believe him.

'Heed me.' He took a chance at touching her arm. 'This has been a most special day. You've shown me sights I would not have seen nor would have appreciated had I been on my own today.'

He probably would have slept half the day and made his way to one of the dancing halls or casinos at night. In her company, he'd lost any interest in either.

One of the glass cases displayed gold lockets and other less expensive pieces.

He pointed to a necklace consisting of a single pearl on a long gold chain. 'Let me buy you a token, then? In thanks for this day?'

She still looked leery, but she said, 'Very well.'

He caught the attention of a clerk and purchased the necklace with the coin in his purse. As the clerk opened the glass case to remove the necklace, he turned to her. 'Earrings to match?'

The corner of her lovely mouth quivered as if she was trying not to smile. 'No. Do not say more or I will change my mind.'

No woman of his acquaintance would threaten to refuse a gift, especially such an inconsequential one. It was even less of a gift he might bring to Jacob's sister or her young daughter.

Nothing about this fascinating lady was like other women he knew.

* * *

Cecilia glanced into Oliver's hazel eyes, so unexpected paired with his darker skin, but so captivating she had to glance away again. He placed the gold chain around her neck, her skin tingling where his fingers touched as he worked the clasp. Stubble shadowed his cheeks, and his scent filled her nostrils. His face was so close she could feel the warmth of his breath.

She knew this feeling, this attraction that made her want to run her hands over his stubble-roughened chin or plunge her fingers into his hair. She'd once felt a similar attraction to her husband as she felt now. This carnal aching inside her.

She'd forgotten that erotic sensation, but she had not forgotten that just because a man attracted her like a moth to a flame did not mean he was decent or honourable. It did not mean he would not change from loving to…hurtful.

'Thank you for the gift,' she managed.

'My pleasure.' His voice turned low.

He finished fastening the necklace and put an inch more space between them, enough that she could see his smile, which had its own power over her.

'It looks fine,' he said. 'In fact, against your skin, it is even more pleasing than against the black velvet of the glass case.'

As compliments went this was a mild one. Did he know that a more flowery compliment would have driven her away even faster than an expensive gift would have done? Was he that clever to know precisely how to chip away at her defences?

For long moments during this day she had been able to believe he was just as he seemed—gentlemanly, kind, generous—but every once in a while her guard flew up again. Like when he asked about her husband. Like when

he wanted to buy her jewels. Somehow, even in those moments, he managed to find a way around the walls she
erected to keep from ever being at the mercy of a man
again.

They left the shop and strolled out to the gardens, where
it seemed there were many gentlemen and ladies engaged
in flirtations. That only made her worry again. Was he
merely charming her or was he what he seemed to be?

'Do you know what I would like to do now?' he asked.

Some wariness crept in. 'What?'

'I would like to walk along the Seine like early this
morning. There is still an hour or so before the sun sets. I
watched it rise there; it would be nice to see it set.'

What man desired walking? Duncan had once seemed
to enjoy the strolls they took away from prying eyes when
he was trying to ingratiate himself with her, but after she
married him, he wanted nothing to do with walking. Just
bedding.

But, then, that was all she'd wanted at first, too.

'I should go home.' Best she part from him while she
could still think and before he did something to burst the
illusion that he was a perfect gentleman.

They left the Palais-Royal.

'I will escort you home, then,' Oliver said.

'It is not necessary.' She did not want him to know that
she lived in a small room near the theatres, casinos, gentlemen's clubs and *maisons closes* or houses of prostitution.

He frowned. 'I would feel remiss to merely send you
on your way alone.'

'I was alone when you met me,' she reminded him.

'Still, I would not forgive myself if any harm came to
you.'

She made a face. 'How would you know? You leave tomorrow. We will never see each other again.' Her throat

tightened at her words and she feared tears would sting her eyes.

He gave her an imploring look. 'All the more reason not to say goodbye so soon. Stay with me to watch the sunset.'

Those captivating eyes seemed to pull her in.

What harm would it do? Besides, she wanted to stay with him; she wanted to keep this lovely illusion that such a kind, handsome, charming man existed, a man who wanted nothing from her but her company.

'Very well,' she said. 'I will stay with you to watch the sunset.'

They walked through the Paris streets to the stairs leading to the Seine. There were walkways on both sides of the river with other couples strolling, street vendors plying their wares, other men and women hurrying to and fro.

'I am glad to walk off my meal.' He patted his stomach.

'It was delicious.' The best meal she'd had since Brussels three years ago when Duncan had taken her to fine restaurants.

Then Duncan received the letter from her father saying he would never provide her dowry or any money at all. After that everything changed.

But it had not changed in a day. Certainly not in an evening. So, perhaps she could pretend Oliver could be trusted to be a gentleman for one evening.

As the sun dropped lower in the sky, the evening took on a magical quality.

Oliver seemed to catch the magic as well. 'I had been told of the beauty of Paris, but I confess I did not believe in it...' He paused and looked down at her. 'Until this day.'

She fingered the pearl that nestled almost between her breasts. 'You have more than paid me back.'

He touched her arm and made her face him. 'This was not a gift for recompense, but for remembrance.'

As if she would be able to forget him. A man who behaved as a friend and stirred her like a lover.

They resumed their stroll. 'I have been here almost three years and I cannot tire of its beauty.'

The conversation that had come so easily to them when they were sharing the sights lost its ease. There was too much she wished to conceal. Let him think she was an English lady living on a small income here in Paris. Sometimes she felt that was exactly what she was.

She did not fit into this Parisian world any better than he must fit into the British aristocracy. Perhaps that was why she was so drawn to him.

'You told me earlier a little of India, but do you remember what it looked like?' she asked, truly wanting to know about the distant foreign land that was in his blood. 'I have read it also is a beautiful place.'

He took several steps before answering. 'I remember lush gardens filled with fragrant flowers and pools of water. My mother's house was filled with colour, woven carpets, fragrant sandalwood, and soft cushions instead of chairs. My father's house, on the other hand, was typically English. He wore his *jama* when with my mother, but on the other side, he dressed like he'd come from his tailor on Bond Street.'

'What is a *jama*?' she asked.

He laughed. 'A bit like a dress, actually. I wore a *jama* as well. They were cooler than British clothes.'

She threaded her arm through his and rested her head against his shoulder. All the wine they'd consumed made her languorous—and loosened her control. 'Tell me something else about India.'

'I remember the streets of Calcutta being crowded and noisy and alternately perfumed and putrid.' He paused. 'I remember elephants and camels and scantily dressed men charming snakes.'

'Snakes.' She shuddered.

He went on talking about spices and tigers and Hindu gods. His voice lulled her and her eyes grew heavy. It was so comfortable to hold his arm, to lean against him.

To not be alone.

He stopped and put his arm around her. 'You are falling asleep. Time to take you to your home.'

Leave him? She should never have agreed to walk along the river with him. The alchemy of the setting sun turned the sky into yellows and oranges, making the water appear to sparkle with gold. She felt its riches and dreaded going back to the emotional deprivation that was her life.

'Not to my home,' she murmured.

'Where to then?' His voice vibrated inside her.

'To your hotel.'

Cecilia knew precisely what she was saying to him. What she was offering. She wanted to pretend a little longer. She wanted everything that she thought she'd have with her husband, even if for only a night.

'Are you certain?' he asked. 'This is not the wine speaking?'

The wine had given her courage. 'I do not want our night to end, Oliver. I want all it can offer us.'

She did not want the magic to end.

Chapter Three

They crossed the Place Louis XV, which had been called the Place de la Concorde after the Revolution, and walked to Rue Saint-Honoré to where Oliver's hotel, Le Meurice, was located. A doorman opened the huge wrought-iron door for them and the attendant in the hall greeted Oliver by name. Other guests passed them without comment.

In London, a gentleman would have had to sneak a woman up to his room or risk being asked to leave the hotel. In Paris, no one took any notice.

Oliver led Cecilia up the three flights of stairs to his room. It was a comfortable space with a sitting area and a separate bedroom and dressing room. His valet stayed in a room next door and would come only if Oliver summoned him.

Oliver opened the door and stepped aside for Cecilia to enter. She walked to the centre of the room and stood as if uncertain she wanted to be there.

He closed the door and removed his hat and gloves. 'Are you wishing I had walked you home instead?'

She turned to him, looking surprised.

He softened his voice. 'It is not too late, Cecilia. I will take you home if that is what you desire.'

She pulled off her own gloves and removed her bonnet. 'I do not desire you to take me home.'

He stepped forward to take her shawl. His fingers skimmed her determinedly squared shoulders.

'Then tell me why you suddenly seem as taut as a bow-string.'

'Do I?' She attempted a smile, which disappeared as quickly. 'I was remembering something…unpleasant.'

He put his arm around her and guided her to the sofa. 'Come sit and do not think of unpleasant things. I will pour us some champagne.'

He was filled with desire for her, which had surged when she proposed coming to his hotel. He'd been on fire ever since. But she was different from other women he'd pursued. She was not a conquest; he liked her too much.

She was mysterious and sad, but strong, as well. He wanted to know why. He wanted to know everything, so he could make her smile again.

She gazed around while he opened and poured the champagne. 'This is a lovely room.'

He recognised, after this whole day, that she relied on typical society conversation when her guard was up. He knew many women who knew of no other kind of conversation, no matter what.

How was he to put her at ease?

He handed her the glass of champagne. 'It looks remarkably like a room in the Clarendon Hotel on Bond Street, but then, Le Meurice is known to cater to British visitors.'

'It is quite comfortable.'

Oliver felt as if he was losing her.

He sat next to her on the sofa. 'Cecilia, nothing will happen here that you do not want. I have enjoyed this day with you. I will not spoil it now.'

She smiled wanly. 'You must think me very absurd.

To offer myself so blatantly, then to act like the silliest ninnyhammer.'

He met her gaze. 'Explain it to me.'

She glanced away and her breathing accelerated. 'I—I do not frequent the hotel rooms of gentlemen by habit.'

He was glad of that, even though he could not say he did not occasionally entertain women in hotel rooms.

She finished her glass of champagne, and he refilled it.

Then he put his hand on top of hers. 'You have promised nothing by coming here, except to spend time with me.'

She gazed at him sceptically.

He smiled. 'Nothing.'

Her eyes softened. 'May I truly believe you?'

He looked her in the eye again. 'I do not lie. I abhor lies.'

She held his gaze for a long time.

He took the champagne glass from her hand and set both glasses on the table next to the sofa. 'So…how do we begin?'

Her lashes lowered and then opened again. She looked directly into his eyes. 'With a kiss?'

He smiled. 'I believe I can comply.'

He gently lifted her chin with his fingers and moved slowly, coming closer and closer until his lips touched hers.

Her lips were soft and warm and they trembled under his. With all his resolve, he held himself back when every fibre of his being wished to pull her body against his and deepen the kiss.

It was she who moved. She wrapped her arms around his neck and came closer. He leaned back and she slid on top of him. Her lips had become hungrier, and he was only too glad to appease her appetite. She opened herself to him, straddling him and pressing against his groin. He was already hard, wanting all of her. He pressed her to him and parted his lips to allow her tongue access. She tasted of champagne, but more intoxicating. His senses reeled.

He could take her here, he realised. Merely unbutton his trousers and free himself to enter her, but he wanted so much more than a speedy release.

He lifted her off him and stood, sweeping her into his arms. 'The bedchamber?' he asked.

She nodded.

He carried her into the bedchamber and lay her on the bed. Making short work of removing his coat and waistcoat, he leaned down for another kiss, which she willingly accepted.

She watched him as he next pulled at his boot, trying to remove it. The boot stubbornly stuck to his foot and he cursed it beneath his breath.

She laughed, a deep, genuine laugh that made his insides quake in joy for it.

She reached for him. 'Let me pull them off for you.'

He climbed on the bed, and she took hold of his boot, twisting and wiggling it before finally pulling. The boot came free.

She grinned at the victory.

She pulled the other boot off with as little difficulty.

He came to his knees. 'Now I shall help you.'

He turned her around and undid the laces of her gown and carefully lifted it over her head, folding it before placing it on the floor. Next he untied her corset and helped her slip out of it. She turned to face him and reached for his shirt, pulling it over his head. He jumped off the bed and removed his trousers and drawers.

She remained seated on the bed, dressed only in her shift, pulling pins from her hair. It tumbled to her shoulders as she watched him, naked before her.

He was accustomed to the appreciative gazes of the women he bedded, but Cecilia set his senses afire.

As she could obviously tell.

He smiled again and twirled his finger at her.

She looked puzzled for a moment, then her brow cleared and she smiled back as she drew her shift over her head. He knew she would be lovely. All creamy skin, narrow waist, full breasts.

'You are a beautiful woman, Cecilia,' he said with complete honesty.

She blushed an appealing pink.

He approached her slowly, climbing back on the bed and lying next to her, drawing her into another kiss, stroking her fine skin, fingering the rich waves of her hair. She touched him, too, placing her palm on his chest, sliding her hand lower to his groin. To his surprise and delight, she wrapped her fingers around his shaft, though it made his resolve to go slow a challenge.

She slithered up to place her lips against his ear. 'How long do you intend to wait?'

Cecilia knew she was behaving wantonly, but she did not care. The wine had loosened her inhibitions and this man had made her yearn for lovemaking. In the early days of Duncan's seduction, he had shown her these erotic delights. She remembered aching for him so acutely she'd have done anything for him. Now she knew it had been his way of making certain she would marry him.

Those early days of lovemaking awakened her to the pleasures of the flesh. She had no doubt she would gladly succumb to such temptations over and over if only she could be certain that the tide would not turn.

Coupling could be transcendental or it could be…brutal.

Since Duncan she'd never taken the risk. Until now.

One night was not too much to ask, was it? One night to re-experience corporeal delights?

'How long?' she whispered again.

He turned his head to face her. 'I should ask first if you have the means to prevent a child?'

She'd not had to worry over that with Duncan. 'I know what to do.'

He smiled teasingly. 'Then have your way with me, Cecilia.'

He rolled onto his back.

She immediately climbed on top of him, but, unlike his words suggested, he was not passive. He grasped her by the waist and guided himself inside her. She gasped at the sensation.

Together they moved, forming a rhythm that built her need. He was a skilled lover, she could tell. He knew just how to move her to intensify her sensations. It seemed to her that he also knew just how long he could draw this out to put her into a frenzy.

A pleasurable frenzy.

She felt the change in him, the moment he lost all thought and was in the throes of lust. His thrusts quickened, pushing her to the brink of frustration until her release came in like a lightning storm. She cried out with the acute pleasure just as his release came. His cry joined hers. He held her tight until the wave of pleasure washed away and her body turned the consistency of soft butter.

She collapsed beside him. 'Well, that was rather nice.'

He laughed softly, but the laugh resonated within her. 'I feel damned with faint praise.'

'And assent with civil leer?' She knew that poem. 'Epistle to Dr Arbuthnot' by Alexander Pope.

He countered. 'And without sneering, teach the rest to sneer.'

She smiled. He knew the poem as well.

'Willing to wound, and yet afraid to strike,' she added.

He finished it. 'Just hint at a fault and hesitate dislike.'

She returned his smile. 'What nonsense, to recite that poem after making love.'

He feigned an innocent look. 'You started it.'

She loved this bantering. Would it not be lovely to have a man who always found some lightness and humour wherever he went?

He reached over to her necklace and fingered the single pearl. 'I do not have faint praise, Cecilia. Mine is rather loud, I fear.'

She grew warm all over again. 'I am glad I accompanied you to your hotel.'

His smile grew slowly. 'As am I.'

He turned on his side and pulled her into a kiss that ignited her senses all over again.

This time he rose over her, entering her again and moving slowly as if savouring the experience. As if trying to make the moment as pleasurable as possible for her.

She was glad she'd allowed herself this liberty, this lapse in the tight control she exerted over herself. She'd lived in the winter of her emotions for too long. How lovely it was to let the sun shine in.

As he moved, her need built slowly, a glorious need because it held the promise of fulfilment at the end. All her senses came alive, awakened after a long hibernation. She was delighted she could still experience this pleasure.

And she was delighted with this lovely man who bestowed it like a gift.

His thrusts accelerated and her thoughts flew out of her head, replaced by sensation. Need. Growing. Nearing its promised end.

Her release shattered inside her, sparkling like the sunlight on the rose windows of Notre Dame. Then the release came again and again. And again when he spilled his seed inside her.

He collapsed on top of her, and she relished his weight upon her for the moment he remained there. Before he made it hard for her to breathe, he rolled off her, pulling her into another kiss and another.

He finally faced her, twirling a lock of her hair in his fingers. 'Ah, Cecilia. Words fail me.'

She merely snuggled against him, relishing the scent of him and the warmth of his skin against hers.

'I wonder,' he began.

She could feel his voice through her body as well as hear him with her ears.

'I wonder,' he said again. 'Perhaps I might extend my visit...'

A *frisson* of fear raced up her spine. No. That was not what she wanted. One day, he'd said. One night. More time together and what could happen?

One night did not seem like enough to her either, though.

She did not answer him, instead closed her eyes and let herself drift into sleep. Another pleasure—sleeping naked next to the man who had just joined with her.

She could still pretend for a few more hours, even if he wished to extend that time into days. She was determined not to let go of this wonderful illusion until she absolutely must.

Oliver, too, drifted to sleep with the thought that he had no real reason to start his journey back to England so soon. What would a few more days hurt? Frederick and Jacob could manage things until he returned. One more week would not matter.

He slept deeply, content to hold Cecilia in his arms.

* * *

When he woke it was to a loud knocking on the door.

'Sir. Sir.' It was his valet knocking. 'The coach is due in an hour. You must rise now.'

Oliver shook himself awake and sat straight up.

He turned to the space in the bed beside him.

Cecilia was gone. Her clothes were gone.

'Sir!' His valet knocked again.

'One moment,' he answered, climbing out of bed.

He searched to see if she'd left him a note, but there was nothing in the bedchamber. He entered the sitting room and searched there. To no avail.

There was nothing to indicate she'd ever been with him.

He had no way to find her. No surname. No address.

Perhaps he could find her on the banks of the Seine, giving coins to the children. He must dress quickly. He ran back to the bedchamber and grabbed his drawers, managing to don them as he started towards the door to let his valet into the room.

A glance towards the window depressed his spirits. The sun was high in the sky. He'd slept through most of the morning. She would not be on the banks of the Seine giving coins to street urchins. She would be long gone.

'Sir! Sir!' his valet cried.

'Coming!' He walked to the door and opened it, and knew he would never see Cecilia again.

Chapter Four

Cecilia had left Oliver's bed at dawn and hurried to the river to pass out the coins to the children who, hungry, flocked to her.

Now when she met the children she would be reminded of him for ever. She'd see him running to rescue her. She'd see his smile and remember his laugh.

How would she be able to sit in Notre Dame, listen to the bells, witness the Mass, without remembering him at her side, seeming to understand the special aura of the place? When she gazed at her favourite paintings in the Louvre, would she not think of him standing next to her, listening to her enthuse about what she loved about the work?

As she'd walked back to her room, she fingered the pearl next to her skin. The memory of him would always touch her if she wore the necklace.

How good it was that the memory of her day with him was a happy one. She so much relished having a happy memory to replace the unhappy ones from her past.

On her way she stopped at an apothecary to buy the items necessary to keep from getting with child. She returned to her room afterwards.

Her room was about half the size of Oliver's sitting

room in the hotel, but it was as clean and as cheerful as she could make it, with a pot of flowers she'd impulsively bought from a vendor and the lace curtains on the window it had taken weeks of saving to afford. She reached behind her to untie her laces so that she could pull her dress over her head and folded it carefully.

Next she removed her corset and set about using the items from the apothecary.

When first married to Duncan, she'd pined for a baby, but it did not take long for her to pray a child would never happen. She'd learned what to do to prevent it. Too many times, though, she could not clean herself afterwards. Still, she did not become *enceinte*. She'd concluded his punches had damaged her and she could not conceive. At the time she thought it a blessing.

After completing her task, Cecilia climbed on her bed and burrowed under the quilt she'd crafted from scraps of cloth collected during her years of marriage. Sewing the quilt had helped her endure. It was her prized possession, her badge of honour.

Her mind drifted as she lay on her bed. She'd slept only briefly the night before. In Oliver's arms. Most of the night she'd gazed out of the window, keeping herself awake so that she could be sure she'd rise before him and make her escape.

She'd waited until the first light of dawn appeared, then slipped out of his embrace where she'd felt warm and safe. As quietly as she could she searched for her clothing, scooping it into her arms and tiptoeing to the sitting room to dress. On a table had been a stack of Oliver's calling cards. She took one as a souvenir of the man with whom she'd spent this wonderful day. When she was fully clothed, except for her shoes, which she still held in her hands, she peeked in the bedchamber one last time, for one last look at him.

So handsome. His face was relaxed in sleep, which only accentuated the perfection of his features. His dark hair was in wild disarray. She stared at him a long time, committing his image to her memory.

As if she could ever forget him.

He'd proposed more days together. He'd tempted her especially when her body had still been humming with the pleasure he'd brought her. But she knew she'd reached her limit with one day. One glorious day.

More time was too great a risk. More time making love with him would only bind her to him, a cord that could bring delight, but also great pain. More time and she'd likely fall under the spell of his charm. More time and she might convince herself that she needed him. Before she knew it, he would be able to control her every move. He'd change. Become brutal.

She'd never go through that again.

Even so, as she lay on her small bed, she yearned to be held by Oliver again. He'd opened a door that she'd thought closed for good—one that Duncan had slammed on her—and how was she to lock those feelings away again?

She would, she vowed. She must.

That night Cecilia entered the club through the rear door. The Maison D'Eros was located near the Palais-Royal, which, at this late hour, became quite a different place from the one she'd strolled through with Oliver. She was glad Oliver would never know she was a part of this world. At night courtesans, departing from the theatre, promenaded with their patrons. Prostitutes strolled, hoping to attract clients.

Cecilia might have been one of those unfortunate creatures had she not been rescued by Vincent, her one French ally. When Vincent found her that first desperate night at the Palais-Royal, she'd spent her last *sou*. Her search for employment had been futile. No Frenchman wished to hire an English lady for any reason—except the most wretched and shameful one. So she'd been reduced to that circumstance that night.

Until Vincent took pity on her.

Dear Vincent, the one man she felt comfortable with. Vincent was like a bosom beau and unlike anyone she'd ever met before. A man who adored womanly things, but preferred men to women. He was the very safest sort of ally. He took her under his wing and brought her to the Maison D'Eros, talking the manager into letting her serve drinks for tips.

'You must flirt with the rich gentlemen so that they buy more drinks and pay you more tips,' Vincent had told her, then he showed her how to do it. She managed it by pretending she was someone else, not Cecilia Lockhart. The men started calling her Coquette, so she became Coquette.

Coquette was brave. Coquette could tease men and put them in their place. Coquette could laugh at their silly jokes and admire their braggadocio. Coquette could sing bawdy songs and dance seductively. Coquette spoke only French.

Soon men were begging for her favours and Vincent devised another plan.

'I have a way you might become the rage of Paris! Paris's most selective courtesan!' he'd said to her one night.

She'd been scraping by on her tips. 'I told you, Vincent, I do not wish to be a courtesan. Bedding strange men is abhorrent to me.'

He'd sighed. 'Abhorrent to you, but my greatest pleasure.' He'd placed his hand to his heart for a moment. 'But, never mind. You will not have to bed anyone.'

'How can one be a courtesan without the bedding?' she'd asked.

He'd explained it to her.

And so Coquette became Madame Coquette, Paris's most selective courtesan, selling her favours a mere two nights a week—without selling her favours at all.

Tonight Vincent greeted her in the back room wearing a purple coat, a deep blue waistcoat and a bright yellow neckcloth—his work costume. His blond hair curled around his boyish face and his lips and cheeks were tinted a pale pink.

'Madame Coquette, *chérie*!' He kissed both cheeks in his flamboyant manner. 'You look ravishing.'

'As do you, *mon cher*.' She kissed him in kind.

'Who do you entertain tonight?' he asked.

'Monsieur Legrand.'

Legrand was a wealthy merchant who had made it a point to ingratiate himself with those in power during the restoration of the monarchy. It was said he courted favour with the Duke of Wellington, but now, with the Occupation near to its end, he'd turned to Frenchmen who were likely to come to power. Procuring a night with Madame Coquette was, no doubt, part of how he intended to impress.

'Legrand,' Vincent repeated. 'He is no challenge at all. You will wrap him around your little finger in no time.'

Her brow furrowed. 'But Hercule will remain nearby, will he not?'

Hercule, large, strong and intimidating, was employed as a flash man to make certain none of the working girls suffered mistreatment. He stayed within shouting distance in case things did not go as planned.

'But of course.' Vincent threaded her arm through his. 'Time to turn yourself into Madame Coquette.'

They walked up the servants' stairs to a room on the

first floor where the dresser arranged Cecilia's hair and applied just a light dusting of rouge on her cheeks and lips.

'What dress today, Coquette?' the dresser asked.

'The red, I suppose.'

The red gown was made of fine silk, its neckline, sleeves and hem trimmed in gold embroidery. The neckline dipped lower than what Cecilia would wish, but it was perfect for Madame Coquette. Her gowns were fine enough for a high-priced courtesan, but they were not hers. The manager of the club paid for them.

Once in her gown and slippers, Cecilia said *au revoir* to the dresser. In the hallway with Vincent, there was nothing left to do but meet her customer.

Vincent held her by the shoulders and looked her in the eye. 'Deep breath!' he commanded. 'Breathe in, Madame Coquette!'

She took a deep breath, closed her eyes and let herself become her alter ego.

Lifting her chin, she opened her eyes again and nodded to Vincent who turned her towards the door that led to the drawing room and gave her a little push.

With a slight sway to her hips that had not been there before, she entered the drawing room and made straight for Monsieur Legrand as if she were eager to be in his company.

He gaped at her as she approached him, almost spilling his glass of wine and only remembering to stand when she drew near.

'Legrand,' she said in a voice deeper than she usually spoke, emphasising the *grand*. 'It is my pleasure to entertain you tonight.'

Legrand was a man in his fifties, who obviously enjoyed the fruits of his labour. His round stomach strained at the buttons of his waistcoat, which was well tailored and made of the finest cloth. His nose had the red hue of someone who enjoyed too much wine and his neck disappeared behind his jowls. Yet he displayed himself to her as if she would find him irresistible. No wonder so many courtesans had their beginnings in the theatre. It took a great deal of acting to convince a man such as this that his company was desired.

He'd paid a great deal for this night with her, although the manager of Maison D'Eros took the lion's share. Her goal was to save enough for a modest living somewhere, ideally back in England, for which she was always homesick—even more so since spending the day with Oliver. It would take her a long time to amass such a sum. Years, perhaps. She'd been building Madame Coquette's reputation over the last year and a half and she had little more than what travel expenses to England would cost her.

'Shall we retire to my room?' she asked, taking his arm.

'Yes. Yes,' he stammered.

She led him up to the second floor to a room that was not exclusively hers. Others, including Vincent, used it on other nights of the week.

She gestured for Legrand to open the door and she swept by him to enter the room, decorated in red-silk drapery on the walls and white and gold damask upholstering the *chaise* and sofa. The tables were mahogany embellished with gold and Egyptian motifs made popular by Napoleon's invasion of Egypt. On the tables were crystal decanters of wine and brandy, bottles of champagne, and plates of grapes and cheeses. Prominent in the room was a large bed, its covers and canopy in a white fabric similar to the upholstered *chaise* and chair, trimmed in gold fringe.

Cecilia's silk red gown was perfect for the room. She looked as if she were part of the room's decoration.

Legrand closed the door and lunged for her, throwing himself at her and slamming his lips against hers.

She pushed him away. 'Monsieur Legrand!' She spoke with great indignation. 'How dare you attack me like—like you are a hound in heat. I will not stand for such disrespect!'

'Forgive me, *madame*.' He grovelled. 'I could not help myself. The mere sight of you lights a fire in me that can never be extinguished!'

She straightened her clothes. 'Well, I suggest you compose yourself immediately. Remember the bargain, *monsieur*. You have paid for my time, but that is all. You must win me over if you want any more of me.'

This was the brilliant ruse Vincent had thought up for her. Her customers were required to make her want to bed them. And if she wanted it, she promised them rapturous satisfaction.

Of course, she never wanted any of them.

'What might I do to please you?' Legrand asked.

She lowered herself onto one of the sofas. 'First you may pour me some champagne and amuse me with your repartee.'

'Yes. Yes.' Legrand nearly tripped over his own feet in his haste to reach the champagne bottle and open it.

The champagne always made being Madame Coquette a bit easier.

Legrand babbled of once meeting and advising Talleyrand, the French politician who'd managed to operate at the highest levels of government through Louis XVI, the Revolution, Napoleon and now the Restoration.

As if Talleyrand would accept advice from such a ridiculous man.

'Talleyrand.' She made a sound of derision. 'He is the one no one trusts completely, is that not so? He is a traitor to France. Am I to admire you for associating with a traitor?'

If Legrand had vilified Tallyrand, she would have praised Tallyrand as a great statesman of France.

Because, no matter what Legrand said or did, she was not going to be pleased by him. He would never win her over. That was the point.

Legrand continued to try, attempting to impress her with his wealth and his success as a merchant. Cecilia could almost feel sorry for him, except he was willing to pay for a woman's favours, merely to impress his compatriots.

Conversation inevitably came to an end and Legrand began spouting flattery. '*Madame*, your beautiful skin makes me long to touch you. You are the most ravishing of Paris courtesans. I would have paid double for this night with you. Triple. And considered it worth every franc.'

Cecilia wished her price had been negotiated higher. This was something to discuss with the manager, who might be underselling her services.

'You flatter me, *monsieur*,' she said, dipping her head and fluttering her lashes the way Vincent had shown her.

His expression turned eager. 'Please, I beg you, *madame*. Sit with me.'

'With pleasure.' Cecilia girded herself and moved to the *chaise*.

Legrand put his arm around her. 'This is much better. Much better.'

She pretended to sigh. 'Would you pour me more champagne?'

'More champagne?' He sounded both surprised and disappointed. 'As you wish.'

'For you as well.' She smiled sweetly.

He opened the second bottle of champagne and poured two glasses, handing one to her.

She tapped her glass against his. 'To this lovely night.'

He puffed up with hope. 'This lovely night.'

He drank the contents in one gulp and put his arm around her again. As Cecilia slowly sipped hers, he stroked her arm, then became bolder and put his hand on her thigh.

'May I kiss you?' he asked while he performed the greater indignity of kneading her thigh.

She took her time to drink the last of her champagne, then smiled. 'Of course you can!'

He placed his dry, thin, fleshless lips against hers and held her in both arms.

She made herself remain still for a moment, before starting to cough. And cough. And cough.

He released her. 'What can I do? More champagne?'

She nodded, still coughing.

His hand shook while he poured another glass of champagne. She grabbed it from his hand and drank as if desperate for it.

When she'd composed herself again, she apologised. 'Forgive me, *monsieur*. I—I tried…' She let her voice trail off.

She positioned herself for another kiss and Legrand eagerly complied. This time he opened his mouth.

She made a sound and again pushed him away. 'Did you clean your teeth, *monsieur*?'

'My—my teeth?' He looked befuddled.

'I am sorry, but your mouth—the taste, the smell—it makes me cough.' She reached for her champagne again.

He cupped his hand near his mouth and exhaled, trying to smell his own breath.

'I cannot kiss you, *monsieur*.' She frowned. 'I am so sorry.'

He moved towards her. 'We can proceed without kissing.'

She allowed him to touch her, to fondle her breasts, to run his hands down her body before pushing away again. 'It is no use, *monsieur*. I am certain you are a very fine gentleman and I am so very impressed by your wealth and your importance, but I must feel something for the men I bed. They must stir me and you—you do not.'

He looked as if she'd slapped him.

This was the dangerous moment. When the man was filled with lust, but spurned. This was when Hercule might be needed.

'I am very certain this has never happened to you before,' she said. 'You are such a fine gentleman. I do not know what is wrong with me.'

He puffed up again. 'Never happened before. Never. Women like me. Many women.'

'I am certain they do,' she said soothingly.

He gave her a hopeful look. 'Perhaps we can proceed anyway? I will not hold it against you if you do not—do not get pleasure from it.'

'Monsieur Legrand!' She pretended to be horrified. 'You wish me to bed you without feeling on my part?'

'Well…'

She shook her head. 'No. That is not what I do. Remember the bargain?' The rules set forth for a night with Madame Coquette were very specific. 'I must want to couple with you and now, I simply cannot. I will have another coughing fit and I know you would not wish me to have another coughing fit.'

'No…' He rubbed his face. 'I told all my friends.'

'You told your friends that you had arranged a night with me?' she asked.

He nodded, looking horror-struck.

She reached over and patted his hand. 'It is not your

fault. It is entirely mine.' She always tried to take the blame. She had no wish to humiliate the men, although with some of the more unpleasant ones, it was tempting.

'No one will believe that.' His lower lip jutted out like a hurt child. 'Some of them are here tonight. In the card room. If they see me leave early—'

'You must not leave early, then!' she reassured him. 'We will stay the whole night, until just before dawn. Will that do?'

He seemed to be considering it. 'Just before dawn. That might work. My wife will expect me home about then.'

The men always had a poor wife waiting at home.

'And you must tell your friends whatever will impress them,' she added. 'I will never say anything but that my time with you was incredibly passionate. I will say I was impressed by your skill—because I am sure I would be, if it were not for my awful cough. Because of the smell.'

'You would be, that is very true.'

She patted his hand again. 'I am very sure I would be.'

He flushed with pride, as if he really had given her incredible passion.

Cecilia was always surprised how easy it was to talk these gentlemen out of bedding her by complimenting their supposed prowess. What the man's friends thought of his night with her was always more important to them than the act itself.

'What will we do all night?' he asked.

She opened a drawer and pulled out a deck of cards. 'We can play piquet!'

Chapter Five

November 1818, three months later

Oliver leaned against the wall in the billiard room of Vitium et Virtus, watching Frederick and Jacob knock the balls in the pockets of the green baize table. The day's weather was cold and drizzling, but the fire in the fireplace kept the room comfortably warm. Frederick was meticulously lining up his next shot, taking long enough that Oliver began tapping his foot.

'Just take the shot, Fred,' he said impatiently. 'This fuss does you no good.'

Frederick ignored him and continued to study the ball some more before placing his cue and executing a perfect shot, sending Jacob's cue ball and the red ball into the pockets.

'That's the game,' groaned Jacob.

Frederick looked up and grinned. 'Does me no good, Oliver?'

'You would have made it without all that fuss.' Oliver picked up his cue and stepped up to the table while Frederick retrieved the balls from the pockets.

Jacob flopped in a chair. 'That is the second game you've won over me.'

'You were distracted.' Frederick turned his grin on the new duke. 'Thinking of your bride, no doubt.'

Jacob laughed.

It was gratifying to see Jacob happy. Oliver had often caught Jacob spending the night hours at Vitium et Virtus, drinking and looking more haggard by the day.

Jacob had been reeling with grief over the accident that killed his father and brother, and lamenting that he was not up to the enormous responsibility of a dukedom.

But then Jacob met his Rose.

Oliver wished them well. He really did.

He wished Frederick and Georgiana well, too.

Both Oliver's friends were obviously besotted with their wives. When Oliver saw them with the women, the loving looks and tender touches between them reminded him of the many gestures of affection he'd long ago witnessed between his mother and father.

But his father had still left his mother behind in India.

Obviously love fled in the wake of expediency. Once gone, love could destroy.

Oliver sincerely hoped the love shared by Frederick, Jacob and their wives would not be so easily shattered. But he would not wager any money on it.

And he was known to wager on almost anything.

Oliver stood next to Frederick and they hit their respective cue balls simultaneously to see who would have the first shot. Oliver's ball stopped closest to the baulk cushion. He went first, hitting both Frederick's cue ball and the red ball.

Oliver concentrated on the billiards. That was what he liked about games or any competition. He could focus on winning and push all other thoughts out of his mind. Unfortunately, Frederick's careful approach to billiards gave Oliver too much time to think.

He frowned and crossed his arms over his chest.

'Back to discussing my wife,' Jacob said in good humour. 'I highly recommend marriage.'

'As do I.' Frederick continued to eye the ball. 'You should try it, Oliver.'

'Not likely.' Oliver's reply came quickly.

'You will change your tune.' Frederick continued to consider the placement of his cue. 'Once you meet the right lady.' He finally hit the red ball and sent it into a pocket.

Did Frederick not see how easily his marriage to Georgiana might have turned to misery? Oliver held his tongue, though.

He took his shot and this time sent Fred's cue ball into a pocket.

'Maybe he already has.' Jacob rose to pour himself some brandy. He turned to Oliver. 'The mysterious Parisian lady.'

Cecilia.

'Nonsense.' He regretted telling them of her, not that he'd said much, and it had taken him some time to divulge even that meagre information. He never discussed the more private elements of his time with women.

'You cannot tell us you do not think of her,' Jacob persisted. 'You've been different since that trip. A veritable malcontent.'

'I dispute that statement.' Oliver tapped his foot, impatient over Frederick's care in executing his shot. Or at least that was the reason he told himself his toe was tapping.

Frederick finally hit the ball. 'I agree with Jake. You've been moodier. And what lady was your last conquest? No one since Paris.'

Frederick was right, of course. 'You assume too much. Perhaps I do not tell you of my every liaison. Perhaps I am discreet.' Oliver took his shot and missed.

His friends exchanged knowing glances.

He played the rest of the game in disgruntled silence. And lost.

Oliver refused to believe that the brief encounter with Cecilia had sent him into this funk. Perhaps the cause was because he'd not accomplished his goal in Paris. He'd not found very much new to offer at their club. Nothing, at least, that was not distasteful to him.

Too much of Vitium et Virtus was becoming distasteful to him.

But that was a worry that had preceded his trip to Paris.

He must admit that the memory of Cecilia did linger in the recesses of his mind. A church bell would call back the image of her in Notre Dame, the sun through the rose windows bathing her face in colour. One of the lady patrons of the club wrapped her Kashmir shawl around her shoulders, just as Cecilia had. Their new French songstress had Cecilia's colour hair.

Reminders were to be expected, were they not? Yet surely that bore no special significance.

'Another game?' Frederick held up a cue ball.

Jacob stood and picked up a cue.

Oliver poured himself some brandy and lowered himself into a chair. The room had been designed for their comfort, his, Jacob, Frederick and Nicholas. The richly carved oak panelling on the walls came from a German monastery. The billiard table, with its fine green-baize surface, filled the room's centre, but around it were the most comfortable chairs in the club and enough tables and cabinets to hold the ever-present brandy. The chandelier's many candles illuminated the billiard table so play could continue all night, if desired.

Very occasionally they offered billiard tournaments, the prize of which was some debauched spree, but most of the time this room was for their own amusement. Oliver preferred it that way. Increasingly he was preferring the days Vitium et Virtus was closed and he had time to himself.

He, Frederick, Jacob and Nicholas began the club back in their Oxford days. It was secret, exclusive and naughtier than the Hell Fire clubs of their grandfathers. Vitium et Virtus also lacked the Hell Fire clubs' anti-religious affectations. No black mass for Vitium et Virtus. No devil worship or paganism or ridiculous rituals. Their club worshipped pleasure and excess, in card-playing, drink and fornication. It had been their highest accomplishment at the University.

When they left Oxford, they brought the club to London.

What did Oliver care that he was not welcome at Almack's? He belonged to Vitium et Virtus.

Life had been good right up until that night six years ago when Nicholas disappeared, leaving only a pool of blood and his signet ring in the alley behind the club.

Oliver, Frederick and Jacob had kept Vitium et Virtus running for Nicholas's sake, but for how much longer? Frederick and Jacob were now married. What honourable gentleman runs a club of Dionysian revels when his wife is waiting at home?

Oliver would keep it going by himself, if necessary. To him, giving up on Vitium et Virtus was like giving up on Nicholas. He refused to believe Nicholas was dead.

He finished his brandy and poured another.

Enough blue devils.

'I do have one new idea for the club,' he began.

Jacob grinned. 'Nothing that involves driving hooks through one's skin and hanging from ropes.'

Oliver had told them of the self-mutilation and flagellation of some Paris clubs.

'Not unless you wish to try it,' he shot back.

Jacob held up both hands. 'Not me!'

'We could have a Vitium et Virtus ball.'

'Oh, that is original,' Frederick said.

'Not the usual sort of ball.' Oliver rose and picked up one of the billiard balls from a pocket. 'We have two baskets of balls like these, only each ball has a number painted on it. There are matching numbers for men and for women. The men pick from the men's basket and the women from the women's. Then they partner up with the person whose number matches theirs. No one knows ahead of time who their partner will be.'

Frederick straightened his spine. 'Georgiana and I will not play.'

Jacob laughed. 'Nor will Rose and I.'

Oliver shook his head. 'Of course not.' In truth, he also had no desire to play that game. 'I think several of our members will relish it, though. We know many married couples who would clamour to be first in line to play.'

Frederick turned back to his game. 'You manage it, if you like, but you had better make certain everyone knows what to expect.'

'What if Bowles shows up?' Jacob asked.

Frederick missed his shot.

Nash Bowles was a nasty fellow they'd known since their Oxford days, who'd joined before they'd become more selective. He'd lately pressed to purchase Jacob's share of the club.

Frederick's lips thinned. 'That reprobate.'

Bowles was the reason Fred had married his Georgiana. Vitium et Virtus had held a virgin auction which was supposed to have been a total farce. The women usually auctioning their wares were certainly no virgins, but instead, those who loved the sexual excess of the club.

Instead, respectable, well-bred Georgiana Knight, a viscount's daughter, had climbed up on the table and offered herself. Frederick had bid on her, intending to protect her reputation.

'Bowles.' Fred spat out the name like a piece of rancid meat. 'He had better behave himself or he will answer to me.'

Bowles had threatened to ruin Georgiana for her escapade at Vitium et Virtus unless she married him as her father wished.

Honourable Frederick married Georgiana instead, to rescue her from Bowles. And somehow Fred and Georgiana had fallen in love with each other.

What were the chances that marriage would remain blissful? Especially since Georgiana was so free-spirited.

And how long would Jacob remain besotted with Rose? He was a duke and she had been a maid here at Vitium et Virtus. How long before Jacob left Rose like Oliver's father had left his mother?

'You two should go home to your wives,' Oliver said. His friends had better do right by those good women or they'd have to answer to him.

'I was thinking the same thing,' Fred said.

Jacob looked pensive. 'I was thinking how lucky I am to have this happiness. And how much I wish Nicholas could share in it.'

'Nick.' Oliver's voice rasped with pain.

He placed his hand palm up on the billiard table. Jacob and Frederick placed theirs on his. 'In Vitium et Virtus,' they recited together.

They'd been schoolboys when they first contrived this oath, resurrecting it after the night Nick vanished to remind them that they were still four. Nicholas was somewhere, Oliver insisted. And somehow he'd find his way back to them.

They broke apart, and Frederick poured more brandy. He lifted his glass in a toast. 'To absent friends.'

Oliver and Jacob raised their glasses.

'Be he in heaven or hell—' Oliver continued, a refrain they'd repeated several times in the six years Nicholas had been gone.

'Or somewhere in between—' Fred added.

'Know that we wish you well.' Jake ended it.

If only words could magically bring Nick back.

They downed their brandy in silence.

After Oliver said goodbye to his friends, he made his way to the back door, the private entrance used only by him and his friends. The drizzle persisted, so he dashed across the garden and out the gate, through the alley and the garden of the town house on Bury Street adjacent to the club. Oliver's town house. How lucky he'd been to be wealthy enough to buy a town house so conveniently located to Vitium et Virtus.

When his father became the Marquess of Amberford and inherited the property and riches to go with the title, he'd settled the fortune he'd acquired in India on Oliver, a fortune great enough that Oliver could live more than comfortably. He could afford many pleasures. Fast carriages, matched horses, beautiful women.

Funny that Oliver used to fear he'd be poor. When he was a boy, his father's wife often threatened to put Oliver out on the streets. Eventually he learned about his fortune and that she could not touch it. When his father was not present, she was always nasty to Oliver. He'd absolutely believed he could be tossed out onto the streets like Cecilia's street urchins—

Cecilia.

Again she popped into his mind unbidden. For the last three months the memory of her caught him at odd moments. Why should she inhabit his thoughts so often? He'd only known her one day.

Perhaps the brevity of their time together had enhanced the experience, made it grander, magical. It had seemed as if she'd appeared out of the mist and disappeared as quickly. No liaison of his had ever begun so unexpectedly and ended so abruptly.

He reached the garden door of his town house and went inside, brushing the raindrops off his coat and hair. He greeted his cook and housekeeper as he passed the kitchen and made his way up to the hall where his butler stopped him.

'Sir, you have a caller,' the butler said.

'A caller?' Oliver rarely had callers. He was not on society's circuit of people whose favour one must court.

His butler, only a decade older than he, leaned closer. 'A lady. She declined to give her name.'

Oliver's brows rose. 'You do not know her?'

Irwin typically had an excellent eye for faces and names, especially ladies' names.

He shook his head. 'She has been waiting over an hour.'

'An hour?' What lady would wait an hour for him? 'Why did you not simply say I was out?'

Irwin appeared affronted. 'I did say you were out. She insisted upon waiting.'

Oliver was always very careful that the ladies with whom he associated knew precisely the nature of the relationship. He did not want any of them to consider him so important they'd waste an hour waiting for him.

Irwin inclined his head towards the drawing room. 'She waits in there.'

Oliver shrugged. He might as well discover who it was.

He opened the door, startling the woman who sat upon the sofa facing the fireplace. She stood and turned to him.

For a moment Oliver could not breathe.

'Cecilia.'

Chapter Six

Cecilia had forgotten how his presence affected her. His handsome face. His masculine grace. His riveting eyes. Unwillingly, her body flared in response to him. She'd not wished to seek him out, but what other choice did she have?

He hurried towards her. 'But why are you here? How did you know—?'

'Where to find you?' She finished his question and felt somewhat embarrassed to admit to the answer. 'I took one of your cards before I left. It gave your direction.'

She was wary of him, of how he would respond to her, of his reaction to what she must tell him.

To her surprise, he softened his voice. 'I am delighted to see you, Cecilia. What is wrong? You seem distressed. Do you need my assistance?'

She had to turn away from him. From his kindness.

'I never intended to come to you. I went first to my parents—my mother—' Her voice cracked and she blinked away tears. The last thing she wanted was to weep in front of him. She wrestled her emotions back in control. 'My mother and father refused to see me. I am dead to them, you see.'

She'd yearned for her mother. When everything fell so completely apart in Paris, she'd desperately yearned for her mother. She'd wanted to be enfolded in her mother's arms and soothed and told everything would turn out all right. So many times after Duncan had beaten her she'd wished for her mother's arms, but when Duncan was alive, it had been impossible. This time, though, with Duncan dead, she thought perhaps her parents would forgive her. She'd travelled first to their country house only to be told they were in London.

She then went to London, but they refused to see her.

You are dead to them, their butler, a man she'd known since childhood, had frostily told her.

So she came here. To Oliver.

She'd always known that her ruse as Madame Coquette would end some day. One night the man who'd paid for time did not fall for her excuses. He'd tried to take what he wanted. For a few frightening moments, it was as if her husband had returned from the dead to again force himself on her. Hercule had burst in and stopped him.

The club manager had not been amused. When he learned what really transpired with Madame Coquette, the manager gave her an ultimatum. Provide what the men desired or leave.

Give the manager control over her? No man would control her ever again. Although a part of her despaired, she'd told the manager she would leave. She begged Vincent to look after the street urchins, sold her meagre belongings and her beloved quilt, and journeyed back to England to a mother who refused to see her.

Now her money was rapidly running out. Now she was forced to put herself at the mercy of another man.

Oliver.

'Tell me how I may help,' he said without hesitation.

She faced him again. 'I need money.'

'Money.' His voice turned cautious. 'Am I to know why you need money?'

She took a deep breath and pressed her hand to her abdomen. 'I am going to have a child.' She fixed her gaze on him. 'Your child. And I do not have funds enough to take care of the baby.'

He looked stunned—and not pleased.

'A baby.' His eyes flashed. His entire demeanour changed. 'You said you would take precautions.'

She lifted her chin. 'I did take precautions.'

'This cannot be!' He began to pace. 'Are you certain?'

'Am I certain?' she shot back. 'Am I certain I took precautions? Yes. Very certain. Am I certain I am with child? Yes.'

So much for kindness from Oliver, apparently. Well, she had endured disappointment before. Kind, loving Duncan had turned violent towards her as soon as life became difficult. Why expect Oliver to be different?

She'd thought nothing could hurt as much as being turned away by her parents. Nothing could make her feel so totally alone, so desolate, but now she realised just how acutely she'd hoped Oliver would not fail her. She'd hoped he'd be that man he'd been for one day and night in Paris.

She should have known he would not. How could he be glad she was carrying his child?

'Heed me, Oliver.' She directed her gaze at him. 'I did not want this to happen any more than you did. I tried to prevent it, but my efforts failed.'

He rubbed his face as he prowled back and forth. 'Are you certain I am the father?'

Cecilia felt her face grow hot. What man would not use this excuse to avoid his duty? 'Yes. You are the baby's father.'

Although, it made sense he would expect her to be with

other men. She'd fallen into bed with him after only a day, had she not?

'Am I to believe you?' he said in an ill-tempered voice. 'One night. Three months ago?'

'I thought this consequence extremely unlikely. I'd never conceived with my husband.' Even when she had not taken precautions. But this time she'd missed her courses and could no longer deny why her stomach felt so unsettled in the morning. 'It took time for me to realise it was true.'

'Did you see a doctor?' he asked as if trying to prove she was lying.

'I did. He confirmed it.' The doctor's examination had been quite unpleasant.

Oliver turned away from her. He faced the fireplace and put a hand on the mantel as if holding back strong emotions. As if his efforts to contain his rage were fraying.

How many times had she witnessed Duncan in such a state?

She should have stayed in Paris, but how could she raise a child there? What work could she do besides what the club manager required of her? Even if she could endure such an occupation, could she bear raising her child in a *maison close*?

Vincent and the other girls at the club told her to visit a physician who would make the problem go away. That idea was worse than becoming a *fille de rue*.

Instead, she'd gone running to her mother. Surely a mother would help her daughter in such a fix. She'd devised a plan. She'd tell her parents the child was Duncan's, pretend he'd been killed three months ago instead of three years. She could preserve her respectability that way. She'd figured it all out, except she had not anticipated her mother would send her away.

Would consider her dead.

Likely Oliver wished she were dead as well.

She fingered the pearl she still wore around her neck. 'You once told me you are wealthy. If you are wealthy, you can support this child you helped create.'

He continued to face the mantel. 'You say you are with child. You say the child is mine. You say you want money for it.'

'Yes.' Although *want* was the wrong word; *need* was more accurate. 'I will be penniless in a few days.'

She touched the pearl again, her only piece of jewellery. What once was a remembrance of a lovely day would have to be sold.

'You say.' He said it in a voice filled with scorn and disbelief.

She knew that tone of voice. Duncan had used that tone of voice. Scorn quickly led to rage.

She'd made the right choice when she'd left Oliver that night in Paris. Their day together had been delightful, their lovemaking glorious, but never would she risk being the recipient of a man's rage ever again.

She'd risk one more try. 'I do not need anything else from you. Merely enough money to support the child. Make an arrangement to provide me the money and I will never plague you again.'

Oliver was whirling with this news, with seeing Cecilia again. She looked so beautiful in a deep green dress that complemented her pale skin and dark hair. Her hair was primly tucked into a bonnet, but he remembered how glorious it had been that night in Paris, cascading over her shoulders in dark silken curls. He remembered how her naked skin had gleamed in the candlelight. How often she'd appeared in his dreams, looking much like that. How often he'd wished to see her again.

Here she was.

With news he never wanted to hear.

A child.

He'd vowed never to bring a bastard child into the world. No child of his would endure the name-calling and rejection he'd lived through. No child of his would be torn between two worlds.

He'd always been so careful, only bedding women who knew the rules of their sensual game, who did not want a baby any more than he did.

He could not think; his emotions were too high.

In his mind he heard the voices of his friends—Frederick, Jacob, Nicholas—cautioning him. Saying to him, *'How do you know it is your child? How do you know there even is a child? Do nothing,'* they'd say, *'until you know whether or not she is lying. You only knew her for a day, after all.'* A day was no time at all.

His father, too, would say to assume a woman lies. Certainly Oliver's stepmother lied at any opportunity, without any qualms. From her, Oliver knew first-hand how duplicitous a woman could be.

Those voices and memories might be crowding his head, but he could not let them matter.

Cecilia was in trouble of some kind. Even if she was lying, her distress was genuine. And he did have the means to help her.

'Do you know something, Oliver?' Cecilia picked up her gloves and cloak from the side table. 'I was mistaken to come here. I do not need anything from you. Forgive me for wasting your time.'

She swept out of the room.

What? First come and ask for money, tell a tale that, unbeknownst to her, was guaranteed to tug at his heartstrings, then run out?

He would not have her disappear again.

'Cecilia! Wait!' He rushed after her.

His butler still attended the hall.

'Where did she go?' Oliver asked.

Irwin lifted his hands. 'Out the door.'

'And you did not stop her?' he growled.

'I was supposed to stop her?' Irwin asked.

'You do not understand, man.' Oliver strode towards the front door. 'I do not know how to find her.'

He opened the door and ran out, sweeping his gaze up and down the street. He did not see her. His house was near the corner, so he hurried to look on Jermyn Street. He could not see her there either. How could she have disappeared so quickly? How was he to find her again? He must.

Because he needed to tell her it did not matter what trouble she was in, he could and would help her. If she were indeed carrying a child, even if that child was not his, he had no wish to make them both destitute, no wish to force her into the terrible choices with which women in her situation were forced to make.

Without a topcoat or hat, he walked in every hotel on Jermyn Street and asked for her, but no one could recall a guest who matched her name and description.

How was he to find her?

He'd mishandled things, become confused by the voices in his head, voices of his friends and his father. But his friends and his father had never met Cecilia, had never spent time with her. He could not believe he had totally misread her character.

He sensed there was much she was not telling him. No wonder he could not instantly believe her, could not immediately decide how to proceed. Besides, his whole life his father had hammered into him to be wary of women, that they would lie and deceive to get their hands on his wealth.

He'd always wanted to ask his father if his mother had

been after his father's wealth. If so, Oliver never saw it. Certainly Oliver's stepmother used his father for his fortune. She relished the heights of society his money and title provided for her—and had always warned Oliver that he would never belong there.

There certainly had been women who were more enamoured of Oliver's money than of Oliver himself, but none had tried to get more out of him than trinkets. None had tried to entrap him with claims they were with child. He'd always supposed the women did not want a bastard half-caste for more than a few passionate nights and some pieces of jewellery, and they certainly did not want the half-caste's child.

Perhaps that was why he'd simply been unprepared for Cecilia and her claim. He'd always believed the women he'd bedded were as eager to prevent a baby as he was.

He'd lost her now, though, so what was he to do?

She thought he'd refused her request. What would she do instead? If she was with child, would she feel forced to give up the baby to the Foundling Hospital? Oliver had visited the Foundling Hospital. He'd donated to it, but, although the hospital did good work raising unwanted children, too many of them died.

The rain had stopped, but the sky was darkening and the air turned even chillier than when he'd dashed out of the town house. Tomorrow he'd go to Bow Street and see about hiring a Runner to track her down. And he'd continue his round of hotels.

Cecilia had hurried into Grenier's Hotel on Jermyn Street, right around the corner from Oliver's town house. Ironic that she should be staying so close to where he lived. The way her luck was transpiring she would encounter him again.

She could not leave it to luck. Tomorrow she would look for somewhere else to live, somewhere cheaper, although how to find such a place, she did not know. She'd only been to London a couple of times when her older sisters were presented at Court.

She pulled off her bonnet and walked to the window overlooking Jermyn Street. Below on the street, Oliver entered the hotel. Her heart pounded. He was pursuing her? Did he see her enter?

Her senses had become finely tuned to other people's moods. Especially men. She'd had to learn to read Duncan or else stumble into something that set him into a rage.

She ran back to her door to make certain it was locked.

Grenier's Hotel catered to French expatriates and she'd registered as a French woman. Coquette Vincent was the name she'd used, although she'd had no good reason to hide her identity. Habit, she supposed. She was glad she had not given her real name. It would make it that much harder for him to find her.

Still, she held her breath when footsteps sounded in the hallway.

They continued past her door.

She hurried back to the window and watched until she saw Oliver leave again, striding down the street away from his house.

Apparently, she was safe.

She walked over to the bed and lay upon it, resting her hand on her abdomen.

'Poor *petit bébé*,' she murmured. 'How am I going to take care of you?'

She refused to say she did not want this baby, now that the baby grew inside her. She knew what it was like to feel unwanted. Her parents had wanted a boy. After two girls,

her older sisters, her parents had been certain the third
child would be a boy.

But Cecilia had been born instead. Her sisters were
never happy they had to share the money for their dowries
or their clothes and such. Her father could not be bothered
with her at all, but when she was a child, she'd thought her
mother cared for her a little.

Until she'd asked to see her mother and father just the
day before and they refused.

Her mother had refused to see her.

She sat up and hugged her knees.

'I'll take care of you, *petit bébé,*' she murmured. 'I'll
never turn you away.'

She needed money. She could still work at something
until her body swelled. She had a few months before that
would occur. She'd survived on her own in Paris and she
would do so here, as well, she vowed.

She could do what she used to do in Paris. All she
needed was a place, a club. She probably did not have
enough time to build an interest in her as Madame Coquette. She and Vincent had worked over the course of a
year to build Madame Coquette's reputation. First by al-
lowing the occasional man a night with her, then gradually
building to more frequent nights as word of her selectiv-
ity spread.

It did not matter, though, because she did not wish to
be Madame Coquette ever again, but she could work in a
club and make the men spend more money there.

Most gentlemen's clubs in London did not allow fe-
males anywhere near their establishments, but she had
heard of a place that was much like the clubs in Paris. On
Jermyn Street, too. She'd met an Englishman at Maison
D'Eros who'd bragged about a club on Jermyn Street that
he intended to own some day. He'd tried to impress her

so she would agree to allow him to have a night with her, but there was something about him she did not trust, so she'd refused.

But she remembered the club and the street it was on. She did not know the number, but how difficult would it be to discover which building was a gaming club?

She rose from the bed, tidied her hair and put on her shoes. She walked down to the clerk of the hotel.

'*Pardon, monsieur.*' She spoke in French. 'I have heard there is a club near here for playing cards where ladies may also play. Do you know where it is?'

'I have heard of it, *madame*,' the man answered. 'It is on this street, they say, but I do not know what house.'

'Are you certain you do not know?' she persisted. 'I will not tell anyone else, if that is what worries you.' Really, how could a man who worked on this street not know this?

'Nothing worries me,' he snapped. 'I know nothing of this club.'

Now he knew nothing of it. Before he knew it was on this street.

'*Merci, monsieur.*' There was no point in pressing him further and making him angry at her.

She would discover the club on her own.

When it turned dark, Cecilia donned her cloak and her half-boots and walked out of the hotel and onto the street.

The pavement was illuminated by the soft glow of gas lamps, an innovation that made this time of night as busy as the day. Pedestrians filled the street, older men with young women on their arms, younger men and their friends, laughing and stumbling from too much drink, women, not unlike herself, unaccompanied, walking with swaying hips and skin exposed. Carriages rumbled by, fine carriages with crests painted on the side and humbler hackney coaches.

It was difficult to discern which of the many houses on the street could be the gaming club for which she searched. She assumed the club would have people coming in and out the door, but people came in and out of several doors.

She walked the street four times and soon received some interested stares from some of the men she passed. Her heart raced. Surely no harm could come to her in such a crowded place?

A man stepped right in front of her. 'How much, doxy?'

She stepped back to get around him and bumped into another man. 'We can pay,' the other man said.

'You are mistaken,' she said in a firm voice. 'I am not game.'

The first man blocked her way. 'I'd say you are as game as they come. What say you, Samuel?'

His companion replied, 'I'd say she ought to give it for free now for causing us trouble.'

She tried to step around, but they would not let her. The first man reached for her.

She jerked back. 'Do not touch me!' she cried in a loud voice. 'Leave me alone and let me pass!'

'Not tonight, doxy.' He seized her arm and she readied her heel to come down hard on his foot.

Suddenly, though, the man was pulled back. Someone had seized his collar and nearly lifted him off the ground.

'Leave her!' a man shouted, shoving her assailant into his friend and knocking them both to the pavement.

Other people stopped to watch.

'Leave,' the man commanded. 'Before you regret it.'

The two scrambled to their feet, pushed their way through the spectators and disappeared down the street.

A woman approached her. 'Are you hurt? They did not hurt you, did they?'

Cecilia wrapped her cloak around her. 'I am not hurt.'

She saw now that her rescuer was a well-dressed gentleman and his lady, a petite young woman with blonde hair and the kindest eyes Cecilia could ever recall.

'Go now,' the gentleman said to the onlookers. 'Nothing to see any more.' He spoke to Cecilia. 'Are you certain you are unharmed?'

Cecilia nodded, though her knees began to shake as the enormity of what could have happened to her struck her.

'You've had a terrible fright,' the lady said. 'Come inside with us and we will get you something to drink.' She turned to the gentleman. 'Won't we, Jake?'

'We certainly will. Come with us.' He walked up to an impressive black-lacquered door and sounded its brass knocker.

A large man opened the door.

'We are back, Snyder,' the gentleman said.

They escorted her inside to a drawing room off a large marble-tiled hall. Cecilia sat in an upholstered chair in front of a warm fireplace.

Almost immediately the blonde lady poured her a glass from a crystal decanter. 'Have some claret.'

The lady sat on a sofa near Cecilia's chair. 'I am Rose,' she said. 'And this is my husband.' She gave him a worshipful look.

He laughed and placed a fond hand on his wife's shoulder. 'You are not yet used to introductions, are you, love?'

'I am perfectly aware of the correct way to do things, but she doesn't need any fancy introductions, Jake,' his wife retorted. 'Not after what she's been through.'

Cecilia looked from one to the other. 'What fancy introductions?'

The gentleman extended his hand. 'Duke of Westmoor.' He inclined his head towards his wife and his voice grew soft. 'And my duchess.'

Cecilia felt her face drain of blood. She'd never before met a duke. 'Your Grace.' She shook his hand. 'I am Mrs Lockhart.' Her real name slipped out instead of her alias in her shock.

The Duke, a handsome man with dark hair and blue eyes, sat next to his wife.

Cecilia glanced around the room, which appeared nothing like she'd expect a duke's house to appear. On the walls were large paintings of naked Roman gods frolicking in lush green gardens. A statue of a nude in a very suggestive pose stood in the corner.

'I know you must wonder why I was out by myself.' Cecilia felt she owed them some explanation. 'I—I am staying in a hotel nearby and I was looking for—for a place I'd heard of.'

'What place?' the Duke asked, looking eager to help.

She took another sip of her claret. 'I was looking for a gentlemen's club. A gaming place.'

The Duke and Duchess exchanged glances.

'I know it sounds scandalous,' she admitted. 'But I am in rather straitened circumstances and I thought perhaps I might find employment there.'

They exchanged glances again.

'Perhaps you have heard of such a place?' she went on. 'I believe its name begins with a V.'

'Vitium et Virtus,' they said in unison.

Her eyes narrowed. 'Perhaps.'

The Duchess laughed. 'You have found it!'

'This is Vitium et Virtus.' The Duke made a gesture that encompassed the whole room. 'It is closed tonight. It is not open every night.'

The Duchess looked sympathetic. 'Tell us about your straitened circumstances.'

'I—I was widowed—my husband was a soldier. He fought at Waterloo.' British people were impressed by Waterloo veterans, even though Duncan's career as a soldier was nothing heroic. 'I was stuck in France for a while, but when I came home, the only relative I counted upon could no longer help me. I am quite alone.' It was all true, but certainly not the whole of her story. 'I've worked at a club before.'

'What did you do at the club?' the Duke asked, with the slightest edge to his voice.

He wanted to know if she was—was what the two men who accosted her thought she was.

'I worked as a hostess,' she said. 'I flirted with the men, eased their time at the club, brought them drinks and food, made them comfortable, urged them to spend more money. The more important the man, the more attention he received. I never sold my favours, though. Never.'

Explaining Madame Coquette would be too difficult and who would believe it?

'A hostess?' The Duke looked thoughtful. 'We've never had a hostess. What do you think, Rose?'

What did he mean *we've* never had a hostess?

His wife smiled, making her look even lovelier. 'I think it sounds like an excellent idea. And it will help Mrs Lockhart.'

The Duke extended his hand once more. 'You are hired, *madame*. We are closed tonight, as you can see, but you may start tomorrow. We have a gambling and entertainment night tomorrow.'

'She should come before then to meet everyone?' His wife turned to her. 'Come around six in the evening. Six would be good, would it not, Jake? We will introduce you to everyone.'

Cecilia shook her head in confusion. 'I am perplexed. Why does a duke hire a hostess for a gentlemen's club?'

The Duke smiled. 'I am part-owner. It is a long story and we do not have time right now. Our carriage is waiting. Tomorrow? Come at six.'

'We cannot allow her to walk back to her hotel alone,' the Duchess protested.

'Indeed we cannot.' The Duke stood and faced Cecilia. 'You must ride in the carriage with us.'

So Cecilia rode back the short distance to Grenier's Hotel in a duke's carriage.

But she had a job and a chance to work out what to do next.

When she lay in her bed a little while later, sleep eluding her, she pressed her hand to her abdomen. 'We'll survive, *petit bébé*. We will survive.'

Chapter Seven

~~~~

The next evening Oliver walked through the public rooms of Vitium et Virtus, checking on the preparations. The game room was set up with several tables for cards, a hazard table and a faro table. It was important to Oliver that the atmosphere be elegant, tasteful, even if unapologetically bawdy in its painted ceiling, a bacchanalian scene they'd commissioned from an Italian artist.

Oliver continued on to the ballroom, which was set up with a stage at one end. There would be musicians in one of the balconies and the songstresses would appear on the stage.

In his youth, Oliver enjoyed the naughty songs sung at the club. The singing had been one of his favourites of the club's offerings. He'd even joined the women, lending his voice to theirs.

She's Tall and Slender,
She's Soft and Tender,
Some God commend her,
My Wit's too low:
'Twere Joyful plunder,
To bring her under,

She's all a wonder,
From Top to Toe.

But now it seemed rather juvenile. Some of the songs were extremely graphic and those were the ones their members liked the most. Some of the club's employees liked to sing them, too. The women used the songs to entice willing gentlemen to spend more money on them. The women poured compliments in the men's ears, making them think it was their manliness that attracted and not their money.

What would happen if Oliver arranged for *Don Giovanni* to be performed here one night? Something beautiful rather than bawdy.

He suspected it would not do well.

Snyder, the porter, came to the door. 'The new woman is here, Mr Gregory.'

'New woman?' He knew nothing of this.

'His Grace hired her last night,' Snyder said. 'Told her to come at six.'

'Hired her? Where is Jacob? Is he here?' Oliver asked. If so, he'd like to speak to him and ask what the devil was she hired for?

'No, sir,' Snyder said.

'Well, where is Mr Bell? Have Mr Bell deal with her.' Mr Bell was, by title, the club's butler, yet in practice more of a manager. He and Mrs Parker, the housekeeper, saw to most of the mundane details of running the club.

'Mr Bell is delayed,' the porter said. 'And Mrs Bell is on an errand.'

'Zounds, is no one else here?' Oliver did not hire the staff.

'You are here, sir,' Snyder said. 'What should I do with the new woman, then?'

He blew out a breath. 'I'll see her, I suppose. Where is she?'

'I put her in the drawing room.' He bowed. 'Must get back to the door, sir.'

Oliver waited a moment to collect himself. If Jacob had hired the woman, then Oliver supposed he'd go along with it, whatever 'it' was, but they usually discussed these matters first.

He left the ballroom and descended the stairs. He crossed the hall, passing Snyder who again stood at his place by the club's entrance. The drawing room was directly off the hall.

Oliver opened its door.

The woman stood with her back to him, staring at one of the paintings, the one where satyrs cavorted with scantily clad nymphs.

He cleared his throat. 'Mrs Lockhart?'

She turned to him and it was as if he'd been punched in the chest.

'Cecilia!'

'Oliver?' Her voice rose an octave.

She wore the same green dress she'd worn the day before, the one that made her skin glow and her whisky-coloured eyes gleam. He wanted to tell her how glad he was to see her here, how he'd searched for her, both the day before and earlier this day, how he'd hired a Bow Street Runner to help find her.

But what was she doing here?

'I expected the Duke and Duchess.' She sounded affronted.

She knew Jacob and Rose? She'd told him she knew nobody. 'How do you know the Duke and Duchess?'

She lifted her chin. 'I met them by happenstance last night.' She took a nervous breath. 'I will tell you, but I hope you honour me with an explanation of your own. I was looking for this club—to ask for work—and I happened upon the Duke and Duchess who agreed to hire me.'

He stared at her, certain she was leaving something out. 'Hire you for what?'

They had their singers and dancers and their maids. Vitium et Virtus needed no more workers. What could Cecilia do? Especially carrying a child.

'To be a hostess.'

'A hostess? What the devil does a hostess do?'

She sighed as if she found explaining this role tedious. 'It will be my job to make the wealthiest of your members as comfortable as possible, to fuss over them, flatter them, bring them drinks, make certain they spend a great deal of money. I should be able to do this for several months until my condition is too evident.' She paused. 'I did this work in Paris.'

'You worked in a club in Paris?' The clubs in Paris he'd visited were gambling dens and brothels. She'd worked in one? That was a great deal to conceal from him.

'That is why I was by the Seine at dawn. I had just left the club.' She spoke as if he ought to have known that. 'You will next want to ask if I slept with the patrons. I did not.'

He'd thought that would go without saying. Not one of the entertainment staff they employed at Vitium et Virtus had refrained from willingly sharing some gentleman's bed.

'You expect me to believe that?' he shot back.

She held his gaze. 'It is the truth. A hostess is not a courtesan.'

What need did Vitium et Virtus have for a hostess? 'Did the Duke explain the nature of our club?'

She glanced around the room. 'I can imagine.'

'No, you cannot,' he insisted. 'We are not a brothel, but

we are a place where men and women can be as free as they desire to seek pleasure in all manner of ways. We take no money from the private arrangements men and women make, even if the women are some of our entertainment staff. We do not allow that licence for the maids, footmen and other kitchen workers. For their protection. They are too vulnerable to being misused.'

'Which would I be, then?' she asked, still sounding defiantly wary.

'You would not be a servant.' He could never see her as a servant.

'So I would be expected to sleep with the members?' Her eyes flashed.

He gritted his teeth. 'You are free to decide for yourself.'

She nodded, as if satisfied.

His anger rose. 'You say you are with child, but you are contemplating—'

She held up a hand. 'I will not sleep with your patrons or with anybody. And after you, I shared no man's bed.'

How could he believe this?

'Now it is your turn for explanations.' She crossed her arms over her chest. 'Why are you running this place?'

'I am part-owner,' he retorted. 'With the Duke and—with two more friends.' Because Nicholas was still part-owner. He stopped himself. 'Wait, Cecilia. We have unfinished business about this baby.'

'I am thinking of the baby,' she countered. 'That is why I need work.'

'You do not need work. I have money to help you. If there is indeed a baby, I will provide for the child.'

Her eyes narrowed. 'What do you mean "if there is indeed a baby"?'

He shrugged. 'I have only your word for it.'

Her eyes flashed. 'And I have only your word that you

will provide for my baby. Your baby! Do not prevent me from working, Oliver. I need this job.'

The desperation in her voice was very clear. It tugged at him.

He softened his voice. 'I won't prevent you from working.' He rubbed his face and changed the subject. 'How did you learn of this place?' he asked. Vitium et Virtus was exclusive and secret.

She took a breath before answering. 'I met a gentleman in Paris who told me of it.'

Oliver's heart pounded. Could she have encountered Nicholas? He took an eager step towards her. 'Who was this gentleman?'

She stepped back. 'Sir Nash Bowles.'

'Bowles!' He spat out the name.

Just when he thought this could not get worse. Sir Nash Bowles. The man who'd nearly ruined Frederick's Georgiana. Bowles always had been a nasty character, even at school.

'How do you know Bowles?' Oliver demanded.

She cast him a wary look. 'I do not know him. He came to the club in Paris. I saw him one time. Why?'

Oliver frowned. 'He is not a good man to know.'

'Then I am glad not to know him.' She glanced towards the door. 'May I see where I will work? Unless you have changed your mind about my employment.'

'I have not changed my mind.' Oliver was a man of his word.

She lifted her chin again. 'I will work only for tips if you do not wish to pay me.'

She was starting to irritate him again. 'Of course we will pay you.'

They paid all their people generously. They could afford to do so. Cecilia would be well compensated.

She looked down at her dress. 'I am not dressed for an exclusive gentlemen's club. Do you provide clothes for me to wear?'

'Yes.' He extended his hand. 'Come. I will show you the club.'

Cecilia flinched when he touched her arm to guide her from the room. He released her, which was good. Even though he was obviously not happy to see her or hear of her condition, he still possessed an allure that made her susceptible to him.

As they approached the stairs, he asked, 'Where are you staying?'

She became wary again. 'Why do you need to know this?'

He blew out a breath. 'Only to inform you that our employees are not allowed to entertain in the house when the club is not open. We are not open every night.'

'I will entertain no one.' How many times must she say so?

They climbed the grand staircase.

He spoke in the tones of a displeased tutor. 'Our club is a secret one. Every member is anonymous, so to attend the club each member must wear a mask. Masks do not always perfectly disguise the wearer, of course. Most members know who is behind a mask, but they are honour bound never to disclose who attends. If you learn the identity of a member, you must swear never to disclose who they are.'

She lifted her hand. 'I swear.'

Masks seemed a bit childish to her. But the British were much more concerned about what other people thought of them than the French had been.

'Do I wear a mask?' she asked.

'Yes,' he said curtly. 'But the masks worn by the female workers are more decorative than disguising.'

He brought her to what looked like a ballroom with sofas and divans arranged for an audience. Like the drawing room she'd just left, the ballroom was decorated with paintings of nude gods cavorting in idyllic gardens. The fireplace mantel was a clever sculpture of two couples engaged in copulation.

'Tonight we will have a concert.' Oliver gestured to a raised platform at one end of the room. 'Our singers will perform before mingling with our guests. I warn you the songs will be bawdy.'

Bawdy songs did not distress her. She'd followed the drum, after all. Soldiers rarely sang hymns.

'We always have gambling,' he went on. 'I'll show you that room. Other nights we feature tableaux.'

'Tableaux?' This was something new to her.

'Our ladies pose—let us say that it is our version of Lady Hamilton's attitudes minus the veils and scarves.'

He meant they posed nude.

'Our ladies dance, as well,' he went on. 'As I said before, the singers and dancers are free to accept arrangements with our male patrons. We also do not interfere with the private decisions of our members who wish to be private with each other.'

She bristled. 'Why do you keep saying this to me? Is this expected of me or not?'

He turned to her and grasped her arm. 'It is not. But you must know how matters exist here. We believe everyone should be free to decide for themselves.'

She averted her gaze. 'That is good, because I decide for myself what I will and will not do.'

His lips thinned. 'As you decided with me?'

Her body flushed with the memory. She pretended to

ignore his question, but the moment seemed to make the air crackle between them.

They continued through the club's elegantly appointed dining room, featuring small tables for intimate repasts. He brought her up another flight of stairs to show her the private rooms, each decorated to fulfil some erotic fancy. One, all red and gold, reminded her of the room in Maison D'Eros. Another looked like it belonged in an Arabian harem. A third was as dark as a dungeon.

Next he took her below stairs to meet the cook, the kitchen servants and the footmen who served the food and drink.

She watched the other workers carefully as Oliver greeted them and they spoke to him. They seemed pleased and comfortable with him and he with them. That was good.

She'd been shocked to see him in the club, to discover he, of all people, was one of the owners. Now she must face him every day she would work, when she'd already decided it was not safe to see him ever again. It made it worse to see him through the admiring eyes of others, to have her body flare in response when he touched her.

But she would endure this. She had a job. She'd earn money. And he said he'd give her more.

She and her baby were safe for now.

He stopped in front of a closed door and knocked.

'We call this the Green Room,' he said. 'It is the dressing room for the singers and dancers and other female workers.'

'Come in,' a female voice said.

He opened the door.

The room was lined with mirrors and there were clothes' presses and rails filled with costumes. Seated in a chair facing one of the mirrors sat a pretty young woman dressed in her shift and a wrapper that was off her shoulders.

She smiled and pulled up her wrapper when she saw Oliver. ''Ello, Mr Gregory.' Her accent was like others Cecilia had heard among ordinary London folk.

'How are you, Fleurette?' he responded.

'Well enough, sir,' she answered brightly. Her gaze turned to Cecilia.

'Let me introduce you.' He looked questioningly at Cecilia. 'How do you wish to be known?'

Fleurette laughed. 'We're none of us using our given names.'

Cecilia gave the name that was foremost in her mind. 'Coquette. You can call me Coquette.' She extended her hand to the girl. 'I am happy to meet you, Fleurette.'

The girl laughed again. 'Fleurette. Coquette. It rhymes.' She accepted the handshake. 'But you can call me Flo. Everyone does.'

'You are getting dressed early,' Oliver remarked.

'Aw, I'm not gettin' dressed yet. I—I bruised my arm on—on a door and I'm trying to cover it up.' She put her hand over her arm, which was already covered by the wrapper.

'Nothing serious?' he asked in a concerned voice.

'Naw. A bruise isn't serious.'

Oliver turned to Cecilia. For a moment his eyes were as warm as when he looked upon Flo, but they quickly turned flinty. She remembered how his eyes had glowed when he'd gazed upon her naked skin. 'I will leave you in Flo's care, then.'

'As you wish,' Cecilia managed.

He spoke to Fleurette—Flo—again. 'She needs a dress to wear tonight. Can you find her one?'

'I can do that,' the girl answered amiably.

'And tell her how things go here?' he went on.

'I can really do that.' She smiled.

He nodded. 'I will leave you to Flo, then…Coquette. But I wish to see you before the club opens. Flo can help you find me.'

'Very well.' She was somehow reluctant to let him go, which was absurd.

At that moment, the door burst open and the Duke and Duchess of Westmoor rushed in.

Flo jumped to her feet. 'Rose!'

'Flo.' The Duchess gave the girl a fond hug. She glanced over at Cecilia. 'I am so sorry we are late.'

'Estate business.' The Duke groaned. 'We got away as soon as we could.'

The Duchess smiled. 'I see Oliver has taken care of you.'

Cecilia curtsied. 'Your Grace.'

Rose released Flo and clasped Cecilia's hand. 'Please do not be so formal with me. Not here, anyway. I am Rose.'

'Rose was one of us, in a manner of speaking.' Flo grinned at the Duchess. 'Before she got so grand.'

Oliver glowered during this display. He turned to the Duke. 'May I have a word with you, Jake?'

'Certainly!' the Duke said jovially. 'Shall I leave you here, Rose?'

'Oh, please do!' She laughed. 'Perhaps some of the costumes need mending!'

This whole exchange meant nothing to Cecilia. A duchess who was not always so grand? Who was one of the hirelings? Who mended costumes?

Oliver left Cecilia without even a nod of goodbye, which only fuelled her wariness of him. Perhaps he would not help her. Perhaps he would turn on her eventually.

'We're to find Coquette a dress for tonight,' Flo told the Duchess.

'Oh, yes.' The Duchess smiled at Cecilia. 'Come, Coquette. Let us look through the costumes and see what might do for you.'

They found her a dress, a lovely indigo confection, which she would don later.

That task complete, the Duchess bade them goodbye. 'I want to say hello to Mrs Parker and cook and the others.' She gave Flo another hug before leaving the room.

'Rose worked as a maid here at the club and then she became companion to the Duke's grandmother,' Flo told her.

She went on to embellish the story with all sorts of drama and romance, ending with a big, envious sigh.

'It is almost time for dinner,' Flo said. 'We eat in the servants' hall.' Her face tensed. 'I—I am going to tend to my bruise, but you can join them now. No need to wait for me.'

Cecilia did not relish walking into a room of other workers alone, even if the Duchess might be there. 'Perhaps I can help you cover the bruises. What are you using for it?'

Flo hesitated before answering. 'Pear's Almond Bloom.' She handed the pot to Cecilia.

Pear's Almond Bloom was a tinted face paint that was supposed to give the face a natural look. Cecilia had used it before.

'Let us try it, then,' Cecilia said.

Flo hesitated again before slipping off her wrapper.

There was not one bruise, but four, all round in shape and reddish-blue in colour. The bruises were on Flo's upper arm. Cecilia's hands trembled. She had seen bruises like this before, in this same pattern. She'd seen them on her own arms.

'Did—did you get the bruises here?' Cecilia asked, trying to sound casual. She opened the pot of Pear's Almond

Bloom and put a little on her finger. She gently dabbed it on one of the bruises.

'No,' Flo answered. 'I was out.'

So someone outside the club had inflicted them?

Confronting Flo so soon after first meeting her would be a mistake. If someone had cared enough to ask Cecilia how she got her bruises, she would have lied. If they'd asked her if her husband had inflicted them, she would have denied it. He'd have killed her if she ever told.

Cecilia vowed she'd find out who did this to Flo, though. She'd bide her time. Look for a safe moment to ask the girl who had held her with a grip so tight it caused bruises.

'Do you have any white powder?' Cecilia asked.

Cecilia had become quite experienced at hiding bruises.

Flo took a powder box and powder puff from a drawer in a nearby dressing table. Cecilia dabbed the powder lightly over the Almond Bloom, then dabbed on some more Bloom followed by more powder until the bruises faded from sight.

'Coquette!' Flo exclaimed. 'You made them disappear! How did you learn to do that?'

'I worked in a club before,' she said, which was no explanation at all.

Flo put on her wrapper and tied it with a sash. 'Let us go to dinner, then,' she said.

Chapter Eight

If they had been anywhere else, a dinner table full of diners would be scandalised by a pretty young woman coming to eat in her wrapper and shift like Flo did. Not in a club such as this. Or in the one in Paris.

Just as outrageous, the Duchess sat at the table with these lowly folk. She did not eat, but did introduce Cecilia to the large group of servants and entertainers. Cecilia could not remember all their names. She made a point of learning the names of Mrs Parker, the housekeeper, and Mr Bell, the butler, who would be present throughout the night, and Snyder, the large man who guarded the door.

After dinner, Cecilia, Flo, and the other girls who would perform that evening donned their costumes, each of which had a mask to match. Cecilia's mask was a lacy gold concoction with paste jewels resembling blue sapphires outlining the eyeholes. As Oliver said, it did not totally disguise her face. Most of the girls wore similar masks that showed more of their faces than they concealed. So the gentlemen members could see how pretty they were, Cecilia supposed.

After she was dressed, Cecilia walked upstairs to report to Oliver as he had requested. She found him in the ballroom standing with another gentleman. They wore black-silk masks, but it took just a glance for her to recognise Oliver. And a second one to see the other man was the Duke. Oliver watched her approach. He, of course, recognised her.

The Duke turned when she came near and smiled. 'Look at you!'

She met Oliver's gaze, made even more intense by the black mask framing his eyes. 'Will this costume do?'

'I think you look lovely,' the Duke said.

Oliver glanced away.

He really did not want her here.

Suddenly he spoke to her. 'Explain how this works. You encourage members to spend more money? There are not many ways this might be done. You might encourage them to play more games of hazard and faro, but that is the extent of it.'

'I will concentrate on the game room, then.' It might be difficult to prove her worth if these were the only ways she could increase revenue. 'I can always challenge them to make larger bets or to linger at the tables a bit longer than they otherwise might have done. I can bring them drinks, so they do not have to take their attention from the games.'

This club was not like Maison D'Eros, where attendance could be gained by paying the price for entrance and where guests were charged for drinks and food and for the privilege of sitting down to a game of cards.

'Have you met everyone?' Oliver asked.

'I believe so,' she responded. 'At dinner.'

The Duke interrupted. 'I beg your pardon. I must bid you goodnight. Rose and I are expected at the theatre tonight.' He took Cecilia's hand. 'I hope this night goes well for you. Welcome to Vitium et Virtus.' He turned to Oliver. 'We seem to be leaving everything to you.'

Oliver's expression softened. 'Go. Enjoy your evening with your wife.'

Cecilia still had difficulty believing that this Duke had actually married a maid.

'The Duchess is below stairs in the servants' hall,' Cecilia told the Duke.

The Duke grinned. 'So I expected.' He seemed besotted with his duchess and she with him.

Cecilia remembered when she had been besotted with Duncan. Before he used his fist on her. She could even admit she'd spent a day besotted by Oliver, but now...

She and Oliver were left standing alone together and she was acutely aware that he might have the power to dismiss her, no matter what his partner, the Duke, might say. She must make herself seem malleable to his desires—at least as far as her duties on the job required.

He turned to her and the softness in his eyes when speaking to the Duke disappeared, replaced by the hard stare that made her feel him a powder keg that was about to explode.

'Shall I place myself in the game room, then?' she asked.

He nodded.

She was about to turn away when he stopped her. 'Are you certain you wish to do this?' His voice seemed earnest. 'Our members will certainly proposition you.'

She forced herself to look into his eyes and hoped she would not weaken in front of him. 'It will not be much different from Paris. I know what to do.'

She would endure the propositions, the lewd remarks, the groping hands, just as she had in Paris.

'Let one of us know—Mr Bell, Snyder, me—if any member becomes too un-gentleman-like.'

She could not read his expression. Did he think this likely? Would he blame her if it happened?

'If there is something I cannot handle myself, I will alert one of you,' she responded.

She turned and walked away from him, feeling his gaze on her back as she did so.

When she entered the game room, her spirits sank. She'd forgotten how much she detested the flirting and flattering. She'd thought she'd left that all behind in Paris. She thought she could return home again.

She shook herself. She must never allow herself to think of home again.

They—her family—must be as dead to her as she was to them.

She lifted her chin and strode into the room, approaching the croupiers who ran the hazard and faro tables, as well as the footmen in attendance in the room, reminding them of what she would be doing there.

At Maison D'Eros there had always been jealousy and competition among the workers, especially between the women who entertained the men. Someone was always feuding with someone else. Vincent taught her to ignore it and simply serve the patrons. She had only been at Vitium et Virtus a few hours, but, so far, everyone seemed amiable and content. At dinner they'd all insisted to her that they were well paid and well looked after by Oliver, the Duke and the third man whom she had not yet met. They all helped each other, too, they'd said.

Each and every worker in the game room offered that very thing. To help her.

It touched her.

The footman in attendance told her, 'If anyone gets out of hand, you signal me. The owners do not allow any tomfoolery.'

It was more reassurance.

'Would you steer me to the wealthier members? Or the more important ones? I will ensure they enjoy losing all the coins in their purses.'

The footman laughed. 'I will indeed.' He called out to the croupiers. 'Let us help Coquette find the wealthy and important fellows.'

The two young women at the faro and hazard tables shouted back their agreement. They were an attraction to the tables themselves, with their pretty faces and low-cut necklines that were almost low enough to cover no part of the breast at all, especially when they leaned over. Which they certainly needed to do in the performance of their jobs.

Cecilia had been fortunate to find this place, lucky to have been hired by the kind Duke and Duchess. Her situation could have been so much worse. Perhaps she could relax a bit.

At that moment voices sounded outside the room and men in masks walked in. Cecilia laughed at herself for thinking about relaxation. She took a breath, straightened her spine, planted a smile on her face and became Madame Coquette.

She strode towards the doorway. 'Greetings, gentlemen,' she welcomed. 'I am Coquette, your new hostess, here to see to your pleasure.'

Oliver did not visit the game room right away, although all his impulses propelled him in that direction. With difficulty he resisted, remaining in the ballroom, mixing instead with the members and guests seeking drinks of whisky and brandy poured one after the other by the butler.

After an hour he could wait no longer. He wandered over to the game room and looked in, his gaze riveted on the young woman dressed in deep blue with her sensuous walk and throaty laugh.

Cecilia.

Several men surrounded her at the hazard table while the croupier gathered their markers or doled out their winnings. She cried aloud for the dice to roll the winning numbers and moaned when they did not. It looked to Oliver as if the entire game was played to attempt to please her. Her gaze drifted from the game and she caught him watching her. Her smile faltered a moment before she returned to the dice.

She had transformed herself into a woman he did not recognise. Openly flirtatious, lively and overtly sensuous, as if she had turned herself into her opposite. Which one was genuine? He could not tell.

One of the footmen came to the doorway. 'The concert begins shortly,' he announced.

Oliver followed him out of the room and back to the ballroom. As one of the owners, he would introduce the singers. The orchestra, seated on a balcony overlooking the room, tuned their instruments while the members filed into the room and found seats on the sofas and divans arranged for their viewing pleasure. Many of the members had already linked themselves to a woman, whether they were those employed at Vitium et Virtus who were not performing this night, or other female guests.

Oliver waited until everyone was settled, then he climbed onto the stage. 'Ladies and Gentlemen!' he shouted over the din of conversation. 'Ladies and Gentlemen! The Vitium et Virtus singers!'

Three young ladies stepped forward, Fleurette in the middle. They immediately burst into a pretty but bawdy song sung in Shakespeare's time.

That was a maid this other day
And she must needs go forth to play.
And as she walked, she sighed and said,
'I am afraid to die a maid.'

When the four friends had been at Oxford, they'd made
a study of bawdy songs. Elizabethan times were particularly fruitful in this endeavour and, truthfully, Oliver had
learned a great deal about that era as he searched.

The ladies continued.

He took this maiden then aside
And led her where she was not spied
And told her many a pretty tale,
And gave her well of Watkins ale.

Oliver glanced over to the doorway of the ballroom
and saw Cecilia standing there, listening to the concert,
the ghost of a smile on her face. She looked more herself
than at any other moment since she'd reappeared to him.
Or, at least, she looked more like the woman she had been
in Paris. His skin warmed at the sight of her relaxed, enjoying the moment, even if she hovered by the doorway
as though she did not belong inside.

He walked over to her and she immediately stiffened.

'The game room is almost empty,' she said defensively.
'I only wished to listen for a minute.'

The Parisian Cecilia had disappeared again. He still did
not know which Cecilia was the real one.

'You are free to go wherever you like in the club,' he
told her. 'I came over to ask what you think of the entertainment.'

She glanced back to the stage. 'Their voices are lovely.
They blend so well. And the song is very pretty.' She

looked at him with a hint of amusement in her eyes. 'Not too shocking.'

He smiled. 'Take care. They are only getting started.'

The singers were skilled at connecting with their audience, so that they made each person feel as if they sang for them. The members loved it. Oliver had attended musicales at his father's house, usually with singers hired from the Royal Opera. Though he appreciated the beauty of their music, it lacked this personal touch.

Sometimes, though, when he listened to music, there drifted in a memory of different rhythms, ones that repeated over and over. Different instruments, making different sounds. Different voices singing words he could no longer make out. Music that touched sympathetic chords deep within him.

He had not thought of India, not with this nostalgia, not since he'd been in Paris. Not since right before he'd first seen Cecilia.

He darted a glance to her. She quickly averted her gaze as if she'd been looking at him. He felt his mood mirrored in the expression on her face, the expression of one who'd lost a great deal of what had been most dear.

Cecilia watched the change in him, saw the moment the sadness enveloped him and felt it resonate within her. Why should she feel this so acutely? Why should this moment bring on his sadness? She did not want to be curious about him, to wonder what had come over him, to wonder what had sparked it. The music? The music was gay, pretty and clever in its use of double entendre. It made no sense that it should depress his spirits.

She forced herself to attend to the singers on stage. Of the three, Flo stood out. It was she to whom one's eye was drawn. Flo was so pretty, so lively. If there was a man hurting her, how long would it take before she'd shrink and cower from everything and everyone?

The singers began a new song, this one sung in the Scot's tongue of Robert Burns.

Come rede me, dame, come tell me, dame,
My dame come tell me truly,
What length o' graith, when weel ca'd hame, Will
sair a woman duly?
The carlin clew her wanton tail,
Her wanton tail sae ready
I learn'd a sang in Annandale,
Nine inch will please a lady.

Cecilia laughed at the last line of the stanza.

Oliver must have heard her, because he emerged from his black cloud to stare at her.

Her guard flew up. Did he object to her finding that funny? Well, she'd told him she'd worked in a club—a brothel, really. Surely he did not expect her to be maidenly. She could never be maidenly again.

At least his sadness evaporated. She could sense it inside herself.

Once Cecilia had learned to be attuned to her husband's moods. That had been a matter of self-preservation. But she could not recall ever *feeling* his moods the way she felt Oliver's.

She mustn't let this draw herself to Oliver, as she had been drawn to him in Paris. She hoped he would make good on his promise to support her and the baby, but she would not even allow herself to count on that. She'd seen his mood change when she told him about her condition; she'd seen his disbelief, his blaming her.

She placed her hand on the doorjamb. Gracious, she

was tired. She could not remember being this weary since marching with Duncan from Belgium to France after Waterloo. In some ways this fatigue was even more pervasive than that.

The club stayed open until two in the morning. She still had two hours to go.

'Are you feeling unwell?' Oliver asked.

He startled her. 'I am merely fatigued.' It would not do for him to think she could not perform her job. She pushed herself away from the doorjamb.

She must have moved too quickly, because a wave of dizziness washed over her. She groped for the doorframe again.

And felt his arms encircle her. 'You are unwell. Come.'

He led her through another room to a door that led to what looked like a completely different place. He brought her to a drawing room and sat her in a chair.

She leaned forward. 'I am so dizzy.'

'Did you eat?' he asked, removing her mask and placing it on a nearby table.

'Yes. With the other staff. I ate.' Although some of the food made her stomach queasy.

'Have you had anything to drink?' He pulled off his mask.

She'd brought many a drink to the gentlemen in the game room, but had no more than a few sips for herself. 'Not since dinner.'

'Wait here.' He left the room.

Cecilia held her head in her hands and prayed the room would stop spinning.

Oliver returned with a tray holding a teapot, cup, sugar and milk. He set it down and poured her a cup, adding milk and sugar.

She took the cup from his hand and sipped it slowly, hoping to keep it down.

She'd heard that women who were going to have babies often felt sick in the morning, but this was the first wave of true nausea and dizziness she'd experienced. And, of all inconvenient things, she had to experience it in front of Oliver.

'Feeling better?' he asked.

She did not feel better, but she smiled and replied, 'Oh, yes. I am quite certain I can return to work.' In a few minutes. She hoped.

'No,' he said emphatically. 'No more work for you for tonight. As soon as you are able to walk, I will see you back to your hotel.'

'Truly, I will be well enough to work.' She tried to stand, but sat down again when the room started spinning.

'See? You are not ready yet.' His voice turned low and soft.

Through the walls they could hear the orchestra. Flo's clear, bell-like voice came through as well.

I'll go no more a roving, with you fair maid.
A roving, A roving, since roving's been my ru-i-in,
I'll go no more a roving, with you fair maid.

She remembered her day of roving with Oliver, how perfect he'd been. Would that day, though, be her ruin? She needed this job. She must not appear weak.

'I am able to work.' She stood again and walked to the door, but could not make it without holding on to the furniture.

He came to her side. 'Stop this nonsense,' he said sharply.

Warning bells sounded inside her.

'You will not work the rest of this night,' he said firmly. 'I'll walk you back to your hotel. Now.'

Her anxiety rose. 'Are you discharging me? I can do the work, Oliver. Believe me, I can do it. Let me return.'

'I am not discharging you,' he said. 'But you are not working any more tonight. If you feel well enough tomorrow come back and I will give you the club schedule.'

'You are not discharging me?'

'No,' he said, his voice lower.

She would have another chance. 'I need to change my clothes.'

'No, you do not. Bring the dress back tomorrow.' He placed her in another chair. 'Where is your hotel? Do I need to summon a coach?'

She shook her head. 'Grenier's. Nearby.'

He gave her a puzzled look. 'I asked for you at the Grenier. They did not know you.'

'I gave them another name, Coquette Vincent.' She switched to French. *'Visite de Paris, France.'*

He did not ask her why. Instead, he said, 'Sit here until I can have Snyder collect your cloak.' He poured her another cup of tea.

She tried sipping it again, but the nausea was worse. All she really wanted was to sleep for a week or more.

He returned, wearing a topcoat and carrying her cloak. He helped her rise from the chair and wrapped her in the cloak. He put an arm around her and supported her while she walked.

They left Vitium et Virtus by a private door that led to the garden. Her dizziness seemed to worsen with each step. Suddenly everything went black. For a moment she could hear the coaches and horses in the street, the music from the club.

Then even the sounds stopped.

Chapter Nine

⁓⁓⁓

Cecilia woke in a strange room dimly lit by daylight peeking through curtained windows. She was in a bed, so comfortable she almost did not care that she had no idea where she was. She forced herself to sit up and look around.

She wore her shift and corset, and was still in her stockings. Her hair was loosened from its pins.

The room was not large, but cheerful with brightly coloured birds painted on vivid blue wallpaper. The chairs and bedcovers were a rich red and the mahogany furniture was accented in gold. She'd never seen a room quite like it.

Where was she?

Still feeling shaky and weak, she climbed out of the comfortable bed and found her slippers nearby. A man's banyan was draped over a chair. The dress she had worn at Vitium et Virtus was folded neatly on a chest.

She donned the banyan and tied it with a sash. There was plenty of fabric to cover her. The garment even reached the floor. Her hairpins were in a dish on a dressing table next to a brush and comb. She smoothed her hair back with the brush, twisted it into a chignon, and secured it with the hairpins.

The room had three doors. One revealed a dressing room, another a cosy sitting room. She walked to the last door and opened it to a hallway across from which was another door, presumably another bedchamber. The stairway was in between.

She paused in her doorway, trying to remember what happened. She remembered becoming dizzy at Vitium et Virtus. She remembered Oliver taking her to some private rooms in the club and insisting she go back to the hotel. She remembered him walking with her. After that, what?

Waking to him carrying her. Taking her inside a house and calling for someone to help him. Being undressed and tucked into that glorious bed.

She started down the stairway. Reaching the landing on the first floor, she could see to the hall below.

A manservant stood there, but looked up at her approach. 'Mrs Lockhart.' His greeting was cordial.

She remembered him. 'I am in Mr Gregory's house?' He'd answered the door the day before.

'That you are, ma'am,' the servant said. 'Mr Gregory asks that you join him for breakfast. I will show you the way.'

The man did not seem to take notice of her unusual dress. He led her out of the hall as if nothing was amiss.

He brought her to a small dining room and announced her presence. 'Mrs Lockhart.' Then left her there.

Oliver, the only person seated in the room, rose.

'Cecilia. You are awake.' His greeting was curt, a mere acknowledgement that she was present.

He walked around the table and guided her to the chair adjacent to his. 'Sit. I will fix you a plate.'

At the mention of food her nausea returned. 'Is—is there toasted bread? Please. That is all I want.'

He turned to the sideboard, which seemed to have a variety of foodstuffs, some emitting smells that were making her stomach roil. He placed a plate with two pieces of toasted bread on it in front of her.

'Butter or jam?' he asked.

'Nothing,' she said too sharply. 'Nothing,' she repeated in a more grateful tone.

He lifted a teapot. 'Tea?'

She nodded.

'Why—why am I here?' she asked him.

He poured her tea and placed the sugar and milk within her reach. 'You don't remember?'

'Only a little.'

He returned to his chair. 'I was walking you to your hotel when you fainted. It seemed wiser to bring you here than carry you to the hotel.'

She took a nibble of the toast and hoped it kept her from vomiting. 'I am not by habit so weak.'

He attended to his food. 'My housekeeper assures me that your symptoms are not unusual for a woman who is with child, but, just in case, I have sent for a doctor.'

'A doctor!' She did not wish to endure another examination. 'I—I am certain I am quite recovered. I do not need a doctor.'

'If you faint in front of me and barely regain your wits, I will consult a doctor.' He spoke in that firm, no-nonsense tone that put her guard up.

She was not about to argue the point and risk making him angrier.

Cecilia took another bite of her toast and chewed it carefully. 'So I am not allowed to leave until this doctor arrives?'

'Not allowed?' He looked surprised. 'You are not a prisoner, Cecilia. But the doctor has already been summoned. When he arrives, I want you to be examined by him.'

She nodded, but she did not like this turn of events. He spoke of freedom, then dictated what he wanted her to do.

They finished the breakfast in near silence. Cecilia concentrated on eating slowly and taking small sips of tea. Oliver read a newspaper.

Before they were finished, the butler announced the doctor's arrival.

She met the man in the drawing room. Oliver came with her and introduced himself and Cecilia to the doctor.

'Dr Ebersham,' the man said, shaking first Cecilia's, then Oliver's hand. If he thought it untoward that a single man asked him to examine an unrelated widow, dressed in a man's banyan, the doctor did not let on. 'Now what seems to be the problem?'

'I—I am going to have a baby,' Cecilia admitted. She recounted her symptoms.

Oliver described her fainting spell and her lack of being fully conscious later and then he excused himself.

His departure surprised Cecilia. She had thought he would want to hear everything she and the doctor said, given his doubting of her before.

The doctor listened to her heart with his wooden tube and pressed down on her abdomen. Thank goodness he did not want to examine inside her. He asked a great many questions about what she ate and drank, how much sleep she'd received, how much worry afflicted her.

When he was finished, he asked her if she wished Oliver to hear his conclusions. Her normal instinct was to keep anything about herself private. And she might have insisted upon doing so had he remained in the room. But because Oliver respected her privacy, she was willing for him to hear what the doctor said.

The doctor left the room to ask for him.

When Oliver and the doctor returned, the physician

said, 'There is nothing serious. All you have experienced is not unexpected when a woman is *enceinte*.' He smiled at Cecilia. 'I do believe you should not exert yourself, though. Only do what feels comfortable for you to do. Do not fatigue yourself or strain yourself in any way. The nausea should pass after a few weeks. The dizziness may persist if you do not eat correctly and achieve sufficient rest.'

All Cecilia could think was that she must work. She could not just rest!

Oliver saw the doctor out and returned to the drawing room.

'Do not tell me I cannot work!' Cecilia cried as soon as he entered the room. 'I have no money.'

That was precisely what he'd been about to say, but the doctor warned about her getting upset.

'I told you, Cecilia, I will support you, as you asked.'

She averted her face as if he'd slapped her. 'And I have told you, I need money of my own in case you do not.'

Perhaps he should settle a sum of money on her right now. If he did so, he was certain his friends—and his father—would consider him a gullible twit.

Besides, if he gave her the funds now, she would leave and he was not ready for that to happen, not until he knew whatever it was she held back from him. And not until he knew her health was restored and she could give birth to this baby safely.

He sat in one of the chairs.

She still stood, her arms folded across her chest. 'Well?'

He tapped his fingers on the table, trying to determine what he should say to her. Something that would keep her healthy—and here—but would reassure her as well.

Finally, she sat as well, tucking the banyan around her.

'The doctor said you need to rest, to not exert yourself,' he began.

'Being a hostess is no exertion,' she burst out. 'All I do is stand around and talk.'

He'd watched her. It took some energy to feign excitement over the roll of dice. And he doubted she'd ever sat in a chair. She'd certainly flagged quickly during the singing.

He held up a hand. 'Let me finish.'

Her lovely lips pressed together in a stubborn expression, but she gave him her attention.

'I cannot discharge you, not when Jacob hired you, but I certainly could attempt to exert some influence over his decision.'

Her eyes flashed. 'You would not dare.'

He met her gaze. 'Believe me, if I felt that was what I must do, I would do it and see it through.'

Her defiance flickered.

'Here is what I propose.' He was making this up as he went along. 'You may work, but you must rest in between. And if you cannot finish out an evening you must stop and leave before you make yourself ill.'

She lifted her chin. 'I'll make it through next time. I'll show you.'

Did she not understand? 'I don't want you to show me, Cecilia. I want you to take care of yourself and the baby inside you.' After the doctor's visit, he at least knew there was a baby. 'If you are worried about money, then it would behove you to leave that expensive hotel.'

'I intend to find a less expensive place to live,' she assured him.

Any place less expensive was likely to be further away which meant she would be travelling the roads of London at two in the morning.

'I can offer you a place to live that will cost you nothing.' What was he thinking? 'You will be close to Vitium et Virtus so if you do get fatigued you can quickly go home.'

'Where can there possibly be a place that will cost me nothing?' she scoffed.

He fixed his gaze on her. 'Here. Come and live here.'

Her eyes widened. 'Here? In this house?'

He nodded. 'In this house. It is not a large town house, but there is room enough for you. You saw the second bed-chamber. It has a sitting room. When you are here, you can be as private as you like.'

She peered at him. 'What sort of payment is expected of me?'

'Cut line, Cecilia,' he said sharply. 'I may not look like a gentleman, but I am one.'

He'd heard his stepmother call him names because of his appearance. Even some of the women with whom he'd had affairs called him savage.

'I am not talking about how you look,' she shot back. 'Gentlemen of all shapes and sizes give gifts so they might get something in return.'

He glared at her. 'You have been around me enough to take that much measure of my character.'

She crossed her arms over her chest. 'Then are you not worried it is too scandalous to share a house with a widow?'

He shrugged. 'By whose estimation? I am a bastard son and you work in a gentlemen's club that I part-own. I do not think anyone expects propriety from either of us.'

Her eyes flashed at him. 'At least you did not say it was my interesting condition that makes me scandalous.'

'Your *interesting condition* makes it sensible for you to live here.'

'I do not see how,' she protested.

'Because it is free and you are close.' He was puzzled by her, but exasperated as well. 'What is your objection?'

Her brow furrowed and she pursed her lips.

'You say it is my child inside you,' he went on, because his doubts about her story were growing again. 'But perhaps it is not and that is why you do not wish to accept my offer.'

'The baby is yours,' she insisted.

'Then live here.' If he was ever to discover the truth about her, he needed her close by. 'You do not need to return to the hotel. I will send Irwin to collect your things and pay your bill.'

'Irwin?'

'My butler,' he explained. 'You stay here and rest.'

'Where will you be?' she asked.

'I need to go to the club for a while.' He did not *need* to go to the club, but her reluctance to share his house kindled memories of his stepmother refusing to live with him as soon as they reached England. He was immediately sent away to school.

She stared at him. 'What will the rules be if I live here?'

'Rules?' He'd always been against rules. He gave her a blank look. 'Do not destroy the furnishings?'

She blew out an exasperated breath. 'I mean, I must be free to come and go as I please.'

'Of course.' He thought more about this, though. 'I may want to restrict who may visit you, however.'

She caught on right away. 'No scores of men in my bed, do you mean?'

He met her eye. 'That is precisely what I mean.'

'That is hardly a worry.' She laughed drily. 'Even if I wished to entertain gentlemen—which I most assuredly do not—who would call upon me?'

Men she met at Vitium et Virtus, perhaps?

She took a breath. 'So… I will abide by your terms.'

He should not be this glad. 'We have a bargain, then?' He reached over to her, extending his hand.

She hesitated. 'Will I have to pay for food?'

'No,' he responded. 'You will not have to pay for your rooms or your food. I offer them at my pleasure.'

She finally clasped her hand with his.

Her touch set off a flare of desire within him and a memory of bare skin against bare skin, of lovemaking and shared pleasure.

He released her and wondered what he had done to himself by inviting the intimacy of sharing this house.

Cecilia could still feel the warmth of his hand on hers even though their handshake was quick. In Paris she'd thought he would merely be a pleasant memory. Never did she conceive of actually living with him day after day. She'd never wanted to live with a man again. Never wanted to be under a man's control again.

But this was simply too tempting an offer. Free food. Free room. She could save every bit of what she made at Vitium et Virtus. And if he did give her enough money for her and the baby to live on, all the better.

But not expecting anything of her in return? That made her suspicious.

'Is there pen and paper?' she asked. 'I will write a note for the hotel.'

He rose and walked over to a table with a drawer. He took out a sheet of paper, an inkpot and a pen. He handed them to her and sat back in his chair.

She leaned over to write the note on the side table. When she was finished she handed it to him. 'I have some coins stitched in my valise. If Irwin could pay the hotel bill, I will pay back the money when he returns.'

Oliver took the note. 'I am well able to afford your hotel bill.'

He would pay her hotel bill? That meant even more obligation to him. She knew how it would be. The more he did for her, the more control he would have over her.

But she must go along with it for the baby's sake.

'Irwin should have no difficulty,' she said. 'My valise is packed with everything I own.' In case she had to leave in a hurry—a habit she'd acquired from living with Duncan.

'I am certain Irwin will have no difficulty,' he assured her.

She stood. 'May I retire to the bedchamber now?'

He stood as well. 'You do not need my permission, Cecilia.'

She nodded. 'It is just that I am suddenly fatigued again.'

'You do not need to explain.' He gave her a concerned look. 'Are you feeling unwell? Do you require anything?'

'Nothing.' She wished he would not be so solicitous. It confused her. And warmed her towards him. 'Sleep, perhaps.' She walked unsteadily to the door.

He came to her side. 'I'll escort you.'

He gave her his arm. Holding on to him did steady her. It also reminded her of their day in Paris when she'd held his arm and they'd seen so many wonderful sights together.

His strength made it so much easier to climb the two flights of stairs to the bedchamber where he'd taken her the night before.

'Who undressed me?' she asked.

His mouth turned up in a half-smile. 'I am tempted to set you into a pique and tell you Irwin and I did it, but Mrs Irwin, my housekeeper, and Mrs Smith, the cook, were the ones.'

This little tease reminded her of his light banter in Paris. She did not want to feel amused by him again.

They reached her room, and he opened the door.

'I'll leave you now, Cecilia, unless there is something I may do for you.' He stepped away.

She crossed the threshold, but turned to see him already at the stairs.

'Oliver?' she called.

He turned.

Her throat felt suddenly tight. 'Thank you,' she managed, though it came out sharper than she intended.

He nodded, turned and descended the stairs.

Cecilia slept until the light dimmed in the room and the clock chimed five o'clock. Five o'clock! She'd slept the day away.

She stretched and sat up, feeling more rested than any time she could remember. Even the nausea had disappeared. Was it the bed? she wondered. Or was it because Oliver had taken away most of her worries?

For the moment.

There was a soft rap at the door. Cecilia jumped out of bed and quickly donned the banyan. 'Who is it?' she asked.

A young woman, little more than a girl, opened the door and peeked in. 'You are awake, ma'am! May I come in?'

'Yes?' Cecilia said uncertainly.

The girl entered, carrying Cecilia's valise. She promptly curtsied. 'I am Mary. Mary Driscoll, ma'am. I'm to be your maid, if you'll have me. Mr Gregory told Mr Irwin you should have a maid and as he is my uncle—Mr Irwin, that is—he asked Mr Gregory if it could be me and Mr Gregory said yes. So I can learn and all.'

Cecilia had not had a maid in years, but this one looked young and fresh and untouched by the world.

'How old are you, Mary?' Cecilia asked.

'Sixteen, ma'am, but I've worked a little here, cleaning and that sort. And I learn fast.' The girl was earnest. 'I want to be a lady's maid, y'see.'

'Oh, Mary.' Cecilia sat down on the chair by the dressing table. 'I do not think that I am the sort of person who can help you be a lady's maid.'

The girl's face turned crestfallen. 'But I love to do hair and mend clothes and such. I am good at it, Aunt Irwin says.'

'It isn't that.' How was she to explain? 'I am simply not the sort from whom anyone would want a reference. In fact, serving me might be an impediment.'

Mary seemed to cogitate on this. 'Do you mean because you are an unmarried lady living with Mr Gregory? Or because you work in the club? Or because you are going to have a baby?'

'You know a great deal about me,' Cecilia said with some dismay.

'Oh, we all do. My uncle and aunt and Cook, at least. Mr Gregory explained it all. None of that worries us, though. My mum was never married to my dad, y'see. And my sister once worked at the club.'

Had Cecilia ever been that unguarded? She supposed she had. Unguarded and naïve and easily manipulated.

Mary went on. 'And Uncle Irwin says when the time comes, Mr Gregory will get me work in the Duke of Westmoor's house and nobody will question a reference from a duke.'

Cecilia was not so certain of this. Rose had been a maid herself. Surely society was less than accepting of her, even if she had married a duke. A commoner duchess was certainly better than a scandalous widow, though.

She smiled. 'Then I would be delighted for you to be my lady's maid.'

Mary gave an excited whoop and jumped up and down. When she settled, she asked, 'May I start right now? I can arrange your hair and put you in a gown.'

The few dresses Cecilia had brought with her would be terribly wrinkled from being in the valise, but she supposed they'd have to do.

'May I suggest the green dress?' She spoke as if she were a lady's maid of vast experience.

'It is here?'

Mary went into the dressing room and brought it out. 'Mr Gregory brought it from the club. I tiptoed in here while you were asleep. I also brought in fresh water for you to wash.'

It had been a long time since a maid had cared for her clothes, helped her bathe and dress and fix her hair. Not since she'd lived at home with her parents and sisters. She'd never had a lady's maid of her own, but she'd always had help with dressing and with her hair. Until she married Duncan.

'Mr Gregory said I was to ask you if you wanted your dinner sent up here or if you would join him in the dining room,' Mary told her while pinning up her hair.

Cecilia did not know what to say. 'I don't know. What do you think he wanted me to do?'

'Why, for you to join him for dinner, of course!' Mary cried, then seemed to question whether she'd been too boisterous. 'Ma'am.'

'Then dress me for dinner with Mr Gregory, Mary.'

'Yes, ma'am!'

Chapter Ten

A week later Oliver and Jacob rose early to give their best horses a good run on Rotten Row. After a friendly race at full gallop on the bridle paths of Hyde Park, the two men cooled their horses at a sedate pace. Rotten Row this early in the morning was a busy place with other riders and groomsmen exercising their masters' horses.

It had been an eventful week and a sad one. Queen Charlotte's death had been announced and the country again plunged into mourning, as they had done the year before for her granddaughter and namesake, Princess Charlotte, the Prince Regent's only daughter, the heir to the throne.

The royal mourning meant that usual social events were suspended or greatly subdued. As a result, more members came to Vitium et Virtus for entertainment. Oliver and his friends did not require the women in their employ to wear black, but they did dress them in various shades of purple and gave them black armbands. Snyder, their porter, always wore black, but he and the other male servants also donned black armbands.

As the Duke of Westmoor, Jacob was expected to participate in the royal funeral. The Queen had died in Kew Palace and there would be a funeral procession from there to Windsor where she would be interred in St George's Chapel.

'I am not made for all this ceremony,' Jake complained. 'I mean no disrespect for the late Queen—she was quite beloved by my grandmother who'd served her in their younger days—but the whole pageant sounds gruelling and tedious. You've no idea how many will participate!'

'It will be elaborate, I am certain,' Oliver agreed. He did not like to dwell too much on the Queen's death. On any death of a mother.

Had his mother had a funeral? Had someone placed her body on a pyre and set it aflame?

Jacob shook his head. 'Enough of the funeral.'

It wasn't as if Oliver brought up the subject. He hadn't started any part of their conversation this morning. The last time he'd seen Jacob, he'd told him about inviting Cecilia to live in his town house. They'd exchanged sharp words over it. Jake warned Oliver that this was bound to cause trouble among the other women at Vitium et Virtus. Worse, he worried that Oliver might not treat Cecilia well, given his history of dalliances with women. Jake did not believe for a moment that there would be no dalliance.

For reasons Oliver could not explain, even to himself, he had not told Jacob or Frederick or anyone that Cecilia was the woman he'd met in Paris, nor had he mentioned she was carrying a child—his child.

Or so she claimed.

'So...' Jake began in a cautious tone. 'How are you faring with Cecilia?'

Oliver did not wish to reopen this discussion.

'Splendidly,' Oliver replied. 'Truly, we see little of each other.'

This was the truth. Cecilia kept to herself in her room and sitting room a great deal of the time. Oliver did not intrude upon her privacy. They did share breakfast occasionally and dinner almost every night.

But he certainly was not going to tell Jacob that sharing meals with her was actually pleasant.

'And at Vitium et Virtus?' Jake persisted. 'Any problems?'

'None of which I have been made aware.' Oliver shook his head. 'I am still not certain a hostess makes any sense at all, though.'

Not any more sense than how much Oliver disliked seeing her in that role.

'Does she help make money?' Jake asked. 'How's the take for the hazard and faro tables? Is it up?'

'Up, but not by much.' His horse lagged behind Jake's and Oliver urged the mare to catch up. 'I will say that the members appear to have taken to her.'

Some of the gentlemen even sought her out. She was attentive to several of them, bringing them drinks and cheering the play at the tables. Sometimes Oliver would spy her seated at a table with one of them, listening intently as the man seemed to prattle on. She had been true to her word, though. She never sought to be private with any of them.

'Does the increased amount cover her wages?' Jacob asked.

'More than covers it,' Oliver replied. At least the part of her wages Oliver took from Vitium et Virtus. That amount was on a par with the singers and dancers. The rest came from his pocket.

'Well, then, as long as we are not losing money, no harm is done to have her there,' Jake said. 'She needed the employment. I would hate to think where she would work otherwise.'

So would Oliver.

This moment was a perfect opportunity for him to tell Jake of meeting Cecilia in Paris.

But he kept his mouth shut.

Jake also did not know Oliver had been discussing with his banker how to set up some sort of annuity for her. Or that he'd indulged her by sending for the modiste the club used for their singers' and dancers' costumes and was having Cecilia fitted for several new dresses, not only for the club, but mourning clothes for day as well. He'd paid extra for them to be completed in a rush. The first of the dresses would be ready tomorrow.

'Will you come to Vitium et Virtus tonight?' Oliver asked.

Jacob looked dismayed. 'Forgive me, Oliver. I cannot. Grandmama has taken to her bed.'

'She is ill?' Oliver was fond of the elderly lady. She'd always been kind to him.

'Mourning more than ill, I am certain, but I think I should stay at home.'

'Of course,' Oliver said.

Jacob turned to him. 'Tonight features the dancers, is that not right?'

The dancers frolicked through the ballroom showing lots of leg and bosom and sensuality in their performance. It was one of the most sought-after entertainments at the club. Oliver would have them subdue their enthusiasm tonight out of respect for the deceased Queen.

They rode a few paces in silence before Jacob said, 'I am ashamed to say I cannot muster much interest in our club entertainments. Not since marrying Rose.'

Oliver could not muster interest in the entertainments and he had no wife.

So much had changed since Nicholas disappeared. The club used to be the friends' shared passion and they relished partaking in whatever boisterous debauchery they'd conceived. But now they were older and Nicholas was gone, and Frederick and Jacob were married. The club had become more of a business venture in Oliver's eyes than his preferred playhouse. There was nothing particularly carefree and daring about a business venture.

They exited the park at Hyde Park Corner, now more crowded with other riders, carriages, and wagons than when they'd set out.

When they reached Park Lane, Jacob said, 'This is where I must leave you.' He leant over and shook Oliver's hand. 'I am sorry we have abandoned you to run Vitium et Virtus alone, Oliver.'

Oliver smiled at him. 'Do not apologise. What else would I do, if not for Vitium et Virtus? Come when you can. Otherwise stay with your family.'

Jake grinned. 'With pleasure!'

That night after a pleasant dinner, Oliver escorted Cecilia to Vitium et Virtus. They walked the back way, through his garden and out of the gate to the alley, then through another gate into the garden of the club. The night was damp and cold and they walked briskly, entering through the door that led to the private part of the building. In the entryway, Oliver helped Cecilia off with her cloak. She felt the touch of his hands on her shoulders even as he turned to hang her cloak on a peg by the door.

She pulled off her gloves and left them on a table where Oliver had placed his hat.

'I will leave you here,' Cecilia told him.

She would paint her face a little and put her mask in place before again becoming Coquette.

To her surprise, he touched her hand. 'Are you feeling well enough tonight?' he asked.

She nodded. 'I am feeling quite well, actually.'

.Perhaps he meant the touch as a goodbye. Whatever his reason, it set her heart dancing.

He had been so kind these last days, ever since she agreed to live in a room in his house. The room, sitting room and dressing room gave her more space than she'd ever lived in since leaving her parents' houses. She told herself that it made sense for her to eat with him, if only to save the servants from climbing the stairs to bring her a meal. She breakfasted in the small dining room for the same reason, although he was often out by the time she rose.

At meals they talked of the events written in the newspapers or chatted about at the club. Cecilia had followed closely the news of the Queen's death and the plan for her funeral, as well as news of financial hardship around the country and of society people and events.

Meals were so comfortable they became her favourite part of the day.

And being Coquette again was her least favourite.

She made her way to the Green Room where the dancers were busy dressing in lavender gowns. Her new lady's maid, Mary, had already arranged her hair and dressed her in her costume, a gown of deep purple.

'There she is,' one of the dancers said scathingly. 'Oliver's choice.'

'Hello, Lanie,' she responded in a friendly tone. 'How are you faring today?'

Cecilia was sorry she upset Lanie, who so obviously wished Oliver favoured her. Lanie's jealousy put a pall on the otherwise genial atmosphere among the workers. Jealousy was so unnecessary. Cecilia kept her distance from Oliver and he seemed content for her to do so.

They might converse comfortably at dinner, but that

was more like a truce than an affair. She could not convince Lanie of that fact, though.

Lanie glowered. 'I'd fare a lot better if I were sharing the boss's bed like you do.'

'Leave her alone, Lanie,' came a voice from the back of the room.

It was Flo.

'Never mind, Flo,' Cecilia assured her. She turned to Lanie. 'I share his house, not his bed, Lanie.' Not now, at least.

'I am not a fool, Coquette.' Lanie flounced past her and left the room.

'Ooh,' the other girls said, laughing.

Cecilia walked over to Flo, who was seated in a chair, but had wrapped her head and shoulders in a shawl. 'I am surprised to see you here, Flo. Are you working tonight?'

Flo shook her head. 'I came to see you.'

'Me?' Cecilia pulled up a chair and sat near her.

Flo glanced at the dancers as if to check if they were watching. She lifted the shawl away from her face. There was a bruise from her temple to her cheek.

'Flo!' Cecilia said in alarm.

Flo covered her face again. 'I—I bumped into a door.'

'You did not bump into a door!' Cecilia touched her own cheek, again feeling the pain of Duncan's fist.

Flo gave her an obstinate look. 'All I want is for you to help me cover it up. I am to visit my mother tomorrow and I do not want her to see it.'

She'd helped Flo cover up bruises on her neck one night, as well as the ones on her arms that first time they met.

'Why? What would your mother think if she saw such a bruise on your face?'

'It—it would make her worry over me and she has enough to worry over feeding my brothers and sisters.'

Cecilia shook her head. 'She'd think someone hit you.'

Flo's hand went to her face. 'Oh, no. I bumped into a door.'

How many *doors* had Cecilia bumped into during her marriage? Her teeth ached as she remembered the pain of Duncan's fist.

Cecilia took Flo's hands in hers and made the girl look into her eyes. 'Heed me, Flo. I know someone hit you. I know, because my husband used to hit me. He used to squeeze my arms until they bruised just like the bruises on your arms when we first met. And the ones on your neck? My husband made marks like that when he choked me.' She released one of Flo's hands and gently touched her face. 'I'll cover your bruise, but we should do it tomorrow morning. What I do tonight will not last.'

Flo's eyes filled with tears. 'Do you think Mr Gregory and Mr Bell would let me stay here tonight? I do not wish to go back to my rooms.'

Cecilia raised her brows. 'Because he knows where you live? Or is he waiting for you there?'

Flo clamped her mouth shut.

There were bedrooms in the club, the rooms where willing men and women could retire and indulge their passions. Or in the case of some of the women, make some money.

'I will ask.' If Oliver refused her, Cecilia would take her to her own rooms to spend the night. 'Will you wait here?'

'Here or in the servants' hall,' Flo said.

Cecilia nodded. 'Tomorrow morning I will come back here and we will cover your bruise.'

They would be alone, then. Maybe when they were alone, Flo would tell her who was beating her.

She hugged Flo and left to put a dusting of powder on her face and tint on her cheeks and lips like Vincent had taught her, with a light touch. She found her mask, made from feathers dyed purple. She filed past the dancers and wished them a good performance.

Lanie waited for her in the hallway. 'How did you manage it, Coquette? Coquette. Such a silly name.'

'I agree,' Cecilia responded, determined not to make an enemy of the girl. 'Coquette is a silly name.'

'That is not my question.' Lanie looked peeved. 'How did you manage to snare Oliver? He has refused any attachment to the rest of us.'

'Lanie.' Cecilia spoke as kindly as she could. 'Do not fret over this. I've explained the nature of my relationship with Mr Gregory. There is no reason to be in such a high dudgeon.'

'The nature of your relationship?' Her voice mimicked someone haughty.

What truly was the nature of her relationship with Oliver, though? Cecilia did not know. His actions were kind and generous, but she often caught him looking at her with anger in his eyes. He did not trust her or believe her.

But if he touched her, even to help remove her cloak, her senses flared in response as if there was still something romantic between them. Like in Paris.

She shook the thought from her head.

'Leave it, Lanie,' she said.

She continued down the corridor to the stairs leading to the hall where Snyder stood guard. At least that was how Cecilia always thought of it. She was pleased the large man was always nearby. Just in case.

She had been propositioned many times by the men in the game room. Some were very displeased she did not accept their offers. Some offered her as much as Madame Coquette earned in Paris.

She passed the ballroom and glimpsed Oliver standing

near the stage. He turned and watched her walk by. She felt his gaze upon her as if it were a touch.

Members and guests were already arriving. The Queen's death increased attendance, as if mourning the Queen was less important than card-playing, gambling and watching bawdy entertainment.

At the door of the game room she hesitated. Taking a breath, she closed her eyes and transformed herself into Coquette.

Oliver walked to the door of the ballroom after Cecilia passed. At the door to the game room her demeanour changed. She became more fluid, her posture more relaxed, her neck looser. When she entered the room, her hips swayed.

She'd become Coquette.

He watched this transformation almost every night the club was open. Could she feign such sensuality?

How could she be two such different women?

Coquette was sensual, approachable, light-hearted. She drew men out so that suddenly they were talking with her, confiding in her. Cecilia was guarded, wary and cool.

No, she was three women, not two. The Cecilia he'd met in Paris was vulnerable, sad and passionately loving.

These changes intrigued him as much as they fed his suspicions of her. Who was she really? And why did she hide her true self?

He entered the game room, but remained at its doorway, pretending to check the room, but really watching her.

She greeted several of the members she undoubtedly recognised and soon was laughing with them and encouraging them to play hazard. Was she pretending to be excited by each roll of the dice? She must be, although she did it so well she had him believing it.

After a few minutes she left the men at the hazard table and walked towards the door. When she saw Oliver there, she seemed to lose Coquette for a moment and become Cecilia.

'Fetching drinks,' she said to him as she passed him.

She brought two of the members at the hazard table glasses of brandy, watched them for a little while and made her way to the faro table. There were only three members there. Two of them greeted her. The third man sidled up to her, effectively separating her from the other men.

Oliver tensed. He recognised a man attempting a conquest. Why should it bother him? He had no claim on Cecilia.

Still, it roused his emotions to think she might accept.

Instead, she stepped away from the man and abruptly left the table. She walked swiftly to the doorway, her expression one of distress.

She passed Oliver without seeming to see him.

He went after her, catching up to her in the hallway. 'What is it, Cecilia? What did that member say to you?'

'Nothing.' She could not look at him, though, and she backed away as if wanting to flee.

He seized her arm. 'Come with me.'

He brought her into the private rooms of the club and removed his mask. 'Now, tell me what happened.'

She pulled her mask off as well. 'Nothing happened. It is just that...' She paused and seemed to have difficulty composing herself enough to speak. 'I—I recognised him.'

'Someone you knew from before?' he asked cautiously.

She laughed with disdain. 'I should say so.'

She'd met Bowles in Paris. But the man who'd spoken to her was not Bowles; Oliver could tell. There must have been other men. 'Who is he?'

Her eyes narrowed. 'You told me never to reveal a member's identity.'

'Cecilia, tell me who it is.'

She met his eye again, but this time hers were full of pain. 'My father.'

'Your father?' Her father was a member? 'Who is your father?'

She glanced away as if considering whether or not to tell him. She glanced back. 'Baron Dorman.'

Dorman? She was Dorman's daughter? A member of the aristocracy?

'He did not recognise me.' Her voice cracked.

Oliver took her in his arms and held her tightly against him. She clung to him and repeated in a more agonised tone, 'He did not recognise me.'

He wanted only to soothe her. 'Of course he did not recognise you. You wore a mask.'

'I recognised him!' she cried.

He probably did not look above her neck, Oliver thought.

She pulled out of Oliver's embrace. 'How dare he gamble! When I was at home, all he did was complain about how much my sisters and I cost him. How he could not afford decent dowries for us. How dare he be so foolish as to play faro!'

Faro was simply a game of chance. The cards were either with you or against you, no skill involved whatsoever.

She paced in front of him. 'I hardly know what to say or do!'

'Would you like me to confront him, Cecilia?' he asked.

She stopped and faced him, obviously considering this. Finally, she met his eye. 'No. Not you. I want to confront him.'

'Then I will bring him to you.'

'Here?' she asked.

'Here.'

She had a look of steely resolve. 'Yes. Bring him here.'

'I will remain nearby.' In case that feeling of panic returned, the one with which she entered the room. Her panic had swiftly transformed into anger, her apparent feelings of weakness, into strength.

She nodded.

He tied his mask on once more and left the room to make his way back to the public rooms and to Lord Dorman who was still at the faro table, losing his money.

'Sir?' Oliver did not call him by name. 'Coquette would like a private word with you.'

The man puffed up like a rooster. 'Coquette? Private? Yes, indeed. Thought she would.' He followed Oliver eagerly. 'Back in the private rooms, no doubt.'

'My private rooms.' Oliver escorted him through the owners' entrance, taking off his mask as he crossed the threshold.

'Should I remove my mask?' Dorman asked.

'If you so desire,' Oliver replied. 'It is entirely up to you.'

Dorman removed his mask and combed his thinning hair with his fingers.

When they reached the door to the drawing room, Cecilia stood with her back to them. She turned as they entered. She'd donned her mask again.

Her father approached her and bowed. 'Lord Dorman at your service, my dear.'

She lifted her chin. 'I know who you are.'

The man simpered. 'Then I am excessively honoured.'

'Are you, sir?' she responded haughtily.

This was yet another Cecilia, Oliver thought. Strong and sure. He could not help but be fascinated.

She smiled at Dorman, slipping back into Coquette's seductive style. 'How has your luck been at the faro table?'

'About to turn at any moment.' Dorman laughed. 'But you must not worry your pretty little head over it.'

'Must I not?' she simpered.

She was playing him with finesse, Oliver thought. He had no idea where she was leading the man, but he admired her for it.

She smiled again. 'Are you pleased that I asked to see you in private?'

Dorman lowered his voice. 'I am very pleased, my dear. I trust you will not be disappointed that you requested me.'

Dorman took another step towards her. Cecilia took a step back and Oliver braced himself to intervene on her behalf, should it become necessary.

'I am disappointed.' Her tone turned sharp.

'Disappointed? But, why? How can I change your mind?' Dorman sputtered.

She fixed her gaze on him. 'You do not recognise me, do you?'

'Should I?' he asked.

'You should.' She pulled off her mask.

Chapter Eleven

It took several painful seconds for Cecilia to finally see recognition dawn on her father's face. Had she truly been so unimportant to him that he had not committed her face to memory?

'You!' he said breathlessly, his face blanched.

Not even using her name.

'I know I am not so altered that a father would not remember me after a little more than three years,' she said. 'A loving father, that is. Not one who declares me dead to him.'

He turned red. 'You disgraced the family!'

'You could have prevented that if you had accepted the marriage.' That had been what Duncan expected. If her father had accepted the marriage, society would have forgiven the elopement and that would have been an end to any scandal.

'Accept the marriage?' Her father huffed. 'He was a nobody!'

She glanced over at Oliver, who stood by the door in the shadows so she could not see his reaction. She'd told him about her marriage, at least about eloping and being disowned.

'Look at you now,' he said scathingly. 'He has you working as a strumpet. I dare say if anyone does recognise you, it will be more scandal for your sisters and your mother.'

'Take care, sir.' Oliver spoke in a sinister tone. 'Your daughter works here as a hostess, nothing else. And, since you were so eager to accept her favours, do not think your hypocrisy is lost on either of us.'

Cecilia added, 'What is more, I would not be forced into this position if you and Mama had taken me in. Mr Gregory was kind enough to hire me so I would not starve.'

Her father laughed derisively. 'What? That no-good husband of yours is not even supporting you?'

'He is dead.'

Cecilia touched her abdomen and thought of the baby growing inside her. She once thought that her parents would welcome her back because of the baby. Now she did not consider her father worthy of learning of the baby's existence.

She went on. 'I wonder how much money you have lost gambling at this club? As much as my dowry would have cost you? How very convenient to refuse to provide that money to Duncan so you could lose it gambling. Tell me, are my sisters still fighting over the dwindling resources?'

'Your sisters married. Respectably,' he shot back. 'But, if it had not been for you, they could have married much higher.'

She ignored that statement. 'Does Mama know you gamble at Vitium et Virtus? Is she still forced to make economies? To deny herself?'

His eyes flashed in panic. 'You would not tell your mother I am a member!'

'Or that you were ready for a dalliance with your own daughter?' she added with sarcasm.

Oliver stepped forward. 'Except you are no longer a member of Vitium et Virtus.'

'What?' Her father sounded outraged. 'You have no cause to expel me.'

'I do not need a cause, except that I do not like the way you treat your daughter,' Oliver said.

Her father took a step towards him. 'Why, you half-caste bastard! Wait until I take this to the Duke. Or to Challenger. We will see who is expelled.'

Oliver stood his ground. 'I implore you to take this to the Duke. Or to Frederick. Do not forget to explain how eager you were to be private with Coquette.'

'I am certain Mama would like to know about that,' Cecilia added. 'As well as about the gambling.'

Oliver extended his arm towards the door. 'Unless Cecilia has more to say to you, let me show you out.'

'I am quite finished,' she said.

Oliver escorted Lord Dorman to the door to the club's rooms.

'Put on your mask,' he ordered, pulling his own from his pocket.

Dorman fumbled for his mask and managed to affix it well enough. When he again wore the disguise required by Vitium et Virtus, Oliver opened the door and led him to the hall where Snyder was in attendance.

'This guest is leaving,' Oliver said. 'And he is not welcome to return.'

'As you wish, Mr Gregory.' Snyder was particularly astute in recognising members under their masks. If he was not certain, he could take them to a more private area and have them remove the mask and verify their identity.

'I'll not forget this, Gregory,' Dorman snapped.

Oliver gave him a contemptuous smile. 'I'll not forget either, Dorman. Neither will my friends. Cause me or the lady trouble and neither will the other members of Vitium et Virtus.'

Dorman's eyes flashed in alarm.

Snyder handed the man his topcoat, hat and gloves. When Dorman had donned them, Snyder walked to the door to the outside and opened it.

'An abomination! That is what this is. An abomination!' Dorman strode out, and Snyder closed the door behind him.

'So what did he do?' Snyder asked.

Since Snyder was the gatekeeper, he needed to know. It helped him bar members if they tried to return.

'Coquette knew something about him, about his mistreatment of his family,' Oliver responded. 'If he tries to return, simply inform him that we will tell his wife all about him.'

Snyder smiled. 'I dare say I could threaten any of them with that statement.'

Oliver answered in the same tone, 'Unless the wives attend, as well.'

'Indeed.' Snyder grinned.

Oliver returned to Cecilia, finding her seated on the sofa, her hands pressed against her abdomen.

Without thinking, he sat down next to her and put his arm around her. 'That cannot have been easy for you.'

She leaned against him. 'I cannot stop shaking.'

He held her tighter.

'I always knew I meant little to him,' she said. 'This was not a surprise.'

But it hurt anyway. Just as his stepmother's cruelty once hurt him. 'He is a detestable man.'

She turned to him so she was able to look him in the face. 'You expelled him. I never expected that.'

He shrugged. 'I could not have him come back.' Not

to hurt her all over again. 'The chances he would cause trouble are too great.'

She shivered. 'He gambles away large sums without blinking an eye. I know that would cause my mother hardship. And I am sure my sisters will have suffered. Their dowries must have been limited by his losses.'

Oliver once relished the excitement of a game of chance, of risking large sums and hoping for the big win. He was lucky that he could always stop himself from risking more than he could afford. He saw it over and over in the game room of other establishments, the men and women whose losses were devastating, but still they could not stop.

She sighed. 'I suppose he will find some other place to gamble.' She leaned against him again. 'I should not care about it.'

But she did no matter what she said.

'You do not need to return to the game room tonight, if you do not wish to,' he told her. 'I will walk you home now, if you like.'

She straightened. 'No. No. I can go back.' She laughed scornfully. 'If I do not, those gentlemen in the game room, who certainly knew my father's identity, will think I went to spend the night with him.'

'You do make a point.'

She put on her mask. 'I wish I knew how my mother and sisters are faring. It sounds like life has been difficult for them.'

'Would you like me to make enquiries about them?' he asked.

She shook her head. 'No. At least I do not think so.'

They walked out of the room and into the hallway.

Cecilia touched Oliver's arm and he faced her.

'I—I did not deserve the kindness and support you

showed me with my father,' she said to him. 'I do not know how to thank you.'

'It was not so difficult a thing for me.'

He found his senses surging at her closeness. He glanced at her neck and noticed the pearl necklace, remembering her thanks in Paris for that trifling gift, remembering what had come after.

He leaned down, closer. Her scent filled his nostrils. He wanted her and her lips were tantalisingly close.

Her eyes dilated.

But he pulled back and continued walking.

'He called you vile names,' she said a moment later. 'I am so sorry. You did not deserve that.'

He smiled. 'I have heard such names my whole life, Cecilia.' Bastard. Half-caste.

'That is dreadful!' she exclaimed.

He lifted a shoulder. 'It is what I am, is it not?'

She resumed walking this time, but he heard her murmur, 'You are much more.'

His heart swelled at that.

They reached the door to the club's rooms, but she stopped again.

'I forgot to ask you something,' she said, her tone changing. 'A favour, really.'

His mistrust was roused. Was she manipulating him? A compliment, then a request? 'What is it?'

A wariness flickered in her eyes. 'Um…when I was in the Green Room…Flo was there.'

'This is not her night to perform,' he said.

'I know.' Cecilia continued. 'She asked me to ask you if she could spend the night here. Alone. Just this once. She cannot go back to her rooms tonight.'

'Why not?' he asked. He'd not expected the request to be on another's behalf.

'She did not tell me, but she seemed…upset…and a little frantic about what she would do.'

It was not something that he could allow on a regular basis, lest the workers move in completely, but it seemed churlish to refuse. Or perhaps it was merely difficult for him to say no to Cecilia.

'Just this once, if she doesn't make a thing of it with the others.' His tone turned sharp. 'I'll tell Snyder and Mr Bell.'

She shrank from him. 'Thank you, Oliver.'

They proceeded to the club's rooms and he walked her to the doorway of the game room. He watched her take a breath and loosen her limbs and again turn herself back into Coquette.

The next morning Cecilia rose early and, with Mary's assistance, dressed in one of her old dresses, her hair in a simple plait down her back. She hurried down to breakfast and learned that Oliver had already gone out.

She ate quickly and told Irwin that she was going over to Vitium et Virtus to help Flo with something.

'As you wish, ma'am,' Irwin said.

She tried the door she and Oliver always used, but it was locked. She crossed the garden again and walked back to the alley and to the front of the house. She sounded the knocker, and Snyder answered the door.

'Coquette,' he said by way of greeting.

'I've come to see Flo,' Cecilia told him.

That seemed to be enough of an explanation for him. He let her enter, even took her cloak.

'Flo is below stairs,' Snyder said.

'Thank you, Snyder.' She walked down the stairs to the dressing room, but Flo was not there. She walked back out to the hallway and saw one of the kitchen workers.

'Morning, Coquette,' the girl said.

'Good morning, Sally,' she responded. 'I'm here to see Flo. Do you know where she is?'

'I do,' the girl responded. 'She's finishing breakfast in the kitchen. Poor thing. She bruised her face. She bumped into a door.'

'Yes,' Cecilia said. 'She told me.'

She came to the kitchen and the cook offered her a cup of tea, which Cecilia gratefully accepted. They all chatted amiably until Flo, hiding her bruised face with her hand, finished eating.

She and Cecilia returned to the dressing room, and Cecilia sat Flo down in front of a mirror and started to work on covering her bruise. Yesterday it had been red and blue; today it was purple.

Flo flinched when Cecilia touched the injured area. Cecilia remembered the pain of a new bruise and she winced in sympathy.

Cecilia started by dabbing Almond Bloom on the bruise. 'A fist made this bruise.' How well she remembered.

Flo tensed.

Cecilia continued. 'I told you. I know how it feels. The fist hitting you. It feels like the pain will explode in your head. Your eyes blur. And then he hits you again.'

She mixed a tiny bit of lip tint to the face powder and put the powder over the Almond Bloom. She repeated this.

And kept talking. 'You wonder what you did wrong. Maybe you should have known not to say what you said, or do what you did. After a while you start to think maybe you deserved to be punched in the face.'

Flo's eyes glistened with tears.

Cecilia put on another layer of powder.

'Won't you please tell me about it?' she asked Flo, keeping her voice low and soft.

''E— 'E is a gentleman,' she began, her accent making her sound like a little girl. 'He gave me presents and said I was pretty and that I was special.'

Cecilia felt a pang of pain.

Duncan's flattery had fallen on grateful ears. Cecilia had been so lonely. Her mother had been preoccupied by money. Her sisters resented and excluded her. She'd been so ripe for someone to pay attention to her and Duncan, so handsome, had told her everything she'd yearned to hear.

Flo went on. 'He asks me about Vitium et Virtus all the time. About Mr Gregory and the Duke and Mr Challenger—they are the owners, you know. He asks if they talk about him and he gets very angry when I say I never hear them say anything.'

This was odd. The man's connection was obviously with Oliver and the other owners, not with Flo.

'Lately I've been thinkin' he doesn't care a fig about me; he just wants to hear about them. But he said he'd never let me go, so I might as well do as he asks, but I can't because I don't ever know anything!' Her words were rushing out now.

And her tears were flowing, washing away Cecilia's handiwork. She started sobbing, and Cecilia took her in her arms and held her, smoothing her hair and trying to soothe her, but instead of being comforted Flo seemed to unfurl her pain and confusion and fear all at once.

There was a loud knocking on the dressing-room door. Cecilia handed Flo a handkerchief and went to answer it.

She opened the door a crack.

It was Oliver.

'What is this?' he asked. 'Snyder said you were here. I heard weeping.'

'Fleurette is a little upset,' Cecilia said.

'Let me talk to her.' He pushed on the door.

She opened it. He walked in, but she hurried to Flo first. 'Mr Gregory wants to see you,' she said.

Flo cowered. 'No! I mustn't talk to him.'

Oliver reached the girl's side. He crouched down so his face was even with hers. 'Why not, Fleurette? Whatever it is that makes you cry so, you must tell me.'

'It is about a gentleman who has been paying her particular attention,' Cecilia said. She did not want to say too much for fear Flo would clamp her lips shut for good.

Oliver handed Flo his handkerchief.

Flo wiped her eyes with the handkerchief and rubbed off the careful cover Cecilia had made over her bruise.

Oliver's gaze darted to Cecilia and back to Flo. He touched Flo's cheek very gently. 'Did the gentleman cause this bruise?'

Flo's eyes grew very wide, but she nodded.

He took Flo's hand. 'We cannot have this, can we? I do not allow anyone to hurt my entertainers, do I?'

''E— 'E would not want me to tell,' Flo said.

'What he wants does not matter a fig, does it?' Oliver responded. 'We cannot have you being hurt. You are too important to the club.'

Cecilia felt tears burning her eyes. She'd remained dry-eyed when her father blatantly rejected her, but Oliver's kindness to Flo was turning her into a watering pot. She knew how much such kindness meant. She'd needed it so desperately when Duncan went into a rage.

''E said he'd hurt me if I told anyone. He'd hurt me and never come back to me,' Flo said, her voice small.

'You cannot want him back!' exclaimed Cecilia. She used to pray Duncan would leave her.

'He wasn't always mean,' Flo shot back. 'Sometimes he was very sweet to me.'

That was how it was at first. The beatings came without

warning, but afterwards Duncan had been so sweet and loving. She'd wanted so much to believe he was sweet and loving. Eventually, though, he beat that out of her as well.

Oliver squeezed Flo's hand. 'You must have a man who treats you well all the time, is that not so? There are many men who admire you. Bide your time and another, better man will love you.'

But, in this club, love would be fleeting. Or soiled by the knowledge that the man had a wife he would never leave.

Oliver made Flo look directly at him. 'Tell me who this man is. I promise you he will not hurt you. He will go away.'

She nodded solemnly. 'He is a member. He wants to own the club.' She swallowed. 'He is Sir Nash Bowles.'

'Bowles?' Cecilia exclaimed.

She felt the emotion in Oliver change. 'Bowles.' His voice turned into a growl. He released Flo's hand and it felt like rancour poured out of him. 'Where is he likely to be?'

Flo shrank back. 'He could be at my room.' She gave him the direction. 'He stays there, waiting for me, lots of times.'

He stood and put a hand on Flo's shoulder. 'Do not fear, Flo. He will leave you alone from now on. He will never hit you again.'

He turned and strode towards the door.

Cecilia caught up to him in the hallway. 'What are you going to do, Oliver?'

'I'm going to take care of Bowles,' he responded in a rough voice.

The rage inside him was palpable. He frightened her, suddenly so violent and untamed.

She could not even say goodbye to him. She fled back to the Green Room.

Flo, though, looked as if a heavy weight had been lifted

off her shoulders. 'I never thought Mr Gregory would be so nice.'

She seemed oblivious of the violent change in him.

'He's going to protect me.' Flo sighed. 'Nobody ever protected me before, not even Mum when that man she lived with made me bed him.'

'Flo!' Cecilia exclaimed. 'How old were you?' She seemed about nineteen now.

'I was eleven.' Her expression changed. 'Do you know Sir Nash?'

'I met him once,' Cecilia responded, her mind horrified by what Flo had just told her. 'That is how I learned about Vitium et Virtus.'

Flo shook her head. 'He sure talks about Vitium et Virtus a lot. Question after question about it, too.'

Cecilia remembered taking an instant dislike to Bowles in Paris. She'd avoided him and was grateful he'd not tried to hire her for the night. Now she wondered if she'd sensed his similarity to Duncan. Both abusive, violent men.

But there was violence in Oliver, too. She'd felt it.

Oliver brought Snyder with him to see Bowles, but they did not find him in Fleurette's room. It took some searching to discover him at the Union Club, reading a newspaper and sipping tea.

Bowles greeted Oliver with a pleased expression. 'Gregory. A pleasure to see you.' He gestured to the second chair at the table. 'Do sit down. Shall I have the servant bring you some tea? Something stronger?' He spoke with that slight lisp that always struck Oliver as a slippery affectation.

Snyder remained standing a few feet away. When Bowles noticed the large man, his friendly countenance momentarily faltered.

Oliver did not sit. 'I'd rather you come with me.'

Bowles looked alarmed. 'Where?'

Oliver signalled to Snyder, who strode over. They flanked Bowles, each taking an arm.

'Not far,' Oliver said.

They lifted Bowles to his feet.

'See here!' the man protested.

They half-walked, half-carried him out.

Once outside Oliver said, 'I learned something about you.'

Bowles blanched. 'What did you learn? It is not true. Not true. Who is talking about me?' His words rushed out.

They carried him to an alley at the back of the club and released him.

He started to back away. 'Two against one, Gregory? That is not a fair fight.'

Oliver didn't heed him. He advanced on Bowles, drew his fist back and punched him in the face.

Bowles fell backwards to the ground, clasping his cheek.

Oliver stood over him. 'How does that feel, Bowles?'

Bowles glared up at him.

Oliver held his ground. 'If I ever hear that you have struck any of the women who work for Vitium et Virtus, Snyder and I will return to finish this job once and for all.'

Bowles looked puzzled, then relieved, which made no sense at all. 'Who has said this?' he demanded.

'Never mind who. I have known you since school, Bowles. I've seen your cruelty.'

Bowles had been behind many a cruel stunt in school, but always slithered his way out of being caught. When they were boys, he'd picked on the younger ones, anyone weaker than he. Now he was older, he'd not changed, obviously.

Bowles's lip curled. 'Boyhood pranks. A long time ago.' He rose to his feet. 'Think, man. I want to own a share of Vitium et Virtus. Why would I damage the goods? Let me buy in to the club. I am certain I could find many creative roles for your beautiful women. If you, Westmoor and Challenger would allow me the opportunity, we could make a fine profit.'

Bowles was one of the men who perceived the club as a brothel, which it was not. It represented freedom, but not profit and certainly not exploitation.

Oliver advanced on him again, seizing him by his coat and lifting him to within inches of his face. 'Heed me, Bowles. You will not approach any of our workers. Unless you want more than this sample of what Snyder and I can do, you will stay away.'

Bowles lifted his hands. 'Easy. Easy. I am a peaceable man. If it pleases you, I will avoid any liaisons with your women. Will that do?'

Oliver released him with a shove. 'Stay away completely. Your membership is revoked.'

'That goes too far, Gregory,' Bowles snapped. 'I have been a member since the beginning.'

They'd made him a member all those years ago so he would keep the club secret, not because they'd wanted him there.

'No matter,' Oliver said. 'You are a member no longer. Do not set foot in the club or Snyder will toss you out. Do not engage with any of our women, or we will both be back.'

Oliver turned away and he and Snyder walked away, leaving Bowles in the alley to stew in his own juices.

They would return to Vitium et Virtus. Oliver would

tell Flo that Bowles promised to leave her alone. He hoped she would inform him if Bowles ever broke that promise.

He also hoped that Cecilia would approve of his action here today.

Chapter Twelve

Cecilia spent that afternoon in her sitting room, mending the purple costume she'd worn the night before. After she'd covered Flo's bruise and the girl went off to see her mother, Cecilia was left with a Gordian knot of emotions inside her. She envied Flo's easy trust of Oliver; she'd believed his word that he could make Bowles leave her alone. She also envied Flo's eagerness to see her mother, who would undoubtedly welcome her. Cecilia was glad of both those things. She was glad Flo's abuse had not escalated to a more dangerous level. She was glad Flo had a loving mother from whom Flo wished to hide her problems. Just because Cecilia could not say the same did not mean she was not happy for Flo.

She was confused about Oliver, which perhaps disturbed her the most. Which was he? A man capable of such kindness and tenderness towards a wounded girl? Or a man with violence inside him?

She'd not sensed that level of anger when he'd spoken to her father, but the fear she used to experience with Duncan returned when Oliver left in pursuit of Bowles.

He'd been angry enough to kill.

She pushed the needle through the fabric and tried to banish that thought from her mind.

A knock sounded at the sitting room door.

'Come in,' she said.

To her surprise, it was Oliver who stepped into the room. She held the needle poised in the air.

'I thought you might wish to know what happened,' he said.

Her hand shook. She immediately stuck the needle into the fabric and set the dress aside.

'Please sit, Oliver,' she managed, but her insides trembled at what she might hear.

He sat in the sofa across from her. 'Bowles was not at Flo's room, but we finally did find him.'

'We?' Who had gone with him?

'I took Snyder with me.'

Snyder, the flash man of Vitium et Virtus. Snyder was intimidating on first sight. Tall. Muscular. Unsmiling. But she was always grateful he was there at the club.

She nodded. 'So what did you do when you found Bowles?'

She sensed the violence again and gripped a fold in her skirt.

'I hit him.'

'You hit him?' She touched her cheek, feeling the memory of Duncan's fist against her face.

'Of course I hit him. I know Bowles. He would not have listened otherwise. I told him if he touched any one of my workers, Snyder and I would finish the job.'

She felt his ferocity. 'Finish the job?'

Oliver nodded. 'Bowles knows I never back down in a fight.'

'You—you've fought him before?'

He laughed drily. 'Not Bowles, but he's seen me fight many times.'

She'd heard of gentlemen who engaged in boxing matches, ridiculous contests of who could hit his opponent until his opponent was knocked out.

'Exactly where did he see you fight?' she asked.

He shrugged. 'On the fields of Eton and in its hallways. There were plenty of other boys who wished to show me my place. At Oxford, as well.'

'In school?' Was that where men learned to punch so hard the victim could see stars? 'You have known Bowles since school?' Was his anger at Bowles that long lasting?

He nodded. 'I knew it would take more than a threat to deter him. He needed to know we meant what we said. But we'll have to be vigilant. Bowles is a snake. He'll slink back as soon as he thinks we are no longer looking. I think I'll warn the entertainers and servants about him. We don't have to mention what happened to Flo.'

Her heart was pounding in anxiety. This image of Oliver striking Bowles roused memories of her husband. Duncan fought everyone, even the man who killed him in a duel.

'Bowles is a member of the club?' she asked.

'No longer,' he replied. He glanced at the door. 'Is Fleurette still at the club?'

Cecilia pulled herself away from memories. 'She is visiting her mother, but she is supposed to return to spend the night at the club tonight.' Cecilia insisted Flo return here and not to her room, just in case Oliver had not succeeded.

'I'll have Snyder tell her she is safe now.' He stood. 'Will I see you at dinner?'

She looked up at him, so tall, so handsome. So strong and powerful. 'Of course.'

'I will see you then.'

When he left the room, she dropped her head onto her hands.

He was a wonderful protector. Why did he also have to frighten her so?

Over the next week, Cecilia settled into a routine, dining with Oliver, walking to the club with him. The nights at Vitium et Virtus had been uneventful, and Cecilia fell into the familiar role of Coquette. Her father, apparently accepting his exile, did not return. There was also no sign of Sir Nash Bowles. Flo moved from her room to one closer to her mother. She'd not seen Bowles since Oliver had intervened. With each day, Flo grew happier and Cecilia allowed herself to be lulled into a comfortable sense of well-being.

Cecilia herself felt physically marvellous. This was her fourth month of pregnancy and she rarely experienced nausea any more. She suddenly had energy again, so much so that she made herself useful in Oliver's house. Helping with the mending. Putting his bookshelves in order. There was not much on his shelves that she wished to read, though. The poetry of Wordsworth and Coleridge was the lot.

Today Oliver invited her to come with him to the shops on Bond Street. She was always suspicious of invitations, but the weather was clear and crisp, making it a fine day for stretching one's legs and exploring the myriad shops that led Napoleon to call England a *nation of shopkeepers*.

She could not resist.

She wore a black dress that had been hastily made after the Queen died, a colour that did not reflect her current feeling of well-being, but was not unflattering. Her bonnet was also black. Both were gifts from Oliver and she was grateful. It meant she would not stand out from the other

Mayfair shoppers, the aristocrats who would undoubtedly respectfully mourn the Queen.

What a great deal that lady had endured, she thought. The madness of her husband. The death of a daughter, a granddaughter and a great-grandchild. The excesses of her sons. No wonder she kept her remaining daughters so confined.

Such motherly devotion. Cecilia dared not dwell on that subject lest she miss her mother all over again.

Never mind. She would have her baby and she'd love her baby with all her heart. She'd devote her life to her child's happiness.

If Oliver fulfilled his promise to support them.

She really was at his mercy as far as the support of her child was concerned and if she thought about that subject too much her feeling of well-being vanished.

She stood in front of the mirror in her bedchamber to check her appearance one more time, pressing the skirt of her dress against her belly to see if it looked as if her belly had swelled. It did.

But not enough to worry about showing under the generous material of her skirt. Enough, though, to remind herself that soon it would become obvious she was carrying a child. She did not know enough about childbearing to say when that would be. Another month? Two? Another worry she tried not to think of.

Instead, she smoothed out her skirt again, picked up her gloves and hurried out to the stairway.

Oliver waited at the bottom of the stairs, dressed in a black coat, waistcoat and black trousers. The dark coat and white linen shirt and neckcloth set off his dark skin and green eyes in a manner that took Cecilia's breath away.

She wished she would not have this reaction to him.

His magnetic eyes followed her down the stairs. Was the expression on his face approval? She could not tell.

'Am I presentable?' she asked warily.

His eyes scanned her. 'Very presentable.'

Irwin helped Cecilia on with her cloak and Oliver with his topcoat and black armband. He held the door as they left the house. Once on the pavement, Oliver offered his arm.

She accepted it. It would seem churlish not to.

'Where would you like to shop?' he asked as they approached Jermyn Street.

'Me?' she responded. 'I will go wherever you wish.'

They turned on to Jermyn Street and walked past the windows of Floris perfumers.

'Do you need some scent?' he asked.

She made do with lavender water. 'I do not like to spend my money on scent.'

He stopped at the doorway. 'I told you in Paris. I am rich. I can buy you scent.'

'Why would you, Oliver?' she asked. Perhaps her lavender water was not to his liking.

'Let us go in. I will purchase a throwaway for you. You can wear it at the masquerade.' He pulled her towards the door.

A throwaway was a small sample of a scent. Perhaps he wished a new scent to be part of her costume. The masquerade was planned to be the last big Vitium et Virtus event before Christmas, when most of the members travelled to their country houses or to house parties.

She acquiesced.

A clerk stood behind a long mahogany case that displayed scent bottles of all shapes, sizes and designs. 'May I be of assistance?' he asked.

'A throwaway for the lady,' Oliver said.

The clerk showed them a variety of scents and offered to make a special blend if she chose. She selected a scent, which was a blend of jasmine and other fragrances that seemed exotic and that met with Oliver's approval. The tiny cylindrical glass bottle was adorned with hand-painted gilt and enamel. It was wrapped in brown paper and tied with string. Oliver carried it in his pocket.

Next they stopped at Hatchard's bookshop, where Cecilia browsed through the first volume of a novel that caught her eye. She'd forgotten the pleasures of reading novels.

'What is that book?' he asked, coming to her side.

'It is two books in one,' she replied. '*Northanger Abbey* and *Persuasion* by the author of *Pride and Prejudice*.'

'Something you would enjoy?'

'I did enjoy *Pride and Prejudice*.' She'd read it an age ago when she'd still had stars in her eyes and dreams of romance and marriage.

'Will you allow me to buy it for you?' Oliver asked.

She closed it. 'No, indeed. Stop offering to buy me things.'

'Why?' he demanded.

Because it made her uncomfortable. Because it reminded her of Paris.

She touched the pearl that hung at her neck. 'It is not economical to buy a novel. One generally reads them just once.'

He shrugged. 'I have no need to be economical.'

What else could she say? 'Gifts come with obligation.'

He sobered. 'I have asked nothing of you. It is you who ask of me. You want me to support you.'

She leaned even closer. 'Not me. The baby.'

Their eyes caught and gazes held and the flush of arousal rushed through her. Like Paris all over again.

She glanced away and put the book back on the shelf.

'Did you find anything for yourself?' she asked.

He gently extended his hand and touched her arm, but just as quickly withdrew it and shook his head.

After they left Hatchard's they passed many ladies and gentlemen of Oliver's acquaintance on the street. He tipped his hat in greeting. The gentlemen tipped their hats in return; the ladies smiled appreciatively.

'I thought you were ostracised from society,' Cecilia said. 'There seem to be many people willing to acknowledge you.'

'I am not entirely a pariah,' he admitted. 'Because of Frederick and Jacob—' and Nicholas '—I actually have mixed in society quite a bit. Even my father has included me in invitations from time to time.'

She laughed. 'And here I thought you as scandalous as I am.'

He did not like to hear her speak of herself that way.

'Oh, I am perfectly acceptable if some young buck wants a phaeton race or a sparring match or sword fight. Or if his father enjoys a high-stakes game of cards or wishes membership in Vitium et Virtus. Or his mother or married sister wishes a flirtation.' He frowned. 'But no one wishes me anywhere near their marriageable daughters. No one wants the family line tainted by a half-caste's blood.' He glanced down at her and made himself smile. 'No vouchers for Almack's for me.'

She gave him a look of sympathy. 'None for me either. I cannot imagine I'd ever receive any society invitation.' She grimaced. 'Except the sort of invitation the patrons of Vitium et Virtus offer me.'

They walked on.

'Does it bother you?' she asked.

'Not always,' he admitted. Not when he could distract

his mind from the memories of the time in India when he'd known love and security.

He did not ask if it bothered her, but she answered anyway.

'Sometimes I wonder what my life would have been like if I had not eloped with Duncan.' She blinked. 'But I will never know, will I?'

He made himself smile again. 'Better to enjoy the fine weather, the exercise—' he felt his skin warm as he gazed at her '—and the company.'

Her gaze met his and held. 'Yes. It is a fine day.'

This moment felt like Paris. He would cherish it.

They crossed Piccadilly and walked down Old Bond Street, stopping in a grocer's to purchase tea and pausing to look at all the prints displayed in Ackermann's windows.

He spied another place. Hookham's. 'Let us go in here,' he said.

She did not realise what sort of establishment it was until they crossed the threshold.

'A Circulating Library!' she cried.

This was one way to give her the pleasure of the book she'd examined in Hatchard's. 'You cannot object to me signing you up for the Circulating Library.'

This ploy worked in Paris. Why not here? She'd refused his offer of jewels, but accepted the necklace with a single pearl. It had worked at Floris, too. No bottles of expensive scent, but she had agreed to a small throwaway.

She would not allow him to purchase a book for her, but how could she refuse a subscription to a circulating library? It only cost one pound and fourteen shillings for a subscription for two persons for six months.

After six months, he did not know what would happen.

He walked her to the counter and arranged for a subscription for eight volumes at a time.

'And what books would the lady like to borrow?' the clerk asked.

He turned to her. 'Do you want the one you looked at in Hatchard's?'

'Very well, Oliver.' She sighed. To the clerk, she said, '*Northanger Abbey* and *Persuasion*.'

'Volume one?' the man asked.

'All volumes,' Oliver said.

Books were often in four volumes. It stood to reason to borrow them all at once.

'Any other?' the clerk asked.

He might as well borrow the book he'd looked at in Hatchard's. '*The Principles of Political Economy and Taxation.*'

'Excellent choices, sir,' the clerk said.

Oliver supposed he said that to every subscriber.

The clerk extended his hand. 'Please have some refreshment while I fulfil your request.'

They left the counter. 'Do you want some refreshment?' Oliver asked.

'No,' she responded. 'But I would not mind sitting for a moment.'

'We can wait in the reading room,' he said.

The reading room was a place where subscribers could pass the time until their books were found. Some read the newspapers, which were made available. Others read the books they'd selected to borrow to see if they really wanted them.

In the reading room were a gentleman engrossed in a newspaper and two ladies standing in conversation. One lady had her back to them and she blocked a view of the other. When the lady moved slightly, the other woman's face was visible for a moment.

Cecilia emitted a small sound of alarm and abruptly pulled away from Oliver. She fled back to the main room and retreated to the front of the shop where there was a window display.

He hurried after her.

'What is it, Cecilia?' he asked.

She appeared to be gazing out the window. 'The lady— the lady in the reading room.' She seemed to have trouble breathing.

'What of her?'

She faced him and her eyes filled with pain. 'She is my mother.'

Her mother?

Cecilia seemed to shrink before his eyes, becoming a frightened child. 'May—may we leave?'

Leave? She'd once gone in search of her parents for their help. Her father had his chance to embrace her and return her to the family. He'd lost that chance.

But she must not give up on the possibility that she might reunite with her mother! What he would give for even one brief moment with his mother.

He gripped her arm. 'You confronted your father. Now confront your mother. Say to her all the things you wish to say. You may not get another opportunity.'

She straightened and he watched her transform herself yet again, this time from weakness to strength. 'You are right.'

He released her.

She strode to the reading room. The two women were still conversing. One was older—Cecilia's mother, he presumed. The other, the one whose back was to them, was younger.

Cecilia walked directly up to them. 'Hello, Mama,' she said.

Her mother gazed at her and it took a moment for her eyes to widen in surprise.

It was the younger woman who spoke first. 'Cecilia!'

'Hello, Agnes.' Cecilia's voice sounded flat.

Her mother took a step forward. 'Cecilia!'

The younger woman stopped her. 'Mama! Remember what Papa said when she eloped?' Cecilia's sister, obviously.

Her mother pushed her aside and came up to Cecilia. Tears were in her mother's eyes. 'My darling daughter! How are you?' She touched Cecilia's arms, as if to test whether they were in one piece. Her gaze swept over her daughter. 'I cannot believe you are here.'

'Mama!' Agnes broke in again.

Cecilia was speechless.

Her mother ignored Cecilia's sister. 'But why did we not hear a word from you? Where have you been all these years?' She seemed to notice Oliver. 'This is not your husband?'

'My husband is dead, Mama.' She turned to Oliver. 'This is Mr Gregory. A—a friend.'

'Lady Dorman.' Oliver bowed. He nodded to Agnes. 'Ma'am.'

He seemed to be too much for the baroness to take in. She turned to Cecilia again. 'My condolences,' she said, not very sincerely. 'Why did you never write to me?'

Cecilia looked puzzled. 'I wrote many times, Mama. I had only the one letter from Papa.'

Her mother stumbled and looked as if she could not keep her balance.

Oliver caught Lady Dorman before she fell. 'Come, you should sit.'

He supported her until she lowered herself onto a sofa. She reached for Cecilia's hand so she would sit beside her. Agnes primly took a seat nearby. Oliver stepped back.

'I—I never received a letter from you,' her mother said.

Cecilia glanced at Agnes, who blinked and turned her head.

'Do you know anything of this?' Cecilia asked her sister.

The sister lifted her nose. 'Papa told Joan and me to consider you dead, so he destroyed any letters from you.'

'He destroyed letters?' her mother cried.

The clerk stood in the doorway, looking hesitant. Oliver was not sure how long he'd been there. The man reading the newspaper was still reading.

'Your books, sir,' the clerk said uncertainly.

Oliver walked over to him and took the books, which were wrapped in brown paper.

'Mama,' Cecilia said gently. 'Do not be distressed.'

Her mother looked at her again, a reverent expression on her face. She stroked her daughter's cheek. 'I thought you were lost for ever.'

'I—I've been living in France,' Cecilia said.

As with her father, she had not mentioned that she was expecting a child. There was much she left out. How much had she left out for him?

Her mother grasped her hands. 'Now you are a widow, you can come home!'

Cecilia winced in pain. 'You must ask Papa about that.' She knew, of course, she was not welcome home. 'But tell me, Mama. Are you in good health?'

Her mother continued to hold Cecilia's hands as she related a list of minor complaints to which Cecilia listened sympathetically. When her mother finished, Cecilia turned to Agnes. 'What of you, Agnes? How do you fare?'

Agnes seemed surprised Cecilia asked about her. 'I am married to Mr Higgins, Sir William Higgins's son.'

'How nice,' Cecilia said. 'Do you have any children?'

Agnes faltered. 'Not yet.' She changed the subject. 'Joan is married, too. To Mr Pottinger, an earl's younger son. She has no children either.'

Cecilia gave her a warm smile. 'I wish you both happy.'

Agnes turned her face away.

'Where are you staying?' Lady Dorman asked. 'Are you living here in London?'

Cecilia glanced to Oliver before answering, 'I rent a room in Mr Gregory's property.'

'How do you live?' her mother asked, then gave an answer. 'I suppose you have a widow's pension.'

Agnes interrupted. 'Mama, can you not see she is in Mr Gregory's keeping? She is his mistress.'

Cecilia paled.

Oliver calmly spoke up. 'She is not in my keeping, Mrs Higgins. She does let a room, however.'

'What a silly thing to say,' her mother chastised Agnes, who gave an obstinate look.

'Mama, we should go,' Agnes said, rising from the chair. 'Lady Ashton is expecting us to call.'

Lady Dorman clasped Cecilia's hands again. 'You will call upon me soon, will you not?'

'Mama,' Cecilia replied. 'I cannot. Papa has forbidden me.'

Her mother looked puzzled. 'You have seen him?'

'I called once,' she prevaricated. 'I was told not to call again.'

Oliver stepped forward and handed Cecilia's mother his card. 'If you should need to speak to your daughter, you can send a message to me. I will see she receives it.'

Agnes gestured with her hand. 'Mama, we must go.'

Cecilia helped her mother to stand.

'I am quite all right now,' her mother said. 'It was the shock, you know.' She embraced Cecilia. 'My darling daughter. You are alive.'

'Goodbye, Mama.' Cecilia's voice cracked.

'Mama!' Agnes demanded.

Her mother bustled out of the room behind her other daughter, turning at the doorway for one more glance at Cecilia.

Cecilia collapsed on to the sofa as soon as her mother left. She was a hair's breadth from bursting into tears. Her mother had not disowned her! Her mother had cared about her.

Oliver sat at her side, but said nothing.

She could not look at him. 'You made me confront her. I would never have known otherwise.' It meant everything to her.

His voice turned soft and low. 'She is your mother.' He cleared his throat and his tone turned more conversational. 'I liked her better than your father. I cannot say the same about your sister, though.'

'She was brought up to despise me.'

Their father had reminded her sisters frequently that Cecilia, the youngest, was the reason they did not have more dresses, more visits to London, a larger dowry. If only she had not been born.

Cecilia suspected her father had not mentioned to them that Cecilia had been given no dowry. That money was certainly lost to gambling.

'I would like to write to my mother again, when—when I go away,' she said.

'Go away?' he asked.

'After the baby is born,' she said quietly. 'I plan to move away where no one knows me.'

He frowned and turned away from her. When he turned back his eyes were filled with resolve. 'If you ever want your mother to receive a letter from you, send it to me. I will make certain she receives it.'

She believed him.

Chapter Thirteen

The next day turned cold and rainy and Oliver could think of no reason to go out, not even to Vitium et Virtus, which would be closed this night. He holed himself in the small room that was his library and opened the book he'd borrowed from Hookham's.

It was hard reading, but intriguing. Oliver had never paid much attention to things like the value of land and how much workers should be compensated. It stimulated his thinking. It also expanded his thinking beyond the offerings of Vitium et Virtus, to ideas about producing food and manufacturing essential items, of paying wages based on the value of the tasks performed, and a concept of minimum wage that provided workers enough for food, clothing and shelter.

Perhaps there was more to life than a scandalous gentlemen's club.

His butler came to the door. 'Sir, do you recall the gentleman you asked me to take heed of?'

Bowles? It would be like Bowles to make more trouble.

Irwin went on. 'The gentleman who might ask for Mrs Lockhart?'

Not Bowles. Lord Dorman.

'Is he here asking for her?'

'That he is,' Irwin said. 'What do you wish me to do?'

Irwin would probably throw the man out if Oliver wanted him to.

'I'll see him,' he said instead. 'Did you put him in the drawing room?'

'That I did, sir. He was complaining all the way.'

Oliver closed his book. 'Tell him I'll be down directly.' He rose from his chair and entered the drawing room a minute behind Irwin.

Dorman swung around to him. 'I asked to see my daughter, not you.'

Oliver raised his brows. 'Now she is your daughter? I thought she was dead to you.'

Dorman huffed. 'You know my meaning.'

'Why call here to see her?' Oliver asked.

Dorman gave him a smug look. 'I asked around. I know she lives here.' He sneered. 'With you.'

There was no use in denying it. 'What is this business you have with Mrs Lockhart?' Oliver asked.

'Why should I tell you?'

Oliver came close to him. 'Because I will not have you distressing her. You have done damage enough.'

'What concern is it of yours?' Dorman persisted.

'She is my employee and my friend,' Oliver said. 'Both mean I care that she is not distressed.'

'Humph!' Dorman's expression was of disdain. 'My daughter Agnes tells me she's more than that.'

'Ah.'

Cecilia's sister informed her father about the meeting at the circulating library. And, of course, his wife now knew he had destroyed Cecilia's letters.

'Perhaps you can tell me what you wish to say to Mrs Lockhart. I will pass on the message...' Oliver paused. 'Unless it is hurtful.'

'She is never to contact any member of this family again!' Dorman cried. 'Tell her that. Or show me where the chit is hiding and I will tell her.'

'I doubt she finds it necessary to hide from you.' In fact, Oliver had no more right to keep her from seeing her father than her father had to order her presence.

It should be up to Cecilia to decide.

'If you care to have a seat, I will ask if she wishes to see you.' He gave Dorman a steely glare. 'But I warn you, if you are not civil, you will be tossed out on your ear.'

'You wouldn't dare!' Dorman lifted his chin. 'A man of my station.'

Oliver gave him a sarcastic smile. 'Ah, but I have no station, as you indicated in our last…encounter. What trouble can you cause me?'

Dorman pursed his lips, no doubt frustrated that he had no clout at all with Oliver.

'If you pardon me, I will speak to Mrs Lockhart.' Oliver did not give Dorman a chance to say another word. He walked out of the room and went in search of Cecilia.

Cecilia sat reading by her window when there was a knock at the door.

Oliver.

The last time he'd knocked on her door had been after dealing with Sir Nash. 'Come in,' she said.

He entered the room and sat in a chair near her. 'Your father is downstairs.'

Her stomach turned to lead. 'My father.'

'He wishes to see you. I almost tossed him out, but the choice should be yours. Do you wish to see him?'

He made it her choice? Considered her feelings? She felt a crack in her resolve not to let down her guard about him.

'Did he say why he came?' she asked.

'I suspect he wishes to speak to you about seeing your mother and sister.'

Of course.

'If you do not wish to see him, I will deal with him for you,' Oliver said.

'I will see him.'

He stood and extended his hand to help her rise. His hand was warm. And strong.

They walked out of her room together and descended the stairs. Irwin, looking serious, was attending the hall.

'Stay nearby,' Oliver told him.

Irwin nodded.

Cecilia hesitated before entering the room. She straightened her spine and lifted her head. Her father would not see how much his rejection wounded her.

She strode into the room. 'You wished to see me, Papa.'

As before, at the club, and at the Circulating Library, Oliver remained by the doorway, but she knew he was there.

Her father turned to her. 'You've caused me more trouble,' he spat out. 'Talking nonsense to your mother.'

'Nonsense?' Her eyes widened.

Her father went on, 'We washed our hands of you, remember.'

She crossed her arms over her chest. 'Oh, I remember. Did you come merely to remind me?'

His nostrils flared. 'I came to forbid you to see your mother or your sisters. You stay away from them. I said you are dead to us. Stay dead.'

She placed her hand on her abdomen for a brief moment, before saying coolly, 'You can no longer order me, Papa.'

He went on. 'I'll not have you filling your mother's head with your stories and making life difficult for her.'

'Do you mean telling her of your membership at Vitium

et Virtus? Of your gambling and debauchery? Of destroying my letters?' She kept her gaze steady. 'Or of sending me away when I came to call upon you?' When she'd felt in such need of her mother.

'You have already told her about the letters,' he snapped.

It was Agnes who had told their mother, but Cecilia did not have the heart to put her sister in her father's black books.

'And I am free to disclose anything I know to my mother or to anyone else. I have been disowned by you. I have been married and widowed. You have no say in what I do.'

He took several steps and leaned into her face, but she did not back away. From behind her she heard Oliver move closer.

Her father shook his finger in her face. 'You will do what I say or else.'

She did not flinch. 'Or else what?'

His expression turned smug. 'I will tell your mother you work in a brothel.'

Oliver stepped up, his eyes shooting fire. 'Enough, Dorman!'

Her father backed off.

Oliver's voice rose and shook with anger. 'You dare to threaten us? Recall that I have powerful friends. You cannot harm me. I will not allow you to harm your daughter. I assure you, I will destroy you if you try!'

Cecilia trembled at Oliver's fierce tone and dangerous expression. She felt his repressed rage. It frightened her.

Her father stormed out without another word.

Oliver still seemed like a powder keg that might explode at any minute. 'He had better not threaten you again.'

She was too shaken to say anything. She nodded and fled the room.

* * *

That evening, for the first time, Cecilia asked to dine alone in her rooms. Oliver's anger had frightened her and she simply could not sit in the dining room with him.

After Mary took away her dinner dishes, however, she'd calmed down and guilt seeped in. Oliver's anger had been in her defence, after all. Running off and avoiding him were shabby ways of expressing her gratitude.

She ought to apologise. She rose with resolve and left her rooms to go in search of him, hoping he had not gone out.

She found him seated at a table in the drawing room, gazing down at it and apparently not hearing her approach.

'Oliver?'

He raised his head. A desolate expression on his face changed to a neutral one. He nodded a greeting.

She walked over to where he was sitting and glanced down at the table. It was made of light and dark wood inlay forming long triangles on two sides, their points meeting in the middle. There were chips of white and black marble on the triangles and two sets of dice, one set white, one black, with cups in which to shake them.

'It is a game!' she exclaimed, glad for something else to talk about than explaining why she'd avoided him at dinner.

He moved one of the pieces. 'Backgammon.'

'I have seen this game before,' she said. 'Some of the soldiers played it.'

He looked up at her. 'Do you know how to play?'

She shook her head.

'Would you like to learn?' he asked.

The anger she'd sensed in him seemed to have been supplanted by a sadness that evoked sympathy, not fear. She ached to dispel it. Perhaps to ease her guilt.

'I'd be delighted to learn,' she said.

He gestured for her to sit and rearranged the game pieces. 'Backgammon is an ancient game, known to the Romans and before, but I'd never heard of it until I found this table. I bought it and found a book about the game— *A Short Treatise on the Game of Backgammon.* I taught myself to play.'

'Can only one person play?'

He gave a soft laugh. 'If one plays both sides. You'll be my first true opponent.'

He showed her the rules by playing a couple of practice games. The game was simple enough, easier than chess where each piece moved differently. It took her a few games—a few losses—to grasp that there was strategy involved. She focused even more on her play, wanting to win.

They began to compete in earnest. Both ignored anything but the roll of the dice and moving the pieces. Cecilia let go of her fear of his anger and forgot her guilt at avoiding him. She merely wanted to protect her game pieces as she moved them around and off the board.

'Gammon!' she cried, taking her final two pieces off. Oliver was left with all his pieces still on the board. Gammon gave her an extra point. 'I won!'

'That you did,' he said with some dismay. He immediately set up the pieces again. 'You caught on quickly.'

'I've played some chess and draughts,' she responded. 'When I was following the drum.'

'Not as a child?' He handed her one of the white die.

'Not really.' She put the die in the cup. 'My sisters hated it when I won, so I rarely had an opportunity to play.'

'You have a talent for this game,' he said.

* * *

Oliver put his black die in the cup, shook it and rolled it onto the table.

Earlier he'd been plunging into depression when she had come into the room, willing to play.

He'd missed her at dinner. He relished her company then and it had been lonely without her.

It would be even lonelier when she left for good. He did not want to think about it. He wanted only to enjoy this moment with her.

She rolled her white die. 'Did you play games as a child?'

From the time he could remember he'd played games. With his friends at school. Occasionally with his father. But his earliest memories were playing games with his mother.

He smiled. 'In India, I used to play a game called Snakes and Ladders.'

'Snakes and Ladders?'

'Snakes and Ladders.'

He closed his eyes and could see the board with its black snakes crisscrossing the squares and ladders. The writing on the board was foreign, but he could remember reading it.

He opened his eyes again. 'The board consisted of squares. Each square was a house and each house represented an emotion. You threw the dice to see how far you could go. The ladders represented good feelings and you could rise to the top of the ladders on good feelings, but if you landed on a snake, a bad feeling, you slid back down the board and slipped further and further from *nirvana*.'

'What is *nirvana*?' she asked.

Another memory, this time of his mother, flashed into his mind. Wrapped in her brightly coloured sari, her face beatific, she told him of *nirvana*. 'It is the highest happiness, but also perfect quietude, oblivious to the world of pain and worry.'

Cecilia looked at him with a sober expression. 'Imagine a game all about emotions where one tries to win happiness and peace.'

He held on to the memory as if it were a precious jewel. Emotions had been free-floating in his mother's house. She displayed them generously. Joy. Love. Anger. Sadness.

Grief.

When he arrived in England, though, expression of emotion was forbidden.

Cecilia reached across the table and grasped his hand. 'You've turned sad, Oliver.'

He blinked. 'I was remembering India.'

She kept her hand in his, and he held on to her until the wave of unbidden and forbidden emotion washed through him.

She did not speak until he relaxed his grip. 'Shall we put the game table away?'

He smiled. 'Not until you give me a chance to win another game.'

She returned a smile, reminding him of Paris. 'If you think you have a chance. I believe I have caught on.'

She won the first move.

Halfway through the game, in which he was ahead, she leaned back and put her hand on her abdomen. 'Oh!'

He dropped his dice. 'What is it?'

Was something wrong?

She looked at him with wonder in her eyes. 'The baby moved! I felt the baby move.'

She took his hand and pulled him from his chair to come closer to her. She placed his hand on her abdomen.

She smiled. 'Can you feel it?'

He knelt on the floor next to her. Her hand covered his, holding it in place. There was the faintest flutter beneath his fingertips. He kept still and the flutter happened again.

He met her gaze, feeling a connection as strong as they'd experienced in lovemaking.

'It is real,' she whispered. 'A real life inside me.'

A real life. Had this life come from that extraordinary night they shared in Paris? Was this new life a part of him?

He did not dare believe it.

He stood abruptly. She pulled her hand from his, her expression wounded and confused.

Chapter Fourteen

The next two weeks settled into a routine. Oliver dined with Cecilia, walked to Vitium et Virtus with her and even played backgammon with her, but he kept himself at a distance. He wanted what he could never possess. He wanted a family with her. He wanted the baby to be his. He wanted them to be together.

Everything she did not want and could not guarantee.

At least there had been enough to keep him busy. Vitium et Virtus was preparing for their annual masquerade ball, the last event before the club closed for Christmas. All members were invited and were encouraged to bring guests, making for larger crowds than the club was accustomed to.

The Queen's death made it the only ball anyone could attend, because no one hosted such a lavish party while the country was in mourning—except for Vitium et Virtus, that is.

In previous years Oliver would have been delighted to flout any of society's rules. That was expected at Vitium et Virtus. But the old Queen had been the mother of the country and it seemed unnecessary, disrespectful and simply juvenile to defy the decree to mourn her.

It was not only up to him, though. Both Jacob and Frederick expected Vitium et Virtus to hold the masquerade. All the members counted on it. Oliver supposed the club did have a reputation of irreverence to uphold.

He decided to honour the Queen by dedicating the ball to her. The Queen loved the bucolic life, so Oliver gave the masquerade that theme. The male workers of Vitium et Virtus dressed as peasants or farmers. The singers dressed as milkmaids; the dancers, shepherdesses and the girls in the game room, peasants. Their costumes were, of course, idealised versions of these characters about whom many bawdy songs were sung. Their skirts were short, showing plenty of ankle, and were made from colourful printed fabric. His workers wore their hair unbound, tied back only with brightly coloured scarves. The singers carried milk pails, the dancers, shepherd's crooks.

Cecilia's costume, a dress of red and white stripes with a huge white apron flounced across her middle, was not as revealing. Her skirts reached the floor, although the neckline dipped low enough to show a tantalising glimpse of bosom. She wore her hair unbound, too, reminding Oliver too much of that night in Paris when her mahogany tresses were splayed across the white bed linens.

Masks, of course, were required and, because of the numbers of non-members attending, many attendees covered their faces more carefully. Oliver knew that the more the attendees' identities were disguised, the looser their behaviour would become.

This was a night to stay vigilant.

Once he would simply have joined in and relished the bacchanalia, but ever since Nicholas's disappearance, he'd regarded the club more seriously. No harm to anyone should come from attending the club. Or from working there. Fleurette had been hurt and Oliver had put a stop to that, but he'd not been able to stop the harm that had come to Nicholas.

Yes, tonight he would be vigilant.

The guests started arriving. Snyder and Mr Bell were busy collecting the vouchers that had been issued for admittance. That task was not too onerous at the moment, but when the guests all arrived at once it would be more difficult.

Oliver walked from the ballroom to the game room, checking on things, watching things. Making certain food was plentiful and the drinks flowed.

The singers and dancers made a show of entering. They would perform during breaks in the dancing. Discordant sounds came from the orchestra as they tuned their instruments. More guests arrived.

Oliver stepped into the hallway and glanced over the stair railing down to the entrance.

What an incongruous sight. Vitium et Virtus masquerade balls typically were a potpourri of finery, of outrageous excess, a contest of who might have the cleverest, most outlandish costume of all. This view from above reminded him more of a county fair. Although costumes were exaggerated—hats were larger, trousers baggier, aprons and caps puffier—it looked more like everyone had come from farms and villages for a market-day festivity. Instead of costumes of brilliant reds, yellows, and blues, or dominoes of the deepest black, the guests' costumes were mostly shades of brown and grey.

Not very festive.

Amidst the stream of faux farm workers entering the hall, he spied Cecilia, who appeared like a flower blossoming out of the bare earth. As she made her way through the crowd, she greeted the arrivals and spoke to them, probably encouraging them to come to the game room and try their luck at the faro and hazard tables.

Although, she was not Cecilia at the moment. She was Coquette, seductively slinking through the crowd, lightly touching men on their arms, leaning close, smiling at them.

He watched her climb the stairs, hips loose, dark hair flowing down her back.

His senses flared. This version of Cecilia was a man's dream.

His dream.

He remembered how she'd looked when she'd asked to come to his hotel that night. He remembered how she'd relished their lovemaking, how he'd relished it.

God help him, he wanted her all over again. He wanted her now. He did not want to let her go, alone to raise a child who could not claim a father's name.

She reached the top of the stairs and started for the game room, but turned back and walked up to him instead. 'Is anything amiss, Oliver?'

He was taken aback by the question. 'No…why do you ask?'

'You looked—I don't know—distressed.'

Not distressed. Aroused.

He attempted a smile. 'Much to think about tonight.'

Her brows knitted. 'Let me know if I can help.'

Impulsively, he put his arms around her and pressed her to him. 'Save a dance for me.'

She nodded, her eyes wide. He released her and she backed away, turned and melted into the crowd.

Cecilia wound her way through the growing crowd, her body still throbbing from Oliver's sudden embrace.

Gentlemen greeted her as Coquette, forcing her to act as Coquette.

She smiled. 'Come see me in the game room,' she said, making the invitation sound seductive.

There would be large quantities of wine and spirits flowing tonight and likely a great deal of money wagered. No doubt there would be sexual excesses of all types. She'd heard from the other workers that Oliver used to indulge in every excess, that he'd been linked with the many women eager to bed him.

She could understand why.

She flushed with the memory of making love with him, of feeling his body against hers in that sudden embrace. A mere touch of his hand brought it all back. How his hand felt on her naked flesh, how his lips tasted, how it felt when he entered her—

She must stop thinking of this.

She'd glimpsed him as she climbed the stairs to the first floor. She felt his unease. The masquerade was supposed to be the foremost event offered at Vitium et Virtus, but she could sense no excitement or enjoyment in Oliver to attest to that impression.

She certainly did not expect to enjoy it.

She'd attended masquerades in Paris as required by the manager at Maison D'Eros. The men in Paris took a costume and a mask as licence to behave in as debauched and depraved a manner as possible. She'd endured many an unwanted kiss and incessant groping at a masquerade. The neckline of her dress tonight was too low for her comfort, especially since her breasts seemed to have grown larger. Wearing her hair down made her feel as if she were getting ready for bed.

In any event, the gentlemen who frequented the game room at Vitium et Virtus were typically well behaved once they understood she was not available for licentious purposes. Tonight, though, she suspected they'd behave just as badly as their Parisian counterparts.

She stood at the hazard table, encouraging the players to roll the dice, pretending to be excited or disappointed, depending upon the roll. One of the gentlemen who wore tight buckskins and tall boots, with just a loose shirt and vest, threw his arm around her. She waited a moment before manoeuvring her way out of it. Another clodhopper patted her derrière when he stepped up to the table. She pretended to be amused. She sidled away, but the man moved closer, this time stroking her behind.

She glanced up and saw Oliver in the doorway. Had he seen that bit of intimate contact? Her face burned at the thought. But why? Was that not why she was hired? So the men would remain at the table and wager their money?

Oliver called loudly so everyone in the room could hear, 'The dancing will begin in the ballroom.'

The card players did not even look up.

The announcement gave Cecilia an opportunity to escape the man with the busy hands.

'Oh, dancing!' she cried. 'I adore dancing.'

She hurried out the door and away from groping fingers, hands and arms.

When she stepped into the hallway, Oliver was there.

'May I watch the dancing for a while?' she asked. 'I need to get away for a bit.'

'I saw,' he said.

He brushed against her as they walked to the ballroom, and her body flared in response. Odd that the men groping her in the game room left her cold, but even the barest of contact with Oliver could arouse her.

When the first set began, he touched her arm.

'Save a waltz for me,' he murmured into her ear before

she left his side and mingled with others who watched the dancers perform the figures of the quadrille.

Cecilia had never been to a London ball, but she'd always imagined it to be an exciting, glittering affair, with beautiful gowns on graceful ladies and gentlemen in exquisitely fitting formal attire. This ball seemed colourless and affected. It made her sad.

She glanced over at Oliver, who frowned as he watched the dancers. Was he feeling the same? Too often it seemed as if she could feel what he felt.

When the set ended, he walked through the crowd towards her. Her insides fluttered.

'The next set is a waltz,' he said, extending his hand. 'Shall we?'

She put her hand in his, her fingers tingling. 'As you wish.'

He escorted her onto the ballroom floor.

To her surprise, the Duke and Duchess of Westmoor stood near them.

'How do you fare?' the Duchess asked her. 'Is Oliver taking good care of you?'

The Duchess's tone was light-hearted, but did she know more than she let on? Did she know about the baby? Would Oliver have told her?

'I am well, thank you,' Cecilia answered politely. 'And you?'

She and the Duke were already facing each other. Her hands were on his shoulders and the Duke's were on her waist.

'I am very well,' the Duchess answered, smiling at her husband.

Oliver regarded them both with a fond expression. 'Will

it not cause a scandal that the Duke and Duchess are seen dancing the waltz at Vitium et Virtus?'

The waltz was still considered scandalous by some, because the man and woman faced each other, touched each other and danced alone rather than doing figures in groups of four or more.

The Duke laughed. 'Nothing matters but we are together and happy.' He smiled. 'Besides, we are in costume and masked. Who will know us?'

Another joke. Certainly both she and Oliver had instantly recognised them.

The music began.

With hands held, Cecilia and Oliver began the dance with a short march, then faced each other. Cecilia curtsied; Oliver bowed. Then Cecilia put her hands on his shoulders; his hands touched her waist. As the music played its sweeping tune, Oliver led her twirling around the room.

Cecilia forgot the Duke and Duchess. She forgot the colourless dancers. She faced Oliver, his hands in near embrace, music transporting them. His black mask intensified his green eyes. She felt his gaze upon her more acutely than his hands at her waist. Her body hummed with wanting him.

How glad she was that he was her baby's father. How she wished she could repeat the lovemaking that had created that child.

'Your thoughts?' he asked, his voice deepening.

She shook her head. 'The dance.'

He gazed down at her, his eyes warming her. Thrilling her. She wished the music would never end.

When it did end, it took her a moment to realise it. She leaned towards him and his head dipped down. But the noise of the other couples leaving the dance floor woke her to where she was. She took her hands from his shoulders and stepped back.

'I—I should return to the game room,' she said.

Before he could respond she turned and fled.

It was a bit difficult, but she turned herself back into Coquette, entered the game room and forced herself to approach each of the tables of card players to ask after their comfort. She brought several men drinks and replenished others with a carafe of brandy. At least busying herself helped pass the time. Helped calm herself.

She walked to the faro table, passing out more drinks and encouraging the players to increase their wagers. A short, thick-set man with dark hair and dark, beady eyes stood watching the play. She'd not seen him before, she did not think, but there was something familiar about him.

'May I get you a drink, sir?' she asked the man.

His eyes shifted as if in alarm, but he finally smiled. 'Some brandy, perhaps, would be very nice, my dear.' He spoke with a lisp.

'My pleasure,' she said, turning away and walking to where the drinks were. She brought another carafe of brandy and a glass and returned to the faro table.

'Here you are, sir,' she said in Coquette's cheerful voice.

She poured him some brandy and refilled the glass of the man beside him.

'Thank you, Coquette,' the man said.

'Coquette?' the stranger piped up. 'Have we met before, Coquette?'

She suddenly knew him. He was Sir Nash Bowles. The man who had beaten Flo. He remembered her from Paris, she was certain.

Her hand trembled, but she poured him more brandy and made herself smile seductively. 'Perhaps we have met, sir. I have been many places. Met many gentlemen.'

He nodded, but looked thoughtful.

Did he remember her as Madame Coquette? The courtesan? What would Oliver think if he knew of Madame Coquette?

She could not worry about that. Bowles posed a danger to Flo.

Cecilia strolled to the hazard table and emptied the carafe in other glasses before returning it to the bar and sauntering out of the room. Once in the hallway, she dashed to the ballroom, searching for Oliver.

She found Flo. 'Have you seen Oliver?'

Flo was arm in arm with some gentleman. 'He was here a while ago.'

Cecilia leaned down to whisper in Flo's ear. 'Stay here. Stay with this man. Do not go in the game room.'

Flo's brow creased in confusion, but she nodded and clutched the man's arm tighter.

Cecilia wound her way through the crowd, which was becoming louder and more raucous. She finally spied Oliver at the door of the ballroom. She had to fight the crowd to reach the doorway again, but he'd already left. She caught up with him on the landing as he was descending the stairs.

'Oliver!' she called.

He turned, and she ran down the stairs to him.

She tried not to raise her voice. 'Bowles is here! I saw him in the game room.'

His gaze caught hers. He bounded back up the stairs, and Cecilia ran behind him. They hurried to the game room, but Bowles was no longer there. They searched in the ballroom, but how could they find him among so many like-costumed men?

From the ballroom, she glimpsed him in the hallway.

'There!' she cried to Oliver, pointing to the door.

They went after him, but as they reached the stairs, he had crossed the entrance hall to the front door.

'Stop him!' Oliver cried, but no one was near. Snyder was not at his post.

Oliver raced down the stairs. Cecilia hurried after him, but he was out the door before she reached the hall. Where was Snyder? She searched for him, but he was not near. What else was there to do but follow Oliver outside? The street was busy enough even at this late hour. She searched up and down the pavement to no avail. When she passed the entrance to the alley leading to the rear of the buildings on Jermyn and Bury Streets, she heard a man's cry. The alley was dark, but she entered it, walking carefully until she could make out two men in the darkness.

One man was beating on the other with his fists.

'Stay away, Bowles!' she heard Oliver shout. 'Did you not think me serious?' He held one of Bowles's arms in one hand and punched him with the other.

'No!' she gasped, but her voice was too soft to carry.

She couldn't breathe. Oliver was beating Bowles! She cowered, remembering how it felt to be hit over and over. *Stop, Oliver!* she wanted to cry, but fear locked her throat. Oliver could kill Bowles with his bare hands, just as Duncan could have killed her. She could not bear to watch and was too frightened to try to stop it. She turned on her heel and ran, her heart pounding wildly.

She could not return to Vitium et Virtus and pretend to be Coquette, not while Oliver might be killing Bowles. She went instead to Oliver's house and pounded on the door until Irwin let her in.

Chapter Fifteen

Oliver pulled off his mask and looked down on Bowles, seated in a puddle in the alley. Blood dripped from his nose and one eye had already swollen shut.

It served Bowles right.

Bowles had pulled a knife on him, but Oliver had been quick enough to deflect the blade from stabbing him in the chest.

He picked up the knife and pointed it into Bowles's face. 'Shall I show you what the blade of this knife feels like?' Oliver growled.

Bowles glared at him, but gave no answer.

Oliver gripped the handle of the knife for a moment, angry enough to consider using it. Blood dripped from his hand, pooling on the ground.

Like the pool of blood they'd found in this same alley six years before when Nicholas disappeared.

'Nicholas,' Oliver murmured.

Bowles rose to his feet. 'Nicholas Bartlett? What of him?'

'Never you mind about Nicholas,' Oliver shot back.

He hurled the knife as far as it would go, over the fence and into someone's garden.

Bowles made an unintelligible sound.

'You won't be pulling that knife again,' Oliver told him. Bowles never heeded the rules of a fair fight.

Oliver's hand throbbed and more blood dripped onto the ground. He pulled a handkerchief from his pocket and wrapped it around his hand.

Oliver spoke low and menacing. 'Stay away from Vitium et Virtus. You cannot best me, so do not try again. Next time I may not let you off so easy.'

'First tell me why you mentioned Nicholas Bartlett,' Bowles demanded. 'He's…he's dead, correct? Everyone says so.'

'Forget Nicholas,' Oliver said sharply. What business was it of Bowles's? 'Leave here now and do not come back. Ever.'

Oliver held the handkerchief tightly against the bleeding cut on his palm as he watched Bowles limp out of the alley. He followed him to the street and watched until Bowles turned the corner at St James's Street.

Oliver walked through the alley again and entered Vitium et Virtus through the private entrance. One of the footmen attending the kitchen was passing by and noticed his bloody hand.

'Sir!' the man cried. 'What happened to you?'

'A cut,' Oliver said.

'Come, sir.' The footman gestured towards the kitchen. 'We'll fetch Mrs Parker. She'll bandage it for you.'

Oliver followed the footman to the doorway of the kitchen, which was a chaos of activity preparing food for the masquerade. The footman strode up to the club's housekeeper and spoke to her, glancing over at Oliver.

Mrs Parker dropped what she was doing and ran over to him. 'Mr Gregory, let us bandage that up.'

She led him to her sitting room where she cleansed the

wound and wrapped his hand in strips of linen. It hurt like the devil.

Oliver thanked her and put on his mask again. He needed to find Cecilia, to tell her he'd caught up with Bowles, who would not likely be bothering them again.

He looked for Cecilia first in the game room, but no one had seen her since she'd left with him. He next searched the ballroom, where Flo approached him.

'Mr Gregory, have you seen Coquette?' Flo asked.

'No. I was about to ask you if you had seen her,' he responded.

'Oh.' She bit her lip. 'She made me worry. Told me not to leave the room.'

He leaned over to Flo's ear. 'Bowles was here, but he is gone now.'

Flo's eyes widened. 'Sir Nash was here?'

He nodded. 'Do not fear. He'd be a fool to return.'

One of the other workers approached Oliver to deal with a drunken guest, and for the rest of the night he was kept too busy to look for Cecilia. When the masquerade was finally over, Snyder told him Irwin walked over to say Cecilia had come home early. Irwin told Snyder she'd appeared upset and Irwin thought Oliver should know.

Oliver left Vitium et Virtus through the private door and walked to his house. He used his key to let himself in. Irwin and the other servants would be abed at this hour. He climbed the stairs to his bedchamber, but paused at his door, turning instead to Cecilia's.

He knocked softly on her door and entered. Coals glowed in the fireplace casting enough light for him to see her in the bed.

How innocent and vulnerable she appeared. Her face was relaxed in repose and, in the dim light from the fireplace, she was almost too lovely to behold.

He made himself call softly. 'Cecilia?'

Her eyes flew open and grew wide with fright. She half rose.

'It is only me.' Oliver wanted to touch her, but held back.

'What?' she said, blinking.

'Sorry to wake you, but are you unwell? You came home early.' Had the commotion about Bowles made her ill? Hurt the baby?

She sat up, holding the bed linens around her. 'I'm fine. I—I just wanted to come home.'

He sensed she was not fine. She was unsettled and disturbed.

He tried to reassure her. 'I came to tell you Bowles will not be a problem any more.'

She clutched the bed linens even tighter. 'Why not?' She seemed even more disturbed. 'What happened to him?'

'I taught him a lesson.' She did not need to hear the details.

'A lesson?' she asked uncertainly.

'He won't be returning.'

Her eyes grew huge and looked frightened. 'What do you mean?'

Her reaction made no sense. 'I mean, I sent him away and he'd be a fool to return.'

The tension in her body eased a little. 'Oh,' she said. 'Very well.'

On the dance floor when he'd almost kissed her, her lips had seemed ready for him. Not now. Something had changed.

'I'll say goodnight, then.' He backed away.

She lay down again, burrowed under the blankets and turned her back to him.

It was near noon by the time Oliver sat alone at breakfast, lingering over the newspapers and cups of coffee, not in any hurry to go over to Vitium et Virtus to survey the damage and disarray that always came in the wake of a special event.

Mr Bell and Mrs Parker would see to the clean-up, but Oliver felt an obligation to be there.

Even if his hand still throbbed from the blade of Bowles's knife.

A knife fight. When had a masquerade included a knife fight?

Could there have been a knife fight the night Nicholas disappeared from that same alley?

Oliver wished he could return to those youthful days when he, Nicholas, Frederick and Jacob conjured up one wild idea after another for their secular version of a Hell Fire club. Even then it had been the camaraderie shared among the four good friends that Oliver valued the most. The belonging. As if they were his family.

When Nicholas disappeared, they lost that. And, with Nick gone, Oliver gradually lost pleasure in Vitium et Virtus.

At least last night he'd had the pleasure of waltzing with Cecilia. Holding her in his arms again.

He wished he'd kissed her.

From her reaction to him last night when he woke her, the chance of kissing her again was somehow lost.

The door opened and Cecilia walked in.

He'd not expected her.

He stood. 'Good morning.'

'Morning.' Her gaze was averted as if she did not wish to look at him.

Why? What had happened between that almost-kiss and now?

He gestured to a chair. 'Sit. I'll fix you a plate.'

She went to the sideboard instead. 'I'll do it.'

She selected her food and poured her tea. He stood the whole time, waiting for her to sit. She finally lowered herself into a chair, not across from him, but adjacent to him. So she would not have to look at him?

He felt as if she were four leagues away.

He returned to his newspaper. What other choice did he have? Until she told him what disturbed her, what else could he do?

She finished her cup of tea and glanced at the teapot, which was not in her reach. She started to rise to walk over to it.

'Allow me.' Oliver picked up the teapot with his bandaged hand.

Her voice rose. 'What happened to your hand?'

He poured her a cup.

'Nothing serious,' he assured her, passing her the cream and sugar. 'A cut.'

She made no effort to fix her cup of tea. 'Last night? How?'

He rubbed the bandage. 'Bowles drew a knife.'

Her eyes grew huge. 'You fought with knives?'

'Bowles pulled a knife. I disarmed him.' *And then pummelled him with my fists*, but she did not need to hear the unpleasant details.

She reached out as if to touch his hand. 'How bad is the cut?'

It still hurt like the devil. 'It will not kill me.'

'May I see?'

Cecilia watched him unwrap his hand, the strips of linen closest to the wound showing new red blood.

Bowles had attacked him with a knife? All Oliver had were his fists. No wonder he used them so fiercely against Bowles.

She moved her chair closer and took his hand in hers. The cut was a long gash across his palm.

'How did Bowles cut your hand?' She had a difficult time picturing it.

Oliver shrugged. 'He was aiming for my heart. I stopped him.'

She shivered. Oliver hadn't been a killer; he'd almost been killed.

The wound's edges were smooth, but there was a gap from which blood still oozed. The skin around the cut was very red and a little swollen.

'I think you need this stitched,' she told him, still holding his hand. 'Would you allow me to sew the sides together? They will heal better.'

His eyes narrowed. 'Do you know how to stitch wounds?'

She nodded and looked directly into his face for the first time this morning. 'After Quatre Bras and Waterloo, the surgeon had me sewing up the easier wounds. I had the needle and thread, you see.'

'You stitched up wounds after Waterloo?' His brows arched.

The sight of wounded men came back to her. 'There were so many.' What she'd done had been such a small thing. 'At first it was a little difficult, but I became accustomed to it.' She examined his wound again, gently touching the edges with her finger. 'Come up to my room. I have needle and thread there.'

She gathered the bloody bandage in her hand. He stood and extended his uninjured hand to help her rise.

As they walked to her room, her emotions were in a jumble. He might have been killed! On the other hand, she'd witnessed him angry enough to kill.

When they reached the top of the stairs, he opened the door to her bedchamber. She led him to her sitting room.

'Please sit, Oliver. I'll gather what I need.' She brought a clean towel, a basin and her bottle of lavender water. When she'd tended to the soldiers at Waterloo, she'd not had the luxury of lavender water.

Her sewing box was on the table in the sitting room.

She sat on the sofa with him and drew one of the tables to the sofa's side. Sitting so close, she felt her body hum again, teasing her with desire. She blinked, trying not to lose focus on his wound.

'Let me wash the blood away.' She held his hand over the basin and poured lavender water on it, carefully wiping off dried blood and new blood with the towel.

If she kept her attention on the task and not on the lime and bergamot scent of his soap, she'd endure this.

She took a needle from her etui and a length of black thread from a spool. She threaded the needle and wet the thread with the lavender water. 'It will go through easier this way.'

'I am delighted to know that.' His voice was strained.

She glanced into his eyes. 'This will hurt, but it will go faster if you do not move.' She folded the towel and placed his hand on top of it on the table. 'Are you ready?'

He smiled at her. 'As ready as I have ever been to have my hand sewn together.'

His good humour reminded her of Paris. That was not going to help her complete this task.

She took a breath and pushed the needle into his skin.

He flinched and gritted his teeth, but kept his hand steady.

She continued, riveting her attention to the wound, as she had managed after Waterloo. She worked quickly, but carefully.

As she was concentrating, the baby inside her moved, startling her into pausing.

'Why are you stopping?' he asked, his voice tight.

'The baby,' she said. 'The baby moved.'

How much tougher could this be? The baby reminding her that Oliver was the father.

'There!' she said when finished.

She glanced up at him. His face was taut. She'd seen that look before on countless men trying to endure pain.

Oliver expelled a pent-up breath and more colour returned to his cheeks.

She rose from the sofa. 'Wait here. I need some bandages. I'll be right back.'

She found Mary down in the kitchen with Mrs Irwin. 'Do we have some strips of cloth to use as bandages?'

'Bandages?' Mary cried. 'Who needs bandages?'

'Mr Gregory cut his hand.' It was enough of an explanation.

'I don't think we have bandages,' Mrs Irwin said.

'But I know some cloth we can use.' Mary popped out of her chair.

They ripped an old, laundered bedsheet into strips, and Cecilia brought the bandages to Oliver, who was lying on the sofa, one arm over his face.

He sat up when he heard her enter and extended his arm.

Cecilia started wrapping his hand, a hand that had once caressed her. A hand that had been capable of a brutal beating.

Oliver felt her withdraw again as she finished bandaging. For a very few moments, they had been as they were in Paris. At ease with each other. That was worth the several minutes of pain he'd endured.

'Do you have plans for today?' he asked, trying to delay having to leave her.

'I planned on returning books to Hookham's,' she responded. 'Do you need any returned? Any you wish me to pick up?'

'No.' He had heard of a book he wanted to read, *The European In India*, but to mention it seemed too revealing a disclosure.

The clock struck one. 'I should go now,' she said, standing. 'Oh,' she exclaimed.

'What is it?' Princess Charlotte died in childbirth. So could Cecilia.

Her smile was beatific. 'The baby moved again. Very active baby today.'

'Is that good?' He hoped so.

'I have no idea.' She put her sewing items back and picked up the basin and lavender water.

A hint he should leave, he believed.

But she did not rush him out. 'What about you, Oliver? What are your plans today?'

'Back to the club. It is likely a shambles today.' He would rather walk to Hookham's with her.

'Well, do not use your hand overmuch.' She nodded towards it.

He pushed himself up from the sofa and started for the door of the sitting room, but turned around before crossing the threshold. 'Thank you, Cecilia.' He lifted his hand. 'That was quite remarkable of you.'

He left her bedchamber and continued down the stairs. There was no reason for him to delay going over to the club. Keeping busy would prevent him from thinking of her.

He crossed through the garden and into the alley where he had tussled with Bowles the night before. In the sunlight he could see a small pool of blood from the bleeding of his hand. He touched his bandages, remembering the flash of silver that warned him of Bowles's intent.

He crossed through the club's garden and entered the building through the owners' entrance. As he passed through the rooms to the door through to the public side, a figure stepped into the hallway.

It took a moment for Oliver to recognise who it was. 'Frederick!' He quickened his step. 'When did you get back?'

When they reached each other, a handshake was ready. Frederick and his wife had been away in the country for a couple of months.

'We arrived this morning.' Frederick's lips twisted in dismay. 'I'd planned to be here for the masquerade, but one of the carriage wheels broke and we tipped over.'

'Good God! Was anyone hurt?'

'With God's luck, no,' Frederick said. 'It was just Georgiana and me inside. One of the coachmen was thrown off, but suffered only bruises.'

Oliver frowned. When Frederick purchased his commission in the army after Oxford, Oliver actually prayed his friend would survive. His prayers had been answered, apparently not only during the war, but also on the road to London.

'Suffice to say,' Frederick went on, 'we were delayed. But I was sorry to leave that chaotic event in your hands alone. I know how hectic it can be.'

'Jake and Rose came, so I was not alone.' Although they had been so wrapped up in each other, he'd not had the heart to disturb them.

'From the disarray I just surveyed, it was a wild night,' Frederick said.

Oliver took a deep, resigned breath. 'I might as well see for myself.'

The two men walked together to the door to the public

part of the club. They entered the hall, which was in reasonable shape.

'The ballroom is what you should see,' Frederick said.

The ballroom floor was filled with scattered oddments. Masks. Gloves. Scarves. Shoes. Broken glasses and spilled drinks. Remarkably, some undergarments, as well. Some maids were already busy with brooms and dustpans. One maid went ahead of the others and picked up the items of clothing. Nothing seemed valuable enough to save for an owner to collect it. The maids would sell the clothing on Petticoat Lane and make a few extra pennies.

'Take care,' Oliver said to the maid gathering up clothing. He pointed to the broken glass.

The maid glanced up and smiled. 'I will, Mr Gregory.'

'Mary?' The girl he'd hired as Cecilia's lady's maid was assisting in the cleaning up.

'My uncle asked Mr Bell if I could help. The extra money will help me a lot.'

Frederick pointed to Oliver's bandaged hand. 'What happened to you?'

'Ah…' Oliver laughed sarcastically. 'It is quite a story. Let us look at the other rooms first and I'll tell you over a drink.'

It appeared that Mr Bell had matters well in hand. He'd hired extra help for the day. So far nothing too alarming had been found, except one hungover gentleman who'd passed out on the floor in one of the bedrooms and had gone unnoticed. The singers and dancers had all taken off and would not return until after Christmas.

Back in the private owners' rooms, over brandy, Oliver told Frederick about Sir Nash Bowles.

'That reprobate!' Frederick banged his fist against the table. 'I thought we'd rid ourselves of him after his treachery with Georgiana.'

'I am reasonably certain he will not return,' Oliver said.

'I think we should be watchful,' Frederick said. 'The singer, Fleurette—will he leave her alone, I wonder?'

'He had better,' Oliver said fiercely. He poured them each another brandy.

Oliver had not mentioned Cecilia. How to talk about her with Frederick? He must, because Fred would eventually see Jake and Jake or Rose would speak of her.

'We have a new worker,' Oliver began. He gave a very short version of the events that led to Cecilia being hired, leaving out any mention of his meeting her in Paris.

'We need a hostess?' Frederick looked sceptical.

Oliver could not disagree, but of course, he knew Cecilia's reasons for wanting to work. And he knew her employment would be temporary.

'One thing more.' Oliver could not leave this out. 'She is living at my house.'

'Your house?' Frederick's brows rose. 'Is there more to this?'

Much more. 'She is an employee and a lodger.'

Frederick laughed. 'Since when do you take in lady lodgers?'

'It is complicated.'

'And you do not want to talk about it,' Frederick added.

'That is so.'

His friend leaned forward. 'Well, here's the thing. Georgiana and I want you to come to dinner. The rest of the family are still in the country, so that should keep things calm. Come to dinner the day after tomorrow. Bring this hostess lodger with you.'

'She will not come.' Oliver was certain of that.

'Then invite us to dinner at your house in two days. I want to meet this hostess.' Frederick grinned. 'We will be showing up on your doorstep, so refusal is out of the question.'

There was no sense in countering Frederick when he acted like that. He took it upon himself to oversee the welfare of Vitium et Virtu and his friends.

'Very well. Dinner in two days' time.'

Chapter Sixteen

Cecilia did not see why she must attend this dinner with
Oliver's friends. Oliver said this Frederick Challenger was
one of the owners of Vitium et Virtus and he wanted to
meet the new hostess. If so, she could merely appear and
be introduced.

They had a little row over it.

'You are making it seem as if we are attached and we
are not,' she protested.

'Are we not? If you claim the baby is mine, does that
not mean we are attached?' he shot back.

'I don't *claim* it,' she countered. 'It is the truth.'

They went on like that for a good quarter of an hour.

Finally, Oliver said. 'I've given you a place to live, allowed you to work at the club and have promised to support you and the child. I think you could do this one thing
for me—attend this dinner with my friend and his wife.'

Cecilia could not counter that argument.

The night of the dinner she wore a purple dress, one of
the ones she wore at Vitium et Virtus, because the black
one he'd bought her was not fancy enough for a dinner
dress. She cared that his friend's wife approve, but, at the
same time, it irritated her that it mattered to her.

Mary finished arranging her hair, stared into the mirror and spoke to Cecilia's reflection. 'Will that do, do you think?'

It looked effortless and not as fancy as she might wear as a hostess, but not as plain as she wore every day. Mary had pulled her hair into a coil at the top of her head and picked out a few tendrils to caress the back of her neck. The only jewellery she wore was the only jewellery she still owned—her pearl necklace.

'It is perfect, Mary.' The girl had done precisely what Cecilia wanted.

She stared at her reflection and frowned. 'The neckline is too low.' It was suitable for Madame Coquette, but not Cecilia.

Mary stepped back. 'I have just the thing!'

She ran out of the room and returned with a piece of black net with black embroidered flowers on it. 'A fichu!' she called triumphantly.

'Where did you come by this?' Cecilia asked.

'At Vitium et Virtus,' Mary responded. 'Uncle Irwin got Mr Bell to hire me to clean up after the masquerade. Mr Gregory let us keep some of the things we found that was not likely to be sought by the owners.'

'This does not fit in at all with the masquerade's costume theme.' But it was perfect for Cecilia.

Mary helped her tuck in the netting around the neckline of the dress. When Cecilia again looked in the mirror this time it made the gown even more elegant.

'It is perfect, Mary. Thank you.' Cecilia stood. 'I suppose I should go downstairs.'

The maid gave her a sympathetic look. 'I do not know why you are so unhappy about this. Mr Challenger seemed like a nice man when he was at the club with Mr Gregory. Maybe his wife will be nice, too.'

Cecilia sighed. 'I am sure she will be nice. That is the problem. What am I doing sharing dinner with nice people?'

To her surprise, Mary gave her a hug. 'You have been more than nice to me, Mrs Lockhart. There is no reason why they should not like you very much.'

Except that she worked in a decadent club and was bearing a child out of wedlock.

'I suppose I should go and find out.'

Oliver said he'd not told his friend and his wife that she was carrying a child. He'd not told anyone outside of this house. Though, they would still assume she and Oliver were a couple, would they not? Especially since she'd be dining with them.

She left the bedchamber and went downstairs with butterflies in her stomach, chastising herself for feeling nervous. She knew they'd already arrived because she saw their carriage pull up while she was dressing. As she approached the drawing-room door she decided to borrow a little confidence from Coquette. She straightened her spine and entered the room.

They all turned to her and rose from their seats.

Mr Challenger, who stood next to Oliver, was tall like Oliver, but he was light to Oliver's dark with light brown hair and brown eyes that did not exactly welcome her as much as they assessed her. His wife had the sort of looks Cecilia always envied as a girl. Blonde with blue eyes, taller than was fashionable, though, but with an elegant figure.

'Allow me to present Mrs Lockhart,' Oliver said. 'Cecilia, Mr and Mrs Challenger.'

They would notice, of course, that Oliver addressed her by her given name.

Cecilia curtsied.

Mrs Challenger stepped forward, extending her hand. When Cecilia accepted it, Mrs Challenger held on in a friendlier manner than a handshake. 'Oh, but you must call us Frederick and Georgiana. Oliver does and it will be so much more comfortable.'

Comfortable for her, perhaps, but it reflected an equality that Cecilia could not feel.

'Yes,' Mr Challenger said less enthusiastically. 'Call me Fred.'

'How do you do,' Cecilia managed. She would endeavour not to address them by name at all.

'Some claret, Cecilia?' Oliver asked, having already poured a glass.

She reached for it. 'Thank you.' She'd take a few sips and leave the rest. Since her pregnancy, wine unsettled her stomach, but she did not wish to call any attention to herself by refusing what everyone else was drinking.

Though why she cared what these people thought of her was a puzzle. And yet she wanted them to accept her as if she'd stepped out of her parents' house, never having met or married Duncan.

'Come sit with me,' Georgiana said.

Could she refuse?

'Where are you from?' Georgiana asked.

'Surrey,' she replied.

'Oh, Surrey?' Georgiana smiled. 'Where in Surrey?'

'Near Haslemere.'

'I have never been to Haslemere,' the lady said.

All the better. Think how hard it would be if Georgiana had lived in Haslemere and knew people she knew. Or maybe she should tell her whole story. What difference would it make? If Oliver supported her as he promised to do, she'd go where no one knew her and never see these people again.

Never see Oliver again.

Cecilia suspected Georgiana wished to ask more about her, but could not do so without showing she was pushing for information like a concerned mother interviewing a woman her son wished to marry.

Except marriage was certainly not what Cecilia and Oliver were about.

'Have you spent much time in London?' This was more conversational.

'Not before this.'

Irwin appeared at the door. 'Dinner is served.'

Cecilia did not expect the evening to improve over the dinner table.

But it did.

Instead of continuing to interview her, they talked of Vitium et Virtus, how it began when Oliver, Frederick, the Duke and another friend were all attending Oxford. The other friend, Nicholas, had originated the idea and put up the most money. This was the first Cecilia had heard of Nicholas. She'd heard talk of Frederick and of his marriage to Georgiana, but no one had ever mentioned Nicholas.

'What happened to him?' she asked.

'To whom?' Oliver responded.

'To Nicholas. I never heard of him before.'

Oliver lowered his head and tension filled the room.

Finally, Frederick spoke. 'Nicholas disappeared six years ago. We do not know where he is or if he is even alive.'

'He is alive.' Oliver's voice turned low and firm.

His was obviously the final word, because a pall spread over the room after he spoke.

Georgiana broke it. 'Cecilia, did you know that Vitium et Virtus is the reason Fred and I married?'

'No, I didn't.' She was glad of the change of subject and disturbed by Oliver's change in mood.

Georgiana told of how she contrived to expose the perverted character of the man her father was insisting she marry.

'I knew he would be at Vitium et Virtus, so I came and set up an auction,' Georgiana said.

Cecilia was not following this logic. 'Auctioning what?'

'Her virginity.' Frederick groaned. 'We do not do such things at Vitium et Virtus. There was nothing for me to do but stop it.'

'So he outbid everyone and ruined everything!' Georgiana cried. 'Then that odious man threatened to expose what I'd done and ruin my reputation—'

'So I had to marry her.' Frederick grinned.

'Do you know who the odious man was?' Oliver asked her.

She was glad he spoke. 'Who?'

'Sir Nash Bowles.'

'No!' She swung a look to Georgiana. 'You are lucky you did not marry Bowles. He would be a brutal husband.'

'Yes, he would be,' Georgiana agreed, going on to let Cecilia know she and Frederick had heard of Bowles's latest escapades.

Cecilia lifted her glass. 'May he stay away for good.'

They all joined her in that toast, finishing the wine in their glasses. Cecilia merely sipped hers.

When the pudding was served and even more wine was poured, Frederick leaned towards Cecilia.

'You look familiar,' he said. 'I wonder if we have met before?'

Her heart started to pound. He did not look familiar to her. She remembered every one of the men who'd sought

Madame Coquette's favours, but there were others who might have seen her at Maison D'Eros. Sir Nash Bowles, for example.

'I think I would remember *you*, sir,' she said cheekily, making herself smile.

Georgiana laughed and the dangerous moment passed.

After the pudding, the ladies returned to the drawing room. Oliver and Frederick stayed in the dining room, sipping brandy.

'She is not what I expected,' Frederick said.

'I was not asking,' Oliver countered.

Frederick grinned. 'I do not care a fig. You'll hear what I have to say about it anyway.'

Oliver took another sip of his drink, letting the amber liquid warm his throat. 'Of course I will.'

Frederick stared into space as if tallying up a list of figures. 'She is a mystery, is she not? Not much for talking about herself.'

'She probably resented the inquisition.' Oliver could share a lot more about Cecilia. About her husband. Her parents. That she was carrying a child. It seemed disloyal to her, though, even with his good friend. 'But, I agree. There is much she holds back.'

Frederick went on. 'I liked her, even so. Georgiana liked her, too, I could tell. She would have persisted in her inquisition, if she'd not liked her.'

Georgiana was fearless when she wanted something. He thought of the virginity auction. Or the reckless curricle race to which she challenged Frederick. A challenge he, of course, readily accepted.

'Something about your Cecilia…' Frederick gazed into the air again.

Oliver lifted his glass to his lips. He wanted to tell Frederick that she was not his Cecilia. Better to just change the subject. 'How long will you and Georgiana be in London?'

'We'll stay through Christmas,' Frederick answered. 'Our primary reason for travel here was for the masquerade, you know. But we thought it would be nice to have Christmas just the two of us here in London.' He finished his brandy. 'Out of the chaos, you know.'

Frederick came from a family who thought drama and discord were everyday events.

Christmas was only days away.

Christmas was not a holiday Oliver looked upon with any eagerness. Growing up, he made the obligatory trip to his father's country house, where his stepmother did not want him. She always planned a house party so, as a boy, he could not attend, and as he got older, he felt no more welcome. His father always managed a nice present, usually presented in haste before going off to the next planned activity for the guests.

Oliver finished his brandy and stood. 'We should return to the ladies.'

Frederick grinned. 'Just in case Georgiana is firing more questions at Cecilia.'

The next day Oliver met Frederick at Vitium et Virtus so they could discuss club business. They'd sent a message to Jacob to meet them there, as well, but one never knew if Jacob would be free of ducal affairs and able to attend.

They met in the drawing room. The ledgers were on the table in front of them, but neither Oliver nor Frederick were particularly interested in figures, costs and profit. That was Jacob's forte.

'So…' Fred began. 'What did Cecilia say about us after we left last night? Will she speak to us again?'

'I cannot say,' Oliver replied. 'She retired to her room

as soon as you left.' And not before giving Oliver a withering look.

She did not come down for breakfast, either.

'I have not seen her today.'

She'd looked so beautiful the night before. So elegant and ladylike. No reason she should not look ladylike; she was a baron's daughter. He'd even admired her skill at evading Georgiana's questions. He respected a sense of privacy.

Even so, it rankled that she held back from him.

Frederick drummed his fingers on the table. 'Will Jake come, do you think?'

'Jacob stops by when he has the time.' Truth was Jacob rarely stayed for more than a few minutes when he was able to come.

Frederick looked around. 'What are we doing with this place? Can we keep it up?'

Oliver gave him a direct look. 'We must.'

It went without saying. They could not sell or end the club, not with Nicholas the owner with the most shares.

Fred took another sip of his drink. 'At least for another year.'

In another year, if Nicholas did not return, he could be declared dead.

They both lapsed into a depressed silence that was not going to help anything.

The silence was broken by loud footsteps in the hall and a voice shouting, 'Where are you?'

They both jumped to their feet. Jacob was here.

Frederick reached the door and threw it open. 'Jacob!'

It had only been a matter of weeks since they had been together, playing billiards, the day that Cecilia showed up on his doorstep, in fact. Like they'd done since they were boys, they hugged each other and laughed at themselves for such an emotional excess.

'I am surprised you made it,' Oliver said.

'Some things are more important than others.' Jacob looked from Oliver to Frederick to a missing space in between. 'Friends, for example.'

They caught up on family matters. The delights of their marriages, the health of their families. Any news.

'How is Eleanor?' Oliver asked.

Eleanor was Jacob's sister, who'd been married to some sort of northern laird and widowed a short time after. A boating accident, Oliver thought. She bore the man's darling daughter whom Oliver and his friends now doted on.

'She's doing well,' Jacob said. 'Busy with Lucy, you know.' He shared the latest antics of the child, now five years old and bright as a copper coin.

'By the way, how is your father, Oliver?' Frederick asked.

Oliver shrugged. 'I assume he is in the country, having their usual house party.' He had not heard from his father since informing him he'd returned from Paris.

Frederick and Jacob knew better than to ask him about the stepmother. Nicholas had long ago told Oliver to simply pretend she did not exist, an idea that worked remarkably well.

They finally settled down to the business of Vitium et Virtus, looking through the books, talking of the events they'd held.

'Did you ever do that idea you had?' Frederick asked. 'You know, the one where men and women pick balls with matching numbers?'

Oliver had forgotten all about it. 'No. Not yet.' He was not even sure he liked the idea any more.

Frederick hit Oliver on the arm. 'Does Jake know about Bowles?'

'Bowles?' Jacob sat up straighter.

Oliver held up his bandaged hand and told the whole saga of Sir Nash Bowles.

'He cut you?' Jake frowned.

'Say it,' Oliver teased. 'Tell me I'm slipping. I let the likes of Bowles cut me.'

The afternoon wore on as they talked over plans for the club after Christmas.

'I'll try to help more,' Frederick said. 'We'll stay in London through the Season. I should be able to come often.'

Jacob shook his head. 'I will try to stop by as much as I can. We leave most of the work to you, Oliver.'

Oliver shrugged. 'Do not worry over it.'

As the sky darkened with the setting sun, they lit one lamp after another, but finally they could not deny that the hour was late and it was time for Frederick and Jacob to return to their wives.

'We should go,' Jacob said.

Without saying a word, Oliver leaned forward and placed his hand, palm up, at the centre of the table they sat around. Jake placed his hand on top of Oliver's, and Frederick lay his on top of Jake's.

'In Vitium et Virtus,' they chorused. In vice and virtue, the words that bound them together.

They broke apart, and Frederick poured them each a glass of brandy. They lifted their glasses.

'To absent friends,' Jacob said.

'Be he in heaven or hell—' Oliver continued.

'Or somewhere in between—' Frederick added.

'Know that we wish you well,' Jacob said, his voice turning low.

Their ritual, their incantation. For Nicholas.

They all stood and made their way to the door. Instead of using the side door, as they were accustomed to doing when the club was open, they entered the public parts of the building to the marble-tiled hall. Snyder, typically a fixture in the hall, was absent and they retrieved their own topcoats, hats and gloves.

Frederick punched Oliver's arm again. 'You've gone the whole afternoon without mentioning Cecilia to Jacob.'

Jacob smiled. 'How is our Coquette doing?'

'Coquette?' Frederick's brow furrowed.

'That is the name she goes by.' Jacob peered at him. 'Did not Oliver tell you she works here?'

'He told me,' Frederick said. 'Not the name Coquette, though.'

Here was another opportunity for Oliver to tell his friends about meeting Cecilia in Paris, that she was the woman he'd told them about when he returned, that she said she bore his child.

But the hour was late and they needed to go home.

'Coquette,' Frederick repeated. 'Coquette.'

'What the devil is wrong with you?' Oliver asked him. 'Most of the singers and dancers use false names.'

'Yes, but something about that one.' Fred looked as if he was struggling to remember. His face relaxed. 'I cannot think. But I do need to return home. Georgiana will believe I fell into the Thames—' He stopped abruptly, realising he was joking about what might have been a real possibility for Nicholas.

He nodded uncomfortably. The three men dressed for the cold, damp evening air and walked outside together.

'Wish I would have arranged for my carriage,' Jacob said.

Frederick gave him a playful push. 'Getting soft in all your ducal splendour, are you?'

They said goodbye and started to walk in the opposite direction from Oliver, who merely needed to turn the corner.

Oliver was about to put his hand on the door handle, when he heard running footsteps behind him. He turned.

It was Frederick. 'Wait, Oliver!'

It had started to drizzle, but Oliver waited for Frederick to reach him. 'What is it?'

'I remembered.' Fred took a moment to try to catch his breath. 'I remembered where I saw her.'

'Saw who?' Oliver asked.

'Your Cecilia.' Fred took a deep breath and expelled it slowly. 'It was when I was in Paris. I went to a club called Maison D'Eros. All the men there were talking about a courtesan, the most desirable courtesan in Paris, they said. Very selective and exclusive. I saw her. She went by the name of Coquette. Madame Coquette!'

Oliver went cold.

'She accepted maybe one or two men per week, they said. And the men paid well for a night with her. They paid for the chance to please her. If they did not please her, she sent them off, but kept the money.' Frederick shook his head. 'I do not know why I did not realise it when I first saw her. Her demeanour was so different at dinner.'

Oliver had witnessed Cecilia's transformation many times.

'It was Cecilia,' Frederick said. 'Did you know? Did you know she was a courtesan in Paris?'

'No.' Oliver's voice deepened. 'I did not know.'

Chapter Seventeen

Oliver stood by the door while Frederick dashed away. The rain thickened, falling like needles in the cold air and still he did not move.

She'd told him there had been no other men since him, yet she'd been a courtesan, selective and exclusive, but a courtesan none the less. Was he to believe she'd stopped her liaisons with men after meeting him?

That was how she earned her money.

Rainwater streamed from the brim of his hat and the wet was soaking through his topcoat. He finally turned and put his key in the lock. The hall was empty, but that was no surprise. The servants had a day off.

He peeled off his wet topcoat and dropped it on to a chair; his hat and gloves he left on the table. He climbed the stairs to the second floor where his bedchamber—and Cecilia's—were located. He paused at the top step, his hand resting on the banister.

With sudden resolve he surged towards her door and, restraining himself, knocked mildly.

'Come in.' Her voice sounded unconcerned.

He opened the door and stepped inside.

'I am in the sitting room,' she called.

He walked to the door of the sitting room.

She sat on the sofa, a book in her hand, her face illuminated by the light of a nearby lamp. Her legs were tucked underneath her, her hair merely tied back with a ribbon. She wore a morning dress, a loose-fitting garment of what might once have been white muslin, but had turned grey with time. Even from the doorway he could see where she'd mended it.

'Oliver,' she said with some surprise, although she must have known the servants were out.

'I am back from meeting Frederick and Jacob at the club.' He could not quite keep all the emotion from his voice.

Her relaxed expression tensed. 'Is something wrong there?'

'Not there,' he said.

Her brows rose.

He meant to ease into this discussion, but his anger pushed words out of his mouth. 'Why did you lie to me, Cecilia?'

Her eyes widened. 'I've never lied to you.'

'You are lying now.' He was burning inside, remembering all the lies his stepmother had told, lies that were meant to make him suffer or to make him look the fool.

Cecilia lifted her chin. 'What is this lie you say I told you?'

He laughed derisively. 'Madame Coquette.'

The colour drained from her face. She uncurled her body and placed her feet on the floor. Her feet were bare. She did not avert her gaze from his.

'Madame Coquette,' he repeated, sarcasm dripping from every syllable. 'The most desirable courtesan in Paris. Very selective and exclusive. Frederick told me all about her.'

She did not flinch. 'There was no need to speak of her. She was not real.'

He laughed again. 'Apparently she took real men to her bed.'

'Did she?' Cecilia stood.

He took a step into the room. 'You said you'd been a hostess, not a courtesan.'

'That was the truth.' She moved away from him. 'I had been a hostess and—and later a courtesan.'

'Later. At the time you met me.' He moved closer, but she edged away.

'Yes,' she admitted.

'So did you seek out those other men, when you found your belly swelling?' This was the lie that hit him hardest. 'Did they laugh at you? So you came to find me?'

'I came to find my mother. You were a last resort.' Her voice trembled. 'But you are the father. Whether you believe me or not!'

'Do not play me for a fool, Cecilia!'

'I am not!' She continued to edge away, trying to circle behind him. She was trying to escape from him, he realised.

Well, they would have this out now, he vowed. He'd not go another day believing her nonsense.

'You will stay here, Cecilia!' he shouted. 'We will deal with this now.'

'No!' she cried.

She made a lunge towards the door, but he was quick. He grabbed her by the arms. 'Now! Cecilia!'

She fought like a dervish to be free of his grip. Twisting. Turning. Pulling away. Her eyes filled with terror. 'No! No! Don't hurt me! Don't hurt me.'

It was as if she was in a different place, a different

time. Too hysterical to see what was around her. Who was with her.

'I won't hurt you!' he cried, loosening his fingers to prove it.

She wrenched from his grip and bolted for the door, slamming it behind her.

He took chase, reaching the stairs as she was nearly to the hall. He slid down the banister, but she'd run to the servants' door, closing that behind her, as well. He opened the door and ran after her down the stairs and through the hallway.

He'd done well in many a foot race, but he was no match for her panicked flight. Her bare feet helped her, while his boots could not gain purchase on the polished floor.

She reached the door to the garden and ran outside into the cold, now pouring rain, nothing covering her but her thin dress.

He finally caught her in the alley, the same alley where he'd fought with Bowles, the alley from which Nicholas had disappeared.

He seized her arms again, but she slipped on the wet surface and they both wound up on the ground.

'No! No! No!' she cried.

He feared someone in the surrounding houses would hear her and think he was attacking her.

She thought he was attacking her.

He held her fast and tried to make her look at him.

'I will never hurt you, Cecilia. Look at me! Look at me!'

She finally focused on him.

'I will not hurt you,' he said, slowly and calmly. 'You are safe. But we must get out of the rain.'

Her dress was soaked through and, even in the dim light in the alley, he could see that it clung to her body. The rain drenched through his coat, waistcoat and shirt. It felt like ice, it was so cold out. Her flight, her terror and the cold rain could not be good for the baby.

He repeated, 'You are safe. Now stop fighting. Calm down.'

She nodded, but her eyes still looked fearful.

'We'll go back to the house now and get you warm.'

She started to shiver, a sign, he supposed, that she was calming down.

'Are you ready?' he asked. 'We'll go back now.'

She nodded.

Afraid to let go of her, Oliver continued to firmly grip one of her arms. He rose to his feet and helped her up. He put an arm around her, but as they walked, her wet skirts caught on her legs and tripped her.

He stopped and made her face him. 'I'm going to carry you. Will you allow it?'

Again she nodded. Her teeth chattered.

He lifted her into his arms and carried her back to the garden behind his town house and through the kitchen door, which he'd left open in his rush to catch up to her. He carried her all the way to her bedchamber and placed her in a wooden chair in front of the fireplace. She was shivering and dazed and he feared she would lose consciousness. He needed to get her out of her wet clothes in a hurry. He tried to untie the laces on the back of her dress, but the knots just became tighter. He took a penknife from his pocket and cut them. He pulled off the dress and cut the laces of her corset, as well. Tossing those soaking garments aside, he peeled off her chemise, which was clinging to her like an extra layer of skin.

Her clothing gone, he carried her to her bed and wrapped her in the bed linens and blankets. He pulled the whole bed closer to the fireplace. Near the washbasin, he found a dry towel and wrapped it around her hair.

Her teeth no longer chattered, but she still had not said a word.

'Stay here,' he told her in a gentle but firm voice. 'I will be back quickly.'

Cecilia remained in her bed as Oliver ordered and gradually the mists in her brain cleared and she was able to keep two thoughts together. The cold made her body ache. She loosened the cocoon of covers enough to place her hand on her abdomen.

The baby was so still.

Please, baby, move. Show me you are unharmed.

What had happened? She vaguely remembered being outside in the alley. Oliver carrying her in his arms. She remembered running.

From Duncan,

But that was impossible.

Baby, please move!

The door opened and Oliver entered carrying a tray. He wore the banyan he'd given her to wear that first night she'd worked at Vitium et Virtus.

'Good. You are awake.' He placed the tray on the table beside her bed. It held a teapot, cup and saucer, cream and sugar. He poured her a cup of tea.

She sat up. 'I can't feel the baby move.'

He paused, holding the teapot in mid-air. Her worry seemed reflected on his face. 'Is—is the baby quiet sometimes?'

She'd never paid attention before. 'I suppose so.'

'Try not to worry.' Although he looked worried. He finished fixing the tea and handed her the teacup. 'Drink. It will warm you.'

The blankets slipped from her shoulder and she covered herself again. She took a sip of tea.

She looked up at him. 'What happened, Oliver? I cannot remember.'

'Do you remember that I learned about Madame Coquette?' he asked in a stiff voice.

That part came flooding back. 'You became angry.' It was like a curtain slowly opening in her mind, revealing a little at a time. Her heart pounded and it became difficult to breathe. 'You hit me!'

'Cecilia, no!' His eyes flashed in alarm. 'I never hit you. I would never do that. I seized your arms, but all I wanted was for you to stay and answer my questions.'

She did not remember it that way. She remembered him being angry and lunging at her. She'd had a flash of a memory of him hitting Bowles in the face the night of the masquerade, and then she'd felt the jarring pain of a fist connecting to her own cheek.

She touched her cheek. There was no pain now. She scrambled off the bed with only a blanket to cover her. The towel covering her hair fell to the floor and her still-damp hair tumbled to her shoulders. She walked to her dressing table. Leaning down, she gazed in the mirror. The light in the room was dim, but there was no bruise. She leaned closer, but still—nothing.

'No bruise,' she murmured to herself.

She'd pulled away and ran, but in her mind she had been fleeing Duncan.

'I did not hit you, Cecilia,' he repeated, his voice soft and low. 'I only tried to stop you.'

She turned to him. 'It was you?' She closed her eyes and tried to remember. She remembered terror. She remembered Duncan. 'I thought you were—someone else.'

'Who, Cecilia?' he asked.

'My husband.' She saw Duncan's face again and her legs started to tremble.

'Your husband?' He walked over to her, crouching down so that she could look directly at him. 'Your husband is dead, is he not?'

She nodded.

He searched her face with his green eyes, so piercing framed by his dark skin. 'Why did you think I was your husband?'

Her brows knitted. All she truly remembered was being terrified that this time he would beat her to death. 'I thought you were going to hit me.'

Understanding suddenly filled his eyes. 'Your husband hit you.'

'Yes.'

One of his arms wrapped around her shoulder. 'Come. Let us sit in a more comfortable place.'

She let him help her rise and he led her to the sofa in her sitting room—where her distorted memory had begun. Where he had been so angry with her.

She wrapped the blanket more tightly around her and tucked her feet beneath her. She was shaking, but not from the cold.

He left the room, but returned immediately, carrying the tea tray from the bedroom into the sitting room. He fixed another cup of tea for her and handed her the cup before settling in a chair.

'Tell me about your husband hitting you,' he said.

She stared into her teacup. He'd not asked her *why* Duncan had hit her. To ask her why would have assumed she'd done something to deserve it. Which she once thought she had. It had taken her many months of freedom from him for her to realise he would have beaten her no matter what she'd done.

'He was charming at first. All charisma and solicitude. The first person I truly believed loved me.' She paused.

'But I was wrong. First he merely complained. Scolded me for something I'd done. Or neglected to do. One day I answered impudently and he hit me. Across the face. After that, he hit me often.'

He stared at the floor, but his whole body tensed and she sensed anger in him. Finally he looked up at her. 'Why did you not leave him?'

'How could I?' That trapped feeling came back to her. 'We'd left Brussels, marching to France. I had no money. I knew no one.'

'Why not tell his commanders?'

'Duncan would have killed me!' She hugged herself. 'He told me so. Eventually he would have killed me anyway. I was merely fortunate that he was killed first.'

He stared at the floor again. 'How many times?'

'How many times did he hit me?' And throw her across the room? And choke her? Goodness. She'd lost count. 'Most of the year we were married.'

The disillusionment hit her again. She'd been so convinced that Duncan loved her like no one else ever had. After all, he'd been the kindest, most devoted suitor a girl could want. She'd searched her mind over and over. Had she missed something? How could she have been so thoroughly duped? There had been no love. It had all been a hoax. How could she ever believe in love again? How could she know a man would not change, would not hit her?

She'd been right to fear Oliver. He'd been angry at her. He'd seized her arm. She had only his word for it that he would not have hit her. He might hit her now if she piqued his anger, but she was not in a panic now, like before, and he deserved an explanation.

Not that he would believe it.

She took a deep breath. 'Shall I tell you about Madame Coquette?'

He glanced up at her, but his sympathetic expression disappeared.

And her nerves fired again.

She pressed her belly again.

Please move, petit bébé.

She must not be distracted. 'I was widowed in Paris. I was alone. No one would hire an Englishwoman for any respectable position. I had no money, no food and was in imminent danger of losing my room. I went to the Palais-Royal…and…and there I met Vincent—'

'Your protector?' His voice was grim.

'Yes. But not in the way you mean. Vincent preferred men.' It had been a shock to learn of Vincent's preferences, but she quickly became used to it. He was not so very different for it. 'He helped me, though. He taught me to be a hostess and he invented Madame Coquette.'

'The most desirable courtesan in Paris,' he said scathingly.

She looked him straight in the eye. 'Madame Coquette never bedded anyone.'

He gave a derisive laugh.

She went on, even though she had little hope he would believe her. 'Madame Coquette was paid for her time, not for bedding. She never promised to bed the men, only to consider it. But Madame Coquette always found some fault in the men and would not bed them. She did, however, promise to tell everyone they were wonderful lovers so they could save face. That was how her reputation was built. No man ever wanted to admit he was the one she'd refused, so they boasted about her and she went along with it.'

He gaped at her. 'You expect me to believe this?'

She closed her eyes and rubbed her forehead. 'No. I expect nothing.' She had learned from Duncan to expect nothing.

A part of her yearned for more from Oliver, but that was folly, too, was it not?

She drank her tea.

'Why would a man not demand his money back?' he asked.

She set down the cup. 'The agreement was very clear. Madame Coquette promised her time, not her favours, but that is not why. No man wanted his friends to know that Madame Coquette did not want to bed him.'

His brow creased. At least he seemed to be considering what she said. 'That was enough?'

She rearranged the blanket around her. 'Such is a man's vanity.'

His mouth twitched.

She wrapped her arms around herself. 'I am not proud of this, Oliver, but I did not starve.' And she'd tried to make certain her street urchins did not starve. 'Really, though, the men were mere victims of their own vanity. They thought it fine to pay money to bed a woman. And most of them left a wife at home to do so.' She pulled up her knees and rested her head on them. 'At least I was not at their mercy.' She sighed.

'Did no man protest?' he asked.

'Take me by force, do you mean?' she responded. 'Only one. The flash man had to intervene. That became the end of the game, though. I was discharged. By then I knew I was with child, so it would have been only a matter of time before I would have had to leave.'

'How long did you get away with this?'

Was he believing her?

'Almost a year. I always knew it would end, though. It always surprised me that the men did not complain to the club owner. When he learned I was not bedding the men, he tossed me out.'

He looked at her with scepticism. 'You say you did not bed the men—'

She interrupted. 'I did not want to bed them. The idea was repugnant to me.'

In a swift movement, he leaned towards her. 'But you bedded me.'

She gave a cry and flinched, curling up into a ball and turning away from him.

He reached out a hand, but she tried to back farther away.

'I will not hit you,' he said in a soft voice.

She realised as much this time, but her body had reacted on its own.

He leaned back again, but she still trembled.

'Why did you bed me, Cecilia?' he asked in that soft, calm voice that helped quell her fears.

She could barely look at him. 'I wanted to bed you.'

His expression turned sceptical again.

How could she explain? 'In Paris, we were having such a lovely day. I wanted to pretend a little longer.'

'Pretend?' He crossed his arms over his chest.

'It wasn't real, was it? That lovely day we shared? It was like a dream. I wanted the dream to last longer. I wanted to pretend for merely one day that love existed and I was worthy of it.'

'But you left,' he accused. 'I would have delayed my departure. We could have had many days.'

'No!' She hadn't meant to speak so sharply. 'No,' she said more mildly.

At the time it had taken all of her courage to trust in that one whole day.

'I—I left before everything changed.' Before he changed. 'Every good thing changes.'

Chapter Eighteen

Oliver gazed at her wrapped in a blanket, hair tumbled down to her shoulders, the very picture of vulnerability. How difficult it was to believe she could have worked in a brothel. Or that any man would hit her with his fist.

His head was still swimming. It was hard to fit the pieces of the day's events together, learning she was a courtesan who did not bed her patrons. A manipulator of men.

A victim of an abusive husband.

He did not doubt her husband hit her. Her terror had been too real. No wonder she'd seen through Flo's excuses; Cecilia had already lived through it.

He had a strong impulse to touch her. Not only touch her, but enfold her in his arms and tell her he'd make everything all right again.

He resisted, still reeling from all she'd withheld from him.

'Has the baby moved yet?' he asked.

She placed her palm against her abdomen and shook her head.

Had her frenzy injured the baby? If so, Oliver was to blame. That idea sickened him.

He rose to put more coal on the fire, to keep the room warm for her. The light from the fireplace made her face glow with golden beauty. He remembered in Paris in his room that same glow on her face.

These weeks she'd lived with him, she'd been different people. One guarded and remote and untrusting. Another the seductive Coquette who could easily have passed as the most desirable courtesan in Paris. Now, though, sad and vulnerable, she seemed the Cecilia of Paris.

'I do not have anything left to say,' she told him. 'You know everything now.'

He doubted that.

She lay back on the sofa. 'I want to rest for a little while. You do not have to stay. I—I'm not cold any longer. I'm not ill. I'll ready myself for bed in a little while. Mary is not waiting on me tonight.'

Oliver had given his valet a long leave to visit family. The Irwins and Mary would stay out late.

'Will you eat dinner?' Cook had left food for them.

She rearranged her blanket. 'No, I want to sleep.'

She clearly did not want him to stay.

He'd endured many rejections in his life, but none wounded him to the quick like this one. She did not want him.

'I'll say goodnight, then,' he rasped, placing her teacup on the tray and carrying it out with him.

Once in the kitchen, he spooned out some mutton stew Cook had left on the hearth. He sat at the kitchen table, dipping pieces of bread in his stew until it had cooled enough to eat with a spoon and fork.

The house seemed deadly quiet. Another night he might have gone out seeking some kind of entertainment. He could not remember when he'd last been alone in the house.

Of course, he was not alone, but Cecilia was as distant as Paris.

Memories came back to him as they inevitably did

when he was alone. Another kitchen smelling much different from this one, a kitchen filled with the scents of exotic spices. He remembered sitting on rich carpets to taste spiced stews made with meat, cream, vegetables, fruit and nuts poured over rice. He could hear his mother saying, 'Eat more, *pyaare bête*. Grow strong.'

He rose and strode to the wine cellar, selecting a bottle of brandy. Finding a glass, he carried both with him to his bedchamber, sat in his comfortable upholstered chair and drank.

The brandy warmed his throat and spread heat throughout his body. He'd still been cold, he realised. No wonder. His feet were bare and the banyan did little more than cover him up.

His thoughts drifted back to Cecilia. He went over her story and her telling of it. He supposed he could verify it. He could send someone to the club where she'd worked, perhaps find this Vincent she spoke of. Would that help him believe the baby was his?

But what did any of it matter? She did not want him.

He started to pour another glass of brandy, but put the bottle aside. Drinking was not the answer. Nothing would stop the whirling thoughts in his mind, especially the one thought he most guarded against.

He loved her.

He loved her more than any other woman he'd been with. He cared about her future and the future of her child. He never wished her to again experience the terror she'd experienced today.

He heard a door slam and the sound of pounding feet. The door to his bedchamber opened and Cecilia burst in. He jumped to his feet and she ran directly to him.

'The baby moved!' She ran into his arms and he held her. 'Oh, Oliver. The baby moved. I didn't hurt the baby.'

Neither had he. He thanked God for that.

'I'm delighted,' he murmured. 'Delighted.'

She pulled away enough to look up at him, smiling. How rare it was for him to see her smile so genuinely, he realised. He wanted to keep her smiling. He wanted to make her happy.

The nightdress she wore was a mere thin layer of cloth, like his banyan, so thin it was as if they were skin to skin. Still, the cloth seemed too great a barrier. His desire for her, held back so long because of the even greater barriers of mistrust and suspicion, slammed into him. He loved her and he wanted—*needed*—to join with her.

But he held back.

The decision must be hers alone. Like it had been in Paris.

Her smile faded, but she continued to stare at him. His arousal was painfully acute, but he held himself in check. Through the thin material of her nightdress she must have felt it.

She pressed against him more tightly, rubbing against him. He held his breath to maintain control over himself. She rose on tiptoe so that her lips were mere inches from his, but she looked into his eyes.

'Would—would you despise it if we made love?' she asked.

Joy burst inside him. He smiled. 'I believe I might be able to tolerate it.'

He took possession of her lips like a man greedy for gold. He poured his need for her into the kiss, as well as his realisation that he wanted her in his life for ever.

Oliver picked her up and carried her to his bed. When he set her down, she pulled his head towards hers and placed her lips on his again.

The kiss set his body aflame, but he banked his desire

and waited to see what she wanted. If a kiss was all she desired, a kiss would be what she'd have. But she broke away long enough to remove her nightdress. Only then did Oliver throw off his banyan. He climbed onto the bed and lay next to her, waiting again to have this lovemaking proceed exactly as she wished. She sat up only to lean down for another kiss. He could not help himself. He lifted her on top of him, but she did not resist. She straddled him and positioned herself to ease him inside her.

He guided her, lifting her on his erection and feeling himself slip inside her. This joining was more than pleasure—this joining was a connection, a belonging to another. This joining banished loneliness.

His need grew even more acute. Still, he strained to hold back, but she took pity on him. She began the primitive rhythm for which he yearned. They moved together with Cecilia setting the pace, moving gradually faster and faster as his need grew stronger. Emotions swirled inside him, his genuine love for her swelled like the urging of his body.

Thought fled and sensation took over with each stroke. Only the quickness of their breath filled the air. His need grew stronger and stronger still until he thought he'd perish if this exquisite agony did not reach its apex soon.

Suddenly she cried out and writhed above him. A guttural sound escaped his lips and he erupted inside her, spilling his seed and slaking this intense hunger for her. Their climax held them suspended in this ecstasy, lasting longer than any he could remember.

Because he shared it with her, he thought.

She slid to his side and lay next to him, one leg still wrapped around him.

'Cecilia,' he murmured. It was as much as he could manage.

He cared so much for her, could he really burden her

with the realisation of his love for her? As in their love-making, should he wait for her to show him what she wanted, what she could safely handle?

He felt her withdraw suddenly, slipping her leg away, crossing her arms over her chest, no longer touching him.

'You must think me wanton,' she said.

He rose on one elbow so he could look her in the eye. 'There is something between us, Cecilia. That is what I think. It was there in Paris and is here now.'

Her forehead creased in concentration. 'I do not understand it. But yes, there is something.'

He dared to draw a finger gently down her cheek. 'I love you, Cecilia. I want us always to be together.'

Her head whipped away from his touch. 'No!' Her eyes turned panicked. 'No, Oliver. Do not say it!'

He felt the distance between them grow once more. He wanted desperately to stop it, to stop the loneliness that would return in its wake.

'Wait,' he said, trying not to sound desolate. 'That is what I feel. What I want. I mean no pressure. You must decide what you want.'

She sat up and hugged her knees. 'I don't want to try to understand it. Or to decide. I merely wish to enjoy it. Enjoy being with you. For the time we have.'

He'd said words similar to this many times to other women. *Enjoy it while it lasts*, knowing he did not wish the liaison to last. She was reminding him that she would leave him.

If he could, would he take another month, another week, or even a day with his mother? He'd take even an instant.

He carefully reached out and touched Cecilia's hair, stroking it with his fingers. 'Very well. Let us enjoy this while it lasts.'

He had no other choice.

* * *

Cecilia lifted her head and gazed into his eyes, his lovely green eyes. They could do this, could they not? Enjoy each other for a little while?

She wanted to feel his arms around her again. To make love with him again. And again.

She moved closer so her lips were near to his. He closed the gap and kissed her, his warm tongue tasting of brandy as it slipped into her mouth. His hand cupped her breast, his palm rubbing against her nipple and creating an ache that could only be eased by his touch.

Or his joining with her.

He held her against him, pressing her against his male member, making her ache even more intense.

'I do not know what is wrong with me,' she murmured. 'It feels so—different. As if I will perish if you do not couple with me right now.'

He rose on top of her. 'I do not wish you to perish.'

He entered her, slowly, almost reverently, and the passionate ache doubled.

'Oliver.' Her voice was a plea.

He complied, moving inside her in a stroking that was at once easing the ache and intensifying it at the same time. It was a glorious, confusing mixture.

He'd said they might merely enjoy this for the time it lasted. She could not do otherwise. He seemed wholly present with her in this moment, ready to relieve her fears and deepen her pleasure. Could she not muster that much courage to stay with him until her condition prevented it?

She tossed away her caution and stopped resisting, stopped trying to comprehend. She gave in to every sensation he created and let the pleasure build even further to impossible heights until the pleasure exploded inside her, like the rockets she'd seen in battle. Oliver spilled his seed inside her once more and collapsed heavy on top of her for only a moment before moving to her side where they both languished in the afterglow of their frenzied act.

She lay still, so relaxed that she doubted her limbs could hold her upright. Her thoughts were quiet, as if the thrill of lovemaking had driven them from her mind. She merely relished the heat of his body next to hers, the sound of his breathing.

She might have drifted off to sleep, except a fluttering inside her roused her.

'Oh!' she exclaimed, touching her thickened belly.

He rose on to an elbow. 'What is it?' His voice was worried.

'The baby moved again,' she whispered. 'I can feel it.'

This time she felt the movement beneath her fingers as well as inside her.

As she had done once before, she took his hand and placed it on her abdomen, holding it still until the fluttering repeated.

'Did you feel it?' she asked.

'Yes,' he rasped.

The baby moved again and she and Oliver exchanged knowing smiles.

She carried life insider her, a life that began with lovemaking much like this. With Oliver.

She turned to him and cuddled against him. Yes. She would enjoy a little more time together with him.

Feeling a new life beneath his fingertips, Oliver experienced a fierce sense of protectiveness towards her and this child. In his mind she and the baby were his. For ever. No matter that she would leave him.

'I feel happy,' she said in a surprised voice.

He held her closer. He felt happy, too.

'I cannot remember when I last felt happy,' she went on.

He could remember. He'd last felt happy in Paris, on that day they shared together. Could they recreate it?

He had an idea. 'Tomorrow would you like to explore London?' As they had explored Paris. 'We could visit St Paul's Cathedral and walk through the city. It would not compare with the Louvre, but we could visit Bullock's Museum. What do you say?'

She moved so they were face to face. 'It sounds like a lovely idea.'

The next day Oliver took Cecilia to St Paul's Cathedral. Like Notre Dame, it dominated the skyline of the city. From almost anywhere in the city, one could turn and see its great dome, which was gleaming white on this rare brisk and sunny winter day. St Paul's had been built over three hundred years later than Notre Dame, replacing a Gothic cathedral on the same site that had been destroyed in the Great Fire of 1666. St Paul's was classical architecture, with its dome, columns, arches and symmetry.

They explored the three naves inside the church and all its chapels, examined the beautiful masonry and ran their fingers over the woodcarving of the choirs. St Paul's lacked the magnificent stained-glass windows of Notre Dame casting rainbows of colour, but its interior was bright, in part due to the windows on the great dome.

Oliver savoured the time with Cecilia—enjoying her while he could. In Paris, he'd known their time together would end—so, too, would it end in London.

Ironically, he'd vowed never to marry, believing no woman would want to marry a bastard half-caste for anything other than his money. Under such circumstances a marriage like that was doomed to unhappiness. It never particularly bothered him not to marry, because he preferred to be free to pursue pleasure and women did not mind his half-caste self in bed, only not as a husband.

But he wanted to marry Cecilia. He wanted to raise the baby as his own. He wanted to spend his life making them both happy.

She did not want it, though. And not because of his birth.

As they walked the long distance of the nave's white-and-black-chequered stone floor, he shook himself out of these musings and decided to enjoy the moment, as she'd asked. As they'd done in Paris.

'What did you think?' Oliver asked her as they reached the great doors of the cathedral to go outside again.

'It is grander than I expected,' she replied. 'But I miss the stained-glass windows of Notre Dame.'

He opened the door. 'It is Christopher Wren's crowning achievement,' Oliver said.

They walked back onto the street in the midday sun. The weather, though much colder, rivalled that beautiful day they'd spent in Paris. It was crisp and cool and windy enough to blow the air clean of the usual veil of smoke that covered the city.

'Could we walk back?' Cecilia asked him. 'It is such a fine day!'

Was she reading his thoughts? 'We could indeed.' He smiled at her. 'I need to let my groom know.'

He'd driven them to the cathedral in his phaeton and his groom waited for them nearby, tending to the horses.

'We have decided to walk,' Oliver said to the man. 'Drive them home, would you?'

'Right you are, sir.'

Oliver and Cecilia started walking along Fleet Street.

'It is not all that far, is it?' she asked.

'Two miles or so.' It felt good to be outside, stretching his legs, walking with her.

She took his arm and they strolled together as they had done in Paris. She did not know London, so he pointed out buildings of interest along the way. St Bride's Church. The various inns of Fleet Street. St Clement's, standing where Fleet Street became the Strand.

'Are you hungry?' he asked.

She did not answer; merely lifted one shoulder.

She must be. '*I* am hungry,' he declared. 'Let us detour to Covent Garden. There will be food there.'

In the early mornings, wagons filled with produce grown outside the city and other wares descended on Covent Garden for a market that had existed for years. It was as rowdy a place as St Paul's had been peaceful. A cacophony of vendors hawked everything from vegetables, fruits and herbs, to hedgehogs.

Oliver spied an old woman tending a still. He pulled Cecilia over to her stand. The old woman was filling bowls with some steaming hot liquid.

'We must have some *salop*,' he said.

Salop was a hot drink made from sassafras wood and infused with milk and sugar. It was like nectar for the gods.

On many a pre-dawn hour Oliver and his friends had soothed aching heads with hot *salop* after imbibing too much liquor at one of the disreputable gambling houses or houses of ill repute in Covent Garden.

Oliver gave the old woman a coin and she poured the steaming liquid into two bowls. Oliver handed one to Cecilia.

She tasted it cautiously, then looked up at Oliver in surprise. 'It is good!'

'Who could dislike it?' Oliver lifted his bowl to his mouth.

The *salop* not only tasted wonderful, it warmed him inside.

They walked on, looking at the displays of vegetables and fruits, stopping at another vendor to purchase ginger cakes.

When they neared the flower sellers, Cecilia exclaimed, 'Oh! Smell the evergreens!'

She hurried to the wagons selling lush cuttings of holly, pine, hawthorn and juniper.

She turned to Oliver. 'Might we purchase some? I have some money with me. It has been so long since I have decorated a house for Christmas. Might we do so?'

She looked as excited as a little girl.

Christmas had never been a happy time for him. He'd either been left at school while his father and stepmother attended a country house party or he'd been stuck staying out of the way when the house party had been at his father's estate. He did remember some enjoyment gathering evergreens to adorn the house on Christmas Eve. He'd been able to climb high in the trees to cut branches or gather mistletoe.

The scent of this greenery reminded him of those days.

'Of course, if you desire it,' he answered her. 'But I will pay.'

She danced in front of him, her cloak coming open. He caught a glimpse of the pearl she wore around her neck, the one he had bought her in Paris. It pleased him that she wore it. It pleased him, as well, that small things like a pearl necklace or fragrant evergreens made her smile.

He'd buy her a forest of greenery if it kept that smile on her face.

He followed her as she flitted from wagon to wagon, trying to decide on what she wanted.

'Buy it all,' he said, laughing. 'I'll pay a lad to bring it to the house.'

While she picked branches of holly, hawthorn and pine, he spied a ball of mistletoe and purchased it when she was not looking. He hired a couple of boys to help them carry the greenery to the house. By the time they neared the town house, Cecilia's cheeks were tinged pink and her eyes sparkled.

Oliver could not have been more gratified.

'I have an errand,' she said suddenly. 'Just a quick run to the shops. I——I want to buy something for Mary. She has been such a help to me.'

'I will come with you if you wait a moment.' All he needed to do was hand off the boys and their bundles to Irwin.

'No. No.' A nervous edge came into her voice. 'It will only take a moment. I'll buy her pretty muslin or something at Harding, Howell and Company, perhaps. And ribbons and things for our decorations.'

She sounded secretive. It raised his suspicions.

'As you wish.' He pulled out his purse and handed her some coin. 'For the decorations.'

She looked at the money in her palm, gave him a smile and dashed off.

Chapter Nineteen

It had been such a lovely day, Cecilia's heart was floating on air. Even more than the cathedral she'd enjoyed the market at Covent Garden, so filled with pretty vegetables and fruits and tantalising treats. She'd loved the *salop* and the ginger cakes, but mostly she adored Oliver for buying all the evergreen cuttings.

She intended to go to Harding, Howell and Company, a linen draper just a couple of streets away on Pall Mall, but her real errand took her first down Jermyn Street to Floris.

She entered the shop and the same clerk, who had served Oliver and her a few days before, greeted her again. 'Good day, madam. May I assist you?'

'Yes.' She stepped forward. 'I would like to purchase a nice gift for a gentleman. Would you help me decide?'

'Some scent?' he asked.

'No. Something more enduring. Something he would use.' She wanted something he would remember her by, like the pearl necklace.

'Let me show you our combs.' The clerk displayed a variety of combs. She selected one made of tortoiseshell and silver. The clerk wrapped it for her.

She hurried to the draper's and purchased ribbons to

adorn the evergreens and a length of a pretty sprigged muslin for Mary.

When she headed back to the town house, she felt like skipping along the pavement as she'd done when a little girl. She was excited about her gift to Oliver, excited to decorate and to share Christmas with him.

But she kept a normal pace. When she turned to walk to the town-house door, a man approached her, taking her by surprise.

Sir Nash Bowles.

'There you are.' He moved towards her with an unsteady gait.

She tried to edge towards the door.

'I remembered you.' His words were slurred, adding even more emphasis to his rasping lisp. 'You are Madame Coquette. From Paris. I know all about you.'

He came close enough for her to smell liquor on his breath.

'Leave me alone, Sir Nash.'

She reached the door, but he seized her arm and pulled her away. She dropped her packages and cried out, 'No! Let me go!'

Bowles cried, 'I want to learn what Gregory knows. You find out or I'll make trouble for you.'

She tried to pull away, but his grip was surprisingly strong.

The door flew open and Oliver charged out. He grabbed Bowles by the collar and wrenched him away from Cecilia.

Bowles came back at Oliver, leaping on him, fists flying. Oliver took some blows before he was able to hit him back. He knocked Bowles to the pavement and the two men rolled on the ground and into the street.

Cecilia screamed.

A carriage narrowly missed running over them. Oliver

made it to his feet first and went to hit Bowles again, but Cecilia could stand it no longer.

'Stop! Stop!' She ran over to Oliver and tried to pull him away.

Oliver backed off, breathing heavily. Bowles got to his feet and limped away.

Oliver turned to Cecilia. 'Are you harmed?' He rubbed the hand that Bowles's knife had cut.

She glanced at his hand in alarm. 'Are you hurt?'

He shook his head. 'I aggravated the cut.'

'I'm not hurt,' she finally responded. 'Frightened, though.' Frightened at his violence.

He put an arm around her shoulders. 'Come inside.'

Irwin was in the doorway, looking alarmed.

'Have Mrs Irwin bring tea up to Mrs Lockhart's room,' Oliver told him.

Oliver walked Cecilia up the stairs and entered the room with her. He untied the ribbons of her cloak. He took it off her shoulders and laid it down on a chair.

'Sit down, Cecilia. There will be tea here soon.' He walked her to the sitting room. 'Or would you prefer some claret? Or brandy?'

'Tea.'

There was a knock on the door. Mrs Irwin brought tea. She placed the tray on the table near the sofa.

'How are you, dear?' she asked. 'That was such a fright!'

Cecilia made herself smile. 'I am a little shaken. Your tea will fix me up.'

Mrs Irwin nodded. 'Nothing tea cannot help.' She patted Cecilia's hand. 'Now you tell us if you need anything else.'

The woman was kind. 'Thank you, Mrs Irwin.'

After Mrs Irwin left, Oliver sat in a chair opposite Cecilia. 'What did Bowles want?'

'He was drunk. Not making sense. He wanted to know what you know.'

He looked puzzled. 'Know what I know? About what?'

'He did not say.' She did not add that Bowles threatened to make trouble for her.

'He's been trouble from the first. I banned him after learning about Flo, but we should have banned him years ago.' He opened and closed his injured hand. 'How many times must I fight him?'

'Do men always fight?' she murmured.

It was not meant as a question for him, but he answered anyway. 'More than not.'

His answer did not reassure her.

Oliver watched her. He'd seen the panic in her face when she pulled him away from Bowles. Now she looked pale and drawn.

What a damnable end to their perfect day.

She pressed her hand to her abdomen and turned even paler.

'What is it?' Something was wrong.

'I—I need to be private for a moment.' She stood.

He left the room, but remained by her doorway waiting, his alarm growing.

She finally opened the door, but clung to the door jamb.

'Oliver…' Her voice shook. 'Find Mary. I am bleeding. I do not know what to do.'

Bleeding?

'Mary!' His voice boomed. 'Mary! Come here this instant!' He put an arm around Cecilia. 'Let me take you to your bed.'

When they reached the side of the bed, he picked her up and placed her on it. 'I'll find Mary.'

He ran out of the door, only to discover Mary hurrying up the stairs.

'What is wrong, sir?' she asked.

'Cecilia is bleeding. Tend to her. I am sending for the doctor.' He bounded down the stairs and found Irwin and his wife at the bottom staring up to see what the commotion was about.

'Get the doctor,' he said to Irwin. 'Quick. She's—she's bleeding.'

'Oh, my goodness!' Mrs Irwin bustled upstairs.

Oliver paced the hall outside Cecilia's bedchamber door while the women tended her.

He'd lost too much already. His mother. His childhood home. His trust. His friend Nicholas. He did not want to lose this baby.

Or Cecilia.

He could give them what he'd lost in India. A name. Security. Love.

He heard voices in the hall below. Irwin had found the doctor quickly.

He leaned over the banister. 'Up here, Doctor!'

The doctor left his coat, hat and gloves with Irwin and hurried up the stairs.

'What seems to be the trouble?' he asked, out of breath from the climb.

'She is bleeding. I do not know how badly or why.' Oliver stepped quickly to Cecilia's door and knocked. He did not wait for permission to enter, but opened the door. 'The doctor is here.'

The doctor strode into the room and someone shut the door behind him.

Oliver was left to wait alone.

Cecilia sat up in bed as the doctor came to her side. Mary and Mrs Irwin had helped her change into a night-dress and they placed rags between her legs.

'You have been bleeding, young lady?' he asked. 'How badly?'

'I—I do not know.'

'It looks a lot like if she started her monthly courses,' Mary offered.

'Still bleeding?' the doctor asked.

'Some, I think,' Mary answered.

Mrs Irwin wiped Cecilia's forehead with a damp cloth. 'The poor dear is very frightened.'

'Well, let me look.'

The doctor examined her, felt her abdomen, and listened for the baby's heart with his wooden tube.

Cecilia's own heart was pounding so loud she did not see how he could hear the baby's. Had she done too much? Walked around London too much? Rushed too fast to the shops? Or was it the tussle with Bowles, her struggle to get away from him?

'Is my baby harmed?' She was afraid to hear the answer.

The doctor touched her hand. 'Your baby seems to be doing very well.'

'But the bleeding?' she asked.

'It could be many things. Not all are to worry over. In fact, I do not believe you have to worry, for now. If you bleed more, send for me. If you have pains, send for me, but, at the moment, I expect you will have no further trouble.'

She released a pent-up sob. Her baby was unharmed.

The doctor stepped away and put his tube back in his bag. 'Stay in bed tonight and do not exert yourself tomorrow, just in case.'

'We'll make certain of that,' Mrs Irwin said in a determined tone.

'I'll bring anything she wants, anything she needs,' Mary added.

Cecilia slid under the covers. Mrs Irwin and Mary tucked her in. She felt suddenly exhausted. 'I promise I will rest.'

The doctor smiled. 'Good day, then.'

Oliver alternately paced the hallway outside Cecilia's bedchamber and leaned against the wall, his eyes riveted on the door.

Finally, it opened and the doctor walked out.

Oliver straightened. 'How is she?'

The doctor gestured for him to move away from her door. Oliver walked with him to the stairs.

'She and the baby are stable now,' the doctor said as he descended the stairs. 'But one never knows about these things. I've seen women who bleed regularly throughout their carrying of the baby and have a normal birth and I've seen others who bleed once and lose the baby.'

'There is a chance she could lose the baby?' A chance they would both lose the baby.

The doctor lifted both shoulders. 'There is always a chance.'

They reached the first floor.

'May I offer you some refreshment before you leave, Doctor?' Oliver asked. 'Some tea? Or brandy.'

The doctor's face lit up. 'Brandy would be most appreciated.'

He brought the doctor to the drawing room and invited him to sit while he removed the decanter of brandy and two glasses from a cabinet. He poured the doctor a glass and handed it to him.

The doctor sipped, then glanced heavenward. 'Mmm. That is a fine brandy.'

Oliver was still too agitated to sit. He stood by the cabinet, fingering his glass. 'What can be done to save the baby?' he asked.

The doctor sipped again. 'Likely she need do nothing, but I do recommend she not exert herself.'

'Should she stay in bed?' He'd keep her in bed if he had to sit on her.

The doctor lifted one hand. 'Not necessary. But it would be best if she remains calm. Nothing to distress or upset her.'

Like fearing another attack.

'She will remain calm.' Oliver would make certain nothing distressed her.

The doctor finished his brandy and lifted his glass towards Oliver, who promptly refilled it.

'I cannot pretend to know the relationship between the two of you,' the doctor said. 'And I am not in a position to judge, but I will tell you that society treats unmarried women with bastard children very badly.' He tasted the brandy and looked over his glass at Oliver. 'I trust you will at least support the woman and her child? A father's duty, you know.'

The doctor had no right to presume anything—except he was correct on all counts.

'I do my duty, sir,' Oliver answered curtly.

'Excellent!' The doctor finished his brandy, this time placing the glass on the table and standing. 'I should take my leave. I am certain someone else will have need of me today.'

Oliver accompanied him to the hall where Irwin brought the doctor's hat and coat.

Oliver shook his hand. 'I thank you for coming.'

'Send for me again if you need me,' the doctor said.

After he left, Oliver took the stairs two at a time, slowing down as he reached Cecilia's door. He knocked softly.

The maid opened the door a crack.

'Good day, sir.' She curtsied.

'Ask if she will see me, Mary,' he said.

She closed the door and returned a minute later.

'Come in, sir.' She stepped aside for him to pass her, then she and Mrs Irwin left the room, closing the door behind them.

Oliver walked up to Cecilia's bed. 'How are you feeling?'

She sat up against the pillows, now wearing a nightdress. 'I feel like nothing happened.'

Her face, however, was taut with worry.

He tried to smile reassuringly. 'The doctor said you should be fine. Just do not exert yourself.'

She raised her knees and hugged them. 'Think how much better it would be if I'd lost the baby.'

'Better?' He recoiled in surprise. 'Do not say you wish you'd lose the baby.'

'No.' She gave him a direct look. 'Not me. You. You must have wished for it, though.'

'Unfair, Cecilia,' Oliver shot back. 'I have never said anything like that.'

'But you thought it,' she persisted.

He tried to remain calm. To keep her calm. 'Cecilia, I will not debate with you on this. What do you need? Would you fancy something special to eat? Shall I ask Cook to fix you something?'

She shook her head. 'I am sorry I snapped at you, Oliver.'

He stepped closer and lightly touched her arm. 'It is forgotten.'

'Will—will it be acceptable for Mary to sleep here in the dressing room tonight?' she asked.

Why be so reluctant? Until this moment he'd given her

whatever she'd wanted. What made her think he would stop now? 'Of course it will. Shall I have Irwin find a cot to set up in there?'

'That would be good,' she murmured, lowering her legs and again leaning against the pillows. 'And tomorrow we can decorate the house?'

Tomorrow was Christmas Eve, a traditional time for arranging evergreens throughout the house. 'If you promise not to overdo it. The doctor said—'

'I know,' she said solemnly.

'I'll bid you goodnight, then, unless you need to summon me for any reason.'

She looked up at him, her eyes wide and still filled with uncertainty.

He leaned down and kissed her on the top of her head. 'It will be all right, Cecilia.'

She did not look so sure.

He left her, although he wanted to stay. He wanted to be the one who stayed with her this night instead of her maid.

Instead, he took his latest book—*Description of the Character, Manners, and Customs of the People of India*—to the drawing room and, lighting a lamp, opened the book to where he'd last read.

He read of how a Hindu girl and her family were expelled from their caste, simply because the young man who she was to marry died before the marriage took place and she married another. According to the rules, she was supposed to live as a widow for the rest of her life.

Oliver closed the book. Had his mother been expelled from her caste for being his father's mistress? When his father took him to England and left her in India, had she been completely banished from anyone who might care for her?

He pinched the bridge of his nose. He must not think of this. Not now.

He glanced around the room and a profound loneliness descended upon him, a familiar loneliness suffered when he was taken from India and many times afterwards when he seemed not to belong.

His typical means of dispelling these feelings was to engage in a torrid affair, or challenge himself to some dangerous escapade, a race, a bout of fisticuffs, a high-stakes card game.

He had no taste for any of those distractions.

What he wanted most at the moment was to be seated at Cecilia's bedside, sharing her fears and her hopes.

Chapter Twenty

Upon waking the next morning, Cecilia immediately checked to see if she'd bled during the night. She hadn't! It was enough to fill her full of energy and vigour. The baby must be safe or why would she feel so well?

Mary was already awake and dressed and carrying in a jug of clean water. 'Good morning,' she said cheerfully. 'I hope you slept well, because I did not hear a peep from you the whole night.'

Cecilia had slept well. Better than many nights here in London.

And before.

'I slept,' she responded. 'And I feel remarkably well this morning.'

'That is good.' Mary poured the water into a basin on a nearby chest of drawers. 'But remember what the doctor said. You mustn't do too much.'

Too much? She felt as if she could dash across fields as she'd done when she was a child. She felt as if she could climb to the highest bell tower of Notre Dame. It would be difficult to force herself to rest.

'Mr Gregory and I are going to decorate the house for Christmas today,' Cecilia said.

She climbed out of bed and pulled off her nightdress.

'Well, you must take care.' Mary sounded much like a concerned mother.

Cecilia had wished for her mother when she discovered the bleeding. She was certain Oliver would have sent for her mother, if she'd asked. But she'd thought of all the trouble it would cause her mother to come to her. It was not worth putting her mother through that.

Besides, her mother did not know of the baby and Cecilia intended to keep it that way.

And Cecilia had Mary, Mrs Irwin...and Oliver to help her. She was no longer alone.

She rose from the bed and washed herself with the fresh water Mary had brought.

Mary stood nearby, holding a towel.

'I think one of my old dresses will do,' Cecilia said. No need to dress up this day, not while working with plant cuttings.

'Oh.' Mary raised her voice more than necessary. 'They—they need mending.' She blinked. 'I'll tend to them today, but you'll have to wear one of the pretty ones now.'

Cecilia could not remember her dresses needing mending, but she supposed it did not matter much. Mary chose a pale rose morning dress Cecilia had not worn yet, since it was unsuitable to be worn during the Queen's mourning, but she would not be going outside the house, so what difference did it make?

Mary helped her into her shift and corset. She put the dress on Cecilia over her head and adjusted the laces in the back.

Cecilia sat at the dressing table and Mary twisted her hair into a knot at the top of her head. She tied a pink ribbon around Cecilia's head. 'There!'

Cecilia rose and glanced at herself in the full-length mirror. 'Thank you, Mary. I'm sure this will do.'

Mary grinned and curtsied.

Cecilia left her room and walked down to the dining room. Oliver was seated there, reading a newspaper.

He stood at her entrance and his eyes scanned her up and down. 'You look beautiful, Cecilia.'

Her cheeks grew warm. She usually detested a man's admiration.

'Thank you,' she murmured.

He cleared his throat. 'I hope that means you are feeling better.'

'I am feeling quite well.' She quickly turned to the sideboard and selected an egg and a slice of bread with butter and jam. She poured a cup of tea.

'Might we still decorate today?' she asked.

She was asking permission, just as she'd done in her marriage. For every little thing.

She spoke with more strength. 'I would like to decorate today.'

He glanced up. 'As you wish, Cecilia.'

'And before you scold me about it, I will not overdo.'

He nodded. 'Good.'

Why did he seem so distant?

'Do you not wish to decorate?' she asked.

He looked up from his paper again. 'Me? No. I am willing.'

'You are not obligated, though, Oliver,' she went on. 'I am certain Mary or Irwin could help me.'

He laid down his paper. 'Would you prefer that?'

'No,' she admitted.

Why was she going on about this? She longed to spend the day with him, as they had done the day before. Decorating his house for him for Christmas day seemed a delight.

Unlike the one Christmas she'd shared with Duncan. That had been a horror. He'd beaten her for mentioning the day. After that she'd been alone on Christmas and her celebration had been confined to attending the services at Notre Dame. This year she would not be alone.

She would share the holiday with Oliver.

When they'd walked through St Paul's or browsed the stalls at Covent Garden, catching a glimpse of him had taken her breath away. He was so handsome, so different and so kind. She longed for his lovemaking again, that singular joy, a connection that made her forget every unhappy event she'd ever experienced. With the bleeding she didn't dare to share his bed again.

She glanced at him and her breath fled. Even in something as ordinary as breakfast, he was extraordinary.

But she must not be seduced by him. Duncan had been charming and kind once upon a time. And Oliver was capable of violence, just like Duncan.

What harm could come from sharing the best of the Christmas festivities with him, though? Just this once.

She gulped. 'I—I want very much for us to decorate your house together. You seem disturbed, though. Perhaps angry at me for causing so much commotion yesterday.'

'Commotion?' He straightened. 'Not commotion. You thought something had happened to the baby.'

That worry came sneaking back. 'Let us not talk about that. I am well today. The baby is well.'

The baby *must* be well.

Something was amiss with Oliver, though. She felt it.

'I am not imagining this,' she blurted out. 'You are not happy. I must be the cause.'

His gaze softened. 'You are not the cause, Cecilia. Sometimes unbidden sadness permeates every part of me. I start thinking of what I've lost.'

She reached over and touched his hand. 'We must not

think of what we have lost. If we do, how can we ever lift our chins from the floor?'

He clasped her hand.

'There is nothing to do but see if we can enjoy today.' How many times had she told herself just think about today? Not tomorrow. Not yesterday. Today.

She ought to heed her own advice.

He smiled, though his smile seemed a sad one. 'Then let us enjoy today.'

She squeezed his hand. 'We shall adorn every room!'

He lifted his cup. 'After we finish breakfast?'

She laughed. 'As *you* wish, Oliver!'

He returned to his newspaper and she finished her egg.

'Is there anything noteworthy in the newspaper?' How nice it was to merely have a conversation.

He looked up. 'Two men were apprehended for the murder in Hornsey.'

'There was a murder in Hornsey?'

'About a week or so ago. A young man was robbed and killed when he walked through Hornsey wood at night.'

'How dreadful.' She shivered. She used to walk through Paris at night. Not in London, though. Oliver always walked her home from Vitium et Virtus.

He put down the newspaper. 'How do you wish to proceed with the decorating?'

'I want to arrange the greenery in each of the rooms. Decorate with lace and ribbon—' She put a hand to her mouth. 'The ribbon! What happened to the packages of ribbon and—and other things that I purchased yesterday?'

After the altercation with Bowles, she'd forgotten all about them. Her gift to Oliver was one of them.

'Irwin collected them,' he said.

She again saw the ferocious fight between Oliver and Bowles, but did not wish to remember it.

She stood. 'I want to find Irwin and get my packages. Then perhaps we can start in the drawing room?'

He smiled and her spirits lightened. 'I will carry up the greenery.'

Oliver walked below stairs to the room where they'd stored the cuttings they'd purchased.

Both Mrs Irwin and Cook stopped him.

'How is our young lady today?' asked Mrs Irwin.

'She says she is feeling very well.' He was touched by their concern.

'I fixed her a posset last night,' Cook said. 'I am certain it was my posset that helped.'

'It very well may have been,' he agreed.

Cook beamed. 'I'll make her another for tonight.'

'She will be grateful.' He looked around. 'I've come for the greenery. We thought to start decorating.' He turned to Mrs Irwin. 'Will you send your husband on an errand for me?'

'I will, sir,' she replied. 'What will it be?'

'I want to procure firewood for the fireplace in the drawing room for tonight and tomorrow. It won't be a Yule log, but at least it will smell like one.' He wanted to fill the house with as many delights as he could think of, all to please Cecilia.

'Well, won't that be the thing.' Mrs Irwin smiled in approval.

She helped him carry up the greenery Oliver and Cecilia had purchased the previous day. He had two projects that needed to be done without her seeing. Hanging the mistletoe and shopping.

He walked into the drawing room. 'Here we are.'

They were laden with holly, ivy, hawthorn and flowering Christmas rose.

'Oh, I'd forgotten how beautiful they are. They smell heavenly.' Cecilia stood by the mantel, which she had cleared of its decorative pieces. 'Put them on the floor. We can select them easily from there.'

Mrs Irwin placed her bundle, wrapped in a sheet, in the middle of the floor. 'Would you be needing any help?'

Cecilia smiled at her. 'Thank you, Mrs Irwin. It is kind of you to offer. I think Mr Gregory and I can manage.'

She glanced at Oliver, who added his bundle to the pile on the floor.

Mrs Irwin gave her a knowing, but cheerful look. 'That is it, then. Ring for us if you change your mind.'

'Thank you. We will.' Cecilia turned to the pile of cuttings. 'Where to begin?'

'We should begin with you sitting and directing me.' He pointed to a chair.

To his surprise she did as he asked without an argument.

She pointed to which piece of greenery he should use and told him how to arrange it. When he finished she rose and added bows and ribbons. They placed greenery on the mantel and window sills and in vases on the tables.

The scent of the hawthorn and pine brought back memories of gathering cuttings from his father's country estate. He always accompanied the footmen charged with the greatest portion of the task. His father, stepmother and their houseguests made a show of collecting cuttings, but he was not encouraged to join them.

His father had sent him an invitation to their Christmas house party this year, as he had every year since Oliver turned twenty-one. Oliver knew his stepmother did not want him to attend. She'd always gone out of her way to make him miserable. Once he reached his majority, he saw no reason to put himself through that ordeal. His father used to profess to missing him, but he quickly became accustomed to Oliver's absence.

Oliver never had any reason to acknowledge Christmas after that. He and Nicholas, who also had been at loose ends on the holiday, used to spend it together, drinking, gambling or carousing.

Until Nick disappeared.

This Christmas was different. He was not alone and Cecilia's delight in filling the house with evergreens was infectious. Had the ancient Celts felt that same enthusiasm for Winter Solstice, the rebirth of the sun?

Oliver knew of rebirth. His life had changed dramatically several times. Leaving India. Being befriended by Nicholas, Jacob and Frederick. The creation of Vitium et Virtus.

Now, with Cecilia, his life had changed again. When the baby was born, Oliver would be reborn into the role of father, reborn into a new family of his own.

Even if she would not allow it.

When the drawing room was finished, he and Cecilia moved on to the dining room and the hall. Cecilia arranged some holly cuttings in a vase and climbed the stairs to weave ivy through the banister.

'Are you certain you are up to finishing that task?' he asked her.

She sat on the stairs, weaving ivy in and out of the wrought-iron banister. 'I'm sitting. That is not too much, is it?' She smiled. 'Does it not look pretty?'

It did dress up the hall.

'What else do you wish me to do?' he asked.

'After this we are finished.' She gestured to the extra cuttings left over. They had plenty. 'Perhaps you could remove what we did not use?'

'I'll take them to the servants. They will want to decorate below stairs.' He picked up the bundle.

She gave him a very approving look that felt surprisingly gratifying.

It was his pleasure to please her.

While Oliver gathered the remainder of the branches and cuttings and carried them to the servants' door, Cecilia finished with the ivy.

The scent of the greenery filled the house, just as it had in her childhood. They always spent Christmas in the country. Had her parents returned to the country house for Christmas? she wondered. Would her sisters and their husbands be joining them?

She would never be a part of their Christmas again.

Oliver re-entered the hall and looked up to where she was seated on the stairs. 'Would you like me to finish that?' he asked.

'I'm done.' She pulled herself up by the banister. 'But I am fatigued. Would you object if I took a rest?'

There she went again, asking permission.

She spoke with more force. 'I mean, I am going to take a rest now.'

'I have no objection.' He frowned. 'Perhaps you have done too much.'

'I've been careful, Oliver,' she assured him. 'But that is why I think I should rest.'

He nodded. 'I have some errands, but I will be back later in the day. Do you need anything? Is there anything I can do for you?'

His concern warmed her heart. She believed he meant it. For now.

She smiled down at him. 'You have done enough by helping me decorate.'

She walked up the stairs, suddenly wishing she could go on his errands with him and remain in his company the whole day.

She entered her room and gasped.

Holly, hawthorn and pine cuttings adorned her mantel and filled a vase near her bed. Ivy vines wound around her bedposts.

Mary came from the sitting room, carrying a basket of cuttings. 'Oh, you are here!'

'Mary, did you do this?' The room was filled with the heady scent of pine.

Mary grinned. 'I did. Mr Gregory set me to the task. I must say, it was a great deal of fun.'

'Thank you,' Cecilia said. 'It is lovely. Very lovely.'

She'd never had many cuttings in her childhood bedchamber. Her sisters took the extra cuttings for themselves and she'd had to pull small pieces from the decorations in the other rooms and sneak them upstairs.

This room was lavish with greenery.

'I am weary. I plan to rest a little,' Cecilia said.

Mary's brow furrowed. 'Are you feeling ill?'

'No.' It was a lovely sort of weariness. 'But I will retire to the sitting room and read for a while, I think.'

'Anything you require from me?' Mary asked.

Cecilia noticed that the basket had more greenery in it. 'I need nothing. Please use the extra cuttings for yourself.'

Mary grinned and left the room.

Cecilia opened a cabinet and removed the fabric that she'd purchased for Mary. It was wrapped in brown paper, but she added a red ribbon and tied it in a bow. She added a green ribbon to Oliver's gift and wished now that she'd found something of even more value to give to him.

She stared at the package and thought about their day. If all days could be like this one, how pleasant life could be.

How pleasant life could be if only one could depend upon another person to be constant, to never change.

She put the gifts back into a drawer and kicked her shoes off, putting her feet on the sofa and hugging her knees.

The baby moved inside her. She lowered her legs and placed her hands on her rounding belly, vowing to be as constant as the sun and moon for her baby.

'I promise, baby,' she whispered.

At least she could give her baby what she could not have.

She let that thought cheer her.

There was a knock on the door and Mary entered. 'Uncle Irwin said this letter came for you.'

'A letter? For me?' She rose from the sofa and met Mary halfway.

Mary handed her the envelope.

Cecilia examined it. It appeared to be from her mother. 'Thank you, Mary.'

Her maid smiled, curtsied and left the room. Cecilia carried the letter back to the sitting room. She sat on the sofa and stared at it. She'd not had one piece of mail since the one from her father three years ago, the one disowning her.

She took a deep breath and carefully broke the seal.

It was from her mother.

She read:

Dear Cecilia,
We are back in the country, but I managed to devise a way to get a letter to you from here without your father knowing.

It will be a quiet Christmas for us. Both your sisters will be spending the day with their husbands, but that is as it should be. We will have our usual

guests over for Christmas dinner. The parson. Squire
Watson. And their wives, of course. They are dull
company, but your father insisted we invite them.

If you could be with us it would make me so very
happy, but I fear your father would never allow it.

We will be back in town for the Season, of course,
and I hope I am able to contrive to see you. Your father was impossible after we met, checking my every
move, but I suspect he will be too busy in the Season
to think of where I am.

My love to you, my dear daughter.

Regards to your friend, Mr G—

Happy Christmas,

Your loving mother

Cecilia refolded the letter and blinked away tears. That
her mother thought of her, cared for her, meant a great deal,
but her mother was so much under her father's thumb,
would Cecilia ever see her again? Perhaps a snatched visit
in a Circulating Library? By then it surely would be obvious she was with child.

It was probably best that she disappear and never see
her mother again.

She put the letter in the drawer with the presents and
returned to the sofa, feeling more fatigued than before.

She'd told Oliver not to think of the past. She should
heed her own advice. Right now, this day, she'd been
happy. That was what mattered. She and Oliver would
share Christmas together and they would be happy in each
other's company.

For as long as it lasted.

Chapter Twenty-One

Cecilia dozed on the sofa, waking when Mary came in to dress her for dinner.

'I suppose I was tired.' Cecilia sat up and waited for her head to clear. She determinedly pushed the thought of her mother's letter out of her mind.

'Do you wish to dress for dinner?' Mary asked.

'Oh, yes.' She would make dinner with Oliver as enjoyable as possible for them both. 'I want to wear something nice.'

Mary grinned. 'Let us make you fancy tonight!'

Cecilia frowned. 'Like a lady, though, Mary. Not like a worker at Vitium et Virtus.' Not like Madame Coquette.

Mary chose an emerald-green dress. Its design was simple with few embellishments, but the silk fabric shimmered in the candlelight. Cecilia's pearl pendant became her only ornamentation. Mary fixed her hair high upon her head and fashioned bands of ribbon for a very Grecian look, elegant and simple.

'I have an idea!' Mary went to the vase and snipped off a sprig of holly and pinned it in her hair.

Cecilia gazed at her image in the full-length mirror. 'I look festive, do I not?'

Mary nodded. 'Very festive.'

She felt an unexpected fit of nerves. 'I suppose I am ready.'

Cecilia left the room and the distinct scent of burning firewood reached her nostrils. A Yule log? It could not be. Not in Oliver's small fireplaces. She hurried down the stairs to the hall to see.

Oliver stood leaning on the doorjamb to the drawing room.

'I smell burning wood!' she exclaimed.

'Reminiscent of a Yule log,' he said. 'Best I could do.'

'It smells wonderful.'

He moved to the doorway of the drawing room. 'Shall we have some wassail before dinner?'

'Wassail?' She laughed. 'You have wassail?'

'I do,' he responded. 'To celebrate our decorations.'

She hurried to the doorway. 'Perhaps just a sip.'

He blocked the doorway. 'Not so fast.'

'What?'

He pointed above them.

She glanced up and then met his eye. 'You've hung mistletoe.'

He nodded. 'You know what that means.'

She rose on tiptoe, and he bent down and touched his lips to hers in a kiss so tender it caused an aching in her heart.

She wound her arms around his neck and deepened the kiss while her body flared with need. He lifted her and carried her into the room, still kissing her. They were prone on the sofa, him beside her, but he broke off.

'We had better stop,' he said, his voice rasping.

She nodded. 'The baby.'

Not after the scare of her bleeding could they do anything that might hurt the baby.

He rose and she sat up, her body still humming with need for him. He walked to the wassail bowl and brought her a cup of the hot mulled cider.

He poured himself a cup and sat in a chair across from her. He looked like she felt. Unsettled. She took one sip before putting her cup down on the table. It seemed wassail made her stomach turn as well as wine.

'The wassail is good.' She did not tell him she could not drink it. She picked up the cup again and let it warm her hands. 'Did you complete your errands?' she asked, trying for conversation instead.

'I did.' He sipped his drink. 'I know wassail is more typical of Twelfth Night, but I felt as if we deserved a reward for working all day.'

He'd also dressed for dinner, wearing an impeccably tailored coat of deep blue, a striped waistcoat and blue pantaloons.

'I enjoyed it, Oliver. Very much. And everything looks so beautiful.' She looked into the fireplace where flames licked the wooden logs and embers glowed bright orange. 'The fire is such a special touch.'

'I am glad you like it.' He smiled. 'Cook has saved the special meal for tomorrow, but tonight we'll still eat well.'

'Like every night.'

She would miss sharing dinner with him. The thought of leaving this little town house and the people in it—Oliver—made her eyes sting with tears.

She blinked them away. 'I am looking forward to Christmas pudding.'

'I know Cook has made some.'

Irwin came to the door and announced dinner.

Cecilia turned to him. 'You had better not tarry in the doorway, Irwin. I might have to kiss you.'

He almost cracked a smile. 'Mrs Irwin would ring a peal over my head if I let that happen.'

'Or more likely over mine.' She smiled.

Oliver rose and extended his hand. She placed hers in his and let him help her up. It brought her close to him, close enough to smell the soap he used and the spice of the wassail on his breath. He threaded her arm through his and they walked towards the door.

He paused under the mistletoe and gave her the lightest, sweetest kiss she had ever received. She touched her lips and thought of all the men she'd been forced to kiss when pretending to be Madame Coquette. Never again. She'd be happy if Oliver were the last man she ever kissed.

Their dinner had been special enough, Oliver thought. Roast lamb and turbot. Parsnips and broccoli. Chestnuts, grapes and walnuts. And cake for dessert. Their conversation had been light-hearted, confined to their experiences of the day before—not counting Bowles—and the decorating they'd done today.

After dinner they returned to the drawing room and played backgammon. Cecilia won most of the games. They laughed and teased each other and Oliver could not think of an evening he'd enjoyed more.

He wanted the feeling to continue.

When it came time for them to retire, they climbed the stairs to their bedchambers arm in arm. At the top of the stairs, Oliver stopped Cecilia and made her face him.

He touched her cheek. 'Come sleep with me, Cecilia. I do not want this day to end.'

Anxiety filled her eyes. 'I cannot. We cannot.'

He held her face in his hands. 'I am not talking of lovemaking. Come be with me. We will sleep and nothing more.'

She looked into his eyes as if searching for her answer. Finally, she nodded. 'I'll come to you after Mary readies me for bed.'

He leaned down and kissed her lips. 'I'll be waiting for you.'

He watched her enter her room before he opened his door. In his room he undressed, washed and donned his banyan, all without the services of his valet, still in Yorkshire with his family. Oliver put on a fresh pair of drawers underneath his banyan, a barrier to help him keep his promise to Cecilia. He poured himself a glass of brandy and waited for her.

He heard a soft knock on his door and sprang to his feet. When he opened the door to her, all he wanted was to pull her into an embrace and taste her, but his body was already humming with desire and he dared not push himself to a point where they would find it difficult to stop.

'Come in,' he said instead. 'Would you like some brandy?'

She shook her head. She wore a long white nightdress that showed the silhouette of her body when she stood in front of the fireplace. 'I have had enough. We—we perhaps should sleep, like you said.'

She was nervous, he could tell. She had taken quite a chance in coming to him and trusting he would not make love to her.

'Come to bed, then,' he said, taking her hand.

They climbed into his bed and he spooned her against him, his arms around her.

'This is nice,' he said. Nice? It was perfect.

'Mmm-hmm,' she said.

Gradually he felt her body relax.

Why should this have to end? he wondered. Why could they not continue this way? Why not really be a family?

He could give the child his name. He could make the child legitimate, something he would never be. He and Cecilia could spend every day together. And every night.

'Cecilia?'

'Hmm?'

'Remember when I said I wanted us to go on this way?'

She stiffened and pulled away, rolling over to face him. 'Do not, Oliver. Do not speak—'

He cut her off. 'I mean marriage, Cecilia. Marry me. We will be a family.' He was never so sure of anything as he was of this.

Cecilia panicked. 'Marriage?'

'Marriage.'

She jumped out of the bed, her heart racing. 'No, Oliver. No marriage. I won't marry you!'

She loved him. She had no doubt of that. She'd even been considering staying with him. But marriage? Marriage changed everything.

He rose from the bed. 'Why not, Cecilia? I love you. I—I believe you have some regard for me. We could be happy together.'

She hugged herself. 'No marriage, Oliver. I don't want to.'

He'd control her. She'd be his property.

His whole body tensed. 'Is it because I am a half-caste? Half-Indian? Too dark for you?'

Too dark? His complexion, his dark hair, only made him more handsome.

'Of course it is not that,' she retorted. 'Do you not know that?'

'Then it is because I am a bastard.'

'Do not be ridiculous,' she shot back. Why would she care about that?

'Then tell me why you do not care for me,' he challenged.

How could she explain?

'I care for you.' She more than cared for him. She loved him. 'But I won't marry. I won't!'

His eyes flashed in pain. 'Consider the baby, then. You profess I am the baby's father—'

She lifted her chin. 'You *are* the baby's father.'

'You make that hard to believe, Cecilia.' His voice turned hard.

'It is true.' Had they not moved past this?

He leaned towards her. 'I do not care if the child is mine or not. I am offering to *be* his father. Or her father. To give the child my name. Would you deprive this child of a father?' His anger was growing; she could tell. 'You would rather the child go through life being called a bastard?'

'He won't be a bastard,' she shot back. 'I plan to tell everyone I am a widow, which I am.'

'You'll pretend that the baby's father was your husband? The man who beat you?' He scoffed. 'Wonderful legacy. Father was a wife-beater. What happens when the child discovers his supposed father died before he was ever conceived?'

There would be records, certainly, but would her son or daughter ever see them?

'That won't happen.' She felt uncertain, though.

'Let me tell you what that child's life will be like, Cecilia.' He stood, arms akimbo, naked from the waist up. 'He will be ridiculed, ostracised, bullied. Servants will consider him beneath them. Tutors will treat him with disdain. No matter where he is, he will never quite belong. Is that what you want?'

Her anger flared. 'I'll tell you what I do not want. I do not want a husband telling me what to do and when to do it. A husband forbidding me, restricting me, confining me. Hitting me if I displease him. I will protect my child.'

'Protect your child?' His gaze pinned her. 'Do you truly believe you will be able to protect your child? I know I can protect you both. I do not want you out there alone.'

'You promised to support us, Oliver. That is all I need.' She'd take her chances on being a woman alone. She'd managed in Paris. She could manage in a small village somewhere in England. 'I have been married. I know what it did to me. I know what it does to my mother. Maybe even my sisters.'

His face flushed with anger. 'I am nothing like your husband. I am nothing like your father.'

She edged towards the door, fearing his escalating anger. 'But you could become like them.'

Oliver was losing *her*.

The familiar ache of loss started deep within him and spread until it hit every part of him.

She put her hand on the door handle. 'I am leaving.'

He would not stop her.

She opened the door, but hesitated, turning back to him. 'In fact, I think it best that I leave completely. Return to the hotel. I should not stay here any more.'

A knife in his gut could not have hurt more.

'You do not have to go to a hotel, Cecilia,' he said. 'We can live separately. I'll stay at Vitium et Virtus, if you like.'

'No.' She looked frantic. 'I need to leave completely.'

She would never allow him to love her, to belong to him. She would always have left him.

He nodded. 'As you wish. I'll have Irwin arrange a room and payment with the hotel.'

She frowned. 'I would pay if I could.'

He held up a hand. 'I gave you my word I would support you and I will. I'll arrange the funds for you and the child.' The child who now would never be his.

'Thank you, Oliver,' she murmured.

She walked out and closed the door behind her.

Oliver strode over to the table where his decanter of brandy stood. He threw it into the unlit fireplace.

She did not want him. He loved her and she did not want him. All he could do now was provide for her and make certain she and the child would want for nothing. Rather than accept him, she'd choose a harder life for herself and especially for the child.

He'd lived that life, a life of loss and exclusion. Even Vitium et Virtus was falling apart. Nicholas was gone and Frederick and Jacob were making their own families.

At least the women they loved had been happy to marry them.

Chapter Twenty-Two

The next morning Oliver rose early. As he walked down the stairs to the hall, Cecilia's bag was already packed and ready to go. Her maid had just carried it down.

'She says she is leaving today and won't take any of the dresses you bought for her.' The maid frowned. 'Just what she came with.'

Foolish gesture. He was going to pay for her clothes for the rest of her life, why not now?

'Can you contrive to pack the new dresses as well?' he asked.

'I believe so,' she said.

'I'll provide a bag to pack them in. We'll send them with her whether she wants them or not.'

The maid nodded. 'Very good, sir!'

He returned to his room and found a bag for Mary to pack the dresses in. As he brought it into the hallway where Mary was waiting, he spied the items he'd purchased the day before, wrapped in paper.

His Christmas gifts.

He wanted Cecilia to have them, no matter what. If he handed them to her, she'd likely refuse them as she'd refused the dresses.

'Here, Mary, this should do, should it not?' He handed the bag to the maid.

'I'll make them fit,' she replied in a determined tone.

He returned to his room, pulled out pen, ink and paper from a drawer and quickly wrote a note, drying the ink with sand. He gathered the gifts and note and brought them downstairs with him.

Irwin stood in the hall, looking grim.

Oliver nodded to him. 'You have heard that Mrs Lockhart is leaving this morning?'

'Indeed, sir.' Irwin frowned. 'Very bad news, sir.'

Oliver agreed. 'Well, it is what she desires. I need you to go to Grenier's Hotel and arrange a room for her and bring her two bags with you—Mary is packing the second bag right now.'

'As you wish, sir,' Irwin said.

'And if you would be so good as to bring me my topcoat and hat before you leave.' Oliver intended to escort Cecilia to the hotel, something she probably would not want.

Mary brought down the second bag.

'That was quick,' he remarked.

She smiled. 'I am quick!' She curtsied and left the hall to go below stairs.

Oliver opened the second bag and placed the packages and note on top.

Irwin returned with coats, hats, gloves and scarves. 'It is cold outside today.'

Oliver took his things and placed them on a nearby chair. He gestured to the second bag. 'I placed two packages and a note in the bag. When you are in her hotel room, take them out and place them where she will see them.'

'As you wish, sir,' Irwin responded while donning his topcoat. He wrapped a woollen scarf around his neck. 'Are you certain of this, sir? I thought—'

Oliver waved a dismissive hand. 'It is what she wants.'

The butler sighed. 'Very well, sir.' He put on his hat, opened the door, picked up the two bags and stepped out.

Oliver walked over to close the door for him. Outside the sky was grey and fat flakes of snow fluttered to the ground, not yet sticking to the pavement, but tingeing the tops of the wrought-iron gates white.

Oliver and Cecilia might have strolled through the snow to St James's Church on Piccadilly to attend Christmas services. He would have liked that. Afterwards, they could have returned to the town house and stayed cosy and warm inside and shared Christmas dinner together.

He did not close the door until Irwin disappeared through the thickening snow, heading to the hotel on Jermyn Street.

Oliver lowered himself into a wooden chair in the hall and waited for Cecilia.

Cecilia stood in the servants' hall, Cook, Mrs Irwin and Mary surrounding her. She'd given Mary the pretty fabric for a dress and gifts of money to them all.

'Yours is to share with Irwin,' she told the housekeeper.

'Did I hear my name?' Irwin's voice came from the corridor. He popped his head in the servants' hall and saw Cecilia. 'Are you in need of me, ma'am?' His eyelashes glistened and he smelled of being outside.

'I am just saying goodbye,' she said, her throat tight.

The butler nodded. 'I know it. Your room at Grenier's is all arranged and your things are already in it. Mr Gregory's orders.'

How unexpected. 'I should go, then.'

Both older women were wiping their eyes with their aprons.

'You cannot stay for Christmas dinner?' Cook asked.

Cecilia shook her head. 'I will miss your cooking very much, though.'

'Then I'll pack you a basket! You should have some pudding—'

Cecilia lifted a hand. 'No. No. Do not disturb the pudding. I will be very cross if you do.'

Cook scowled. 'I'll find something else to give you.' She hurried back to the kitchen.

'How will we know about the baby if you leave?' Mrs Irwin asked. 'You should stay and let us take care of you.'

'I must go,' Cecilia insisted. 'But I will send word about the baby. I'll—I'll write you a letter.'

Mrs Irwin tried over again to convince her to stay. Cecilia wished she could. She'd loved being in this house, cared for by these servants.

And Oliver.

Cook returned with a basket. 'I've packed some bread and cheese and some of my jam.'

'That will be lovely.' Cecilia's voice cracked. She'd known them such a short period of time, but leaving them was turning out to be painfully difficult. She turned to Mary, who'd been silent during this exchange. 'I must go.'

Mary blinked rapidly. 'I think you are acting like a witless ninny!'

'Mary!' Mrs Irwin scolded.

'Well, she is!' Mary protested. 'Mr Gregory is a nice man! He loves you. Any fool can see that.'

Cecilia shook her head. 'I—I cannot explain. I simply must leave.'

She gave Mary a quick hug, grabbed her cloak and rushed away, climbing the stairs to the hall. When she entered the hall, things only became worse.

Oliver was there.

'Irwin arranged the room,' he told her, his voice stiff. 'I have the key. Your things are already there.'

She could not look at him. 'Thank you, Oliver.' She put on her cloak and pulled on her gloves. 'I'll be leaving then.' She put her hand out for the key.

He did not give it to her. 'I will escort you. See you safely there,' he said. 'One last time.'

She wanted to grab the key and run out, but that seemed childish. What harm in having him walk with her?

He donned his coat, hat and gloves and opened the door for her.

'Oh!' she exclaimed. 'It is snowing!'

The pavement and street were white with about an inch of snow, making everything look new and clean.

'Hold my arm,' Oliver insisted. 'It will be slippery.'

This would be her last time to touch him.

He did not talk to her, except to caution her about a slippery spot or to warn of a curb. The street was empty of people and carriages and the scent of Christmas cooking wafted from kitchens along the way.

She'd be alone this day and so would he.

She could not marry him, though, and she could not stay, because all she wanted was to be with him. It was a splendid trap, loving him, but being shackled with velvet ribbons would still mean being shackled.

They reached the hotel, and she released his arm.

'I am seeing you to your room,' he said to her.

She took his arm again and they entered the hotel. He announced her to the clerk in the hall of the hotel, the same man who had been so unhelpful to her when she'd needed to search for Vitium et Virtus. The clerk directed them to her room on the first floor, one flight up.

Oliver put the key in the door and opened it. 'I will say goodbye to you here.'

She looked up at him, words failing her.

He turned quickly and walked away. She waited until he descended the stairs.

Her last glimpse of him.

She swung back to the doorway. It was better this way. She was better for being free.

She entered the room and removed her cloak and gloves. This room was much more lavish than the one she'd rented before and much more than she needed. Oliver was generous. She fingered the pearl she still wore at her throat. He'd been generous that first day she met him.

Two bags were in the room. She opened the one that was not hers and saw all the dresses Oliver had purchased for her, more reminders of his generosity.

On a table nearby were two small packages and a folded piece of paper. She picked up the paper and unfolded it.

A note from Oliver.

Dear Cecilia,
Do not refuse these gifts. I want you to have them
to remember me. They are trifles. The dresses, too.
Those are yours. My man of business will be in touch
with you within days. You and the baby will be com-
fortable. I promise.

I beg a promise from you. If you are in any need,
send word to me. I will come. I want no harm to
come to you or the baby ever. Do not hesitate to ask
for my help.

Remember that I love you and that fact will not
change.
Yours, O.

A tear slid down her face.

She tore open the larger package, opened the box and

gasped. Inside was a teething rattle. Not just any teething rattle. The finest sort, made of exquisitely engraved sterling silver with silver bells all around and a red handle of coral for the baby to teethe on. The other side was a whistle. She placed it on her mouth and blew softly, producing a shrill sound. It was the finest object she'd ever possessed and it was for her baby.

Oliver's baby.

She put the rattle down on the table and picked up the smaller package, untying the string and removing the paper. Its box was covered in blue velvet. She opened it. Inside were two pearl earrings, a match to her necklace. Not precious. Not even as valuable as the rattle, she guessed, but so personal a sob escaped her mouth.

What sort of man would do this? Send gifts after she rejected him, such dear, perfect gifts? What sort of man would make certain she had a comfortable room after she'd walked out of his? Or agree to support her and a baby he did not even believe was his? A baby to whom he offered to give his name?

Ever since she met Oliver, he'd been kind and generous to her, unfailingly so. He'd been there for her when she confronted her father. When she saw her mother. He'd protected her from Bowles—

She inhaled sharply.

He'd protected her. He'd fought Bowles for Flo's protection. Twice. And was stabbed for it.

He wanted to protect her and the baby. He did not want to confine or control her. When had he ever tried to control her? He'd always given her the choice.

She stared at the rattle and the earrings. She read the note again.

If you are in any need, send word to me. I will come...

Even after she'd rejected him, he'd come to her aid.

She lifted the paper in which the gifts were wrapped. What of her gift to him? It was still in the drawer in the sitting room. She'd hurriedly grabbed Mary's gift from the drawer, but not Oliver's.

Cecilia picked up her cloak and gloves and quickly put them on. She hurried out of the room, locking it behind her and putting the key in her pocket. She ran down the stairs and out the hotel door.

Even in this short period of time, the snow had deepened. She wanted to rush, but the snow impeded her. It fell so thick now she could hardly see two feet in front of her. Her half-boots quickly became caked with snow and her feet felt like icicles. Only a short walk, a couple of streets. The wind picked up and blew the hood of her cloak from her head. She reached Bury Street and tried to walk faster, but it was too hard.

It was Christmas day and she needed to give Oliver his gift.

After leaving Cecilia at the hotel and returning home, Oliver had gone straight to his bedchamber and closed the door.

He imagined he'd figure out a way to put one foot in front of the other again, but for the moment all he could think to do was stand in front of his window and watch the snow fall. He watched it accelerate and thicken, watched the wind toss the flakes into erratic swirls. The pavement was covered with snow and growing deeper. A carriage drove by and was nearly silent. Everything was quiet.

He tried to empty his mind and was fairly successful, except for one thought.

Cecilia was gone. The world was empty. Bleached white. Something moved at the end of the street. He watched a figure emerge from the white curtain. A woman. In a cloak. Barely visible in the falling snow.

He ran out of the room, down the stairs. He flung open the door as the snowy figure faced the house.

He ran to her and she flew into his arms.

'You came back!' he rasped.

She was weeping into his shoulder and she clung to him.

Finally, she looked up and brushed snowflakes from his hair. 'You do not have a hat or coat.'

'I do not care. You came back.' He held her tighter.

He lifted her into his arms and carried her inside, putting her down and removing her snow-caked cloak.

'I need to go upstairs,' she said. 'I forgot something.'

He released her. He'd got it wrong. She'd merely forgotten something.

He would have to endure her leaving all over again.

He followed her upstairs but stood in the hall while she went into what he would always think of as her room. She emerged as quickly.

'This is for you.' She handed him a package tied with a ribbon.

He opened it and discovered a silver-backed tortoise-shell comb.

'It is a silly gift, I know,' she said. 'But I wanted something you would use every day so you would not forget me.'

He met her gaze. 'I will never forget you, Cecilia.'

Her breathing accelerated. 'I—I learned something. Or rather, I finally put pieces of a puzzle together the correct way.'

He had no idea what she was talking about. 'What is that?'

'You protect; you don't hurt. You give; you don't take. You release who you love; you don't confine them.'

Why was she speaking so? 'I love you, Cecilia. I want you to be safe and happy.'

'I know,' she said. 'I am so sorry. I was wrong.'

'Wrong?' His insides twisted. This felt riskier than a carriage race on a twisting country road.

'I was wrong to believe I cannot trust anyone. I can trust you.'

He narrowed his eyes. 'Be clear, Cecilia. I will be. I love you. I still want to marry you. I will never hurt you and I will not control you. I'll protect you and the baby with my life.'

Her eyes widened. 'Do you mean it? You are not angry with me after—after all I've said and done?'

'I am not angry with you.' Wounded, not angry. 'Marry me.'

She flew into his arms once again. 'Yes! Oliver, yes! I've been afraid to love you, but I do. I do.'

He swung her around in a circle, laughing, the knot inside him loosening and releasing joy. He took her face in his hands and kissed her, a kiss full of the promises he'd made to her.

She kissed him back.

He held her tightly against him, but suddenly released her. 'I felt it!' he cried. 'I felt the baby move.'

'Yes. The baby moved.'

He hugged her again. 'A family,' he murmured.

Epilogue

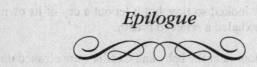

May 1819

Oliver stood in the hallway of his town house while behind the closed door of Cecilia's room, the doctor, Mrs Irwin and Mary attended Cecilia.

His wife.

Her labour had started three hours before, but in the last few minutes her cries of pain grew louder and longer. Each one reached into him with a mirroring pain.

He paced back and forth.

Princess Charlotte died in childbirth. Both her and the baby. Lots of women died in childbirth.

Cecilia cried again and he could not bear it. He entered the room.

'Sir!' Mrs Irwin scolded. 'You should not be in here!'

'I'm not leaving,' he growled.

The doctor did not take notice of him. Neither did Cecilia.

'Push!' the doctor cried.

Cecilia cried again, her face red with strain.

'The baby's coming!' Mary cried. 'I see the head!'

'When the next pain comes, push again,' the doctor said.

The pain came immediately. Cecilia cried and pushed.

Oliver was riveted to the scene. He could see the top of the baby's head.

All of a sudden the baby's whole head emerged and the baby slipped out into the doctor's hands.

'A boy!' the doctor cried.

A boy?

The baby looked so tiny, but it let out a cry of its own and Oliver exhaled a relieved breath.

Half an hour later the baby and Cecilia were cleaned up and resting on clean bed linens. Cecilia gazed adoringly at her baby boy and Oliver gazed in wonder at both of them.

'Little Nicholas,' she murmured.

There'd been no other name to consider for a boy. Oliver wanted to honour his friend.

Cecilia examined every finger and toe on little Nicholas and rewrapped him in his blanket. She traced her finger over the baby's cheek and forehead.

She laughed. 'Look, Oliver!'

He came closer.

She traced her finger over the baby's ear. 'His ear is just like yours.' The ear came to a tiny point, hardly noticeable. 'Look in the mirror. Your ear is the same.'

Oliver walked over to the mirror. She was right! His ear was the exact same shape.

She sobered for a moment. 'Now do you believe me? You are Nicholas's father.'

He walked over to her and kissed the top of her head. 'It has not mattered for a long time,' he told her. 'I belong to both of you. We are a family. I am content.'

She pulled him down into a kiss.

* * * * *

If you missed the first and second books in
THE SOCIETY OF WICKED GENTLEMEN *quartet*
check out

A CONVENIENT BRIDE FOR THE SOLDIER
by Christine Merrill
AN INNOCENT MAID FOR THE DUKE
by Ann Lethbridge

And look out for the final novel in the quartet
A SECRET CONSEQUENCE FOR
THE VISCOUNT
by Sophia James
Coming in December 2017

COMING NEXT MONTH FROM

ℍHARLEQUIN®

ℍISTORICAL

Available November 21, 2017

All available in print and ebook via Reader Service and online

THE RANCHER'S INCONVENIENT BRIDE (Western)
by Carol Arens
William English rescues Agatha Magee from being shot out of a cannon, and the potential scandal means they must get married! Can Agatha make this more than a marriage in name only?

A SECRET CONSEQUENCE FOR THE VISCOUNT (Regency)
The Society of Wicked Gentlemen • by Sophia James
Viscount Bromley returns to London with no memory of his one night with Lady Eleanor and no knowledge of the daughter he fathered. But now, as he regains his lost memories, there's no hiding from the past!

SCANDAL AT THE CHRISTMAS BALL (Regency)
by Marguerite Kaye and Bronwyn Scott
Join *the* Christmas party of the Season in these two closely linked stories of forbidden Regency romance. Will Lord and Lady Brockmore's guests find true love when they embark on a scandalous affair to remember?

BESIEGED AND BETROTHED (Medieval)
by Jenni Fletcher
A marriage bargain is brokered to bring peace between two enemies: warrior Lothar the Frank and Lady Juliana Danville. But is blissful wedded life possible with a dangerous secret hidden within the castle walls?

AN UNLIKELY DEBUTANTE (Regency)
by Laura Martin
To win a wager, Lord Alexander Whitemore is to take Lina Lock from gypsy dancer to perfect debutante. As Lina takes Alex up on his offer, she learns she must curb her rebellious instincts *and* the unexpected passion he awakens in her...

RESCUED BY THE FORBIDDEN RAKE (Regency)
by Mary Brendan
When Faye Shawcross's younger sister goes missing, alluring viscount Ryan Kavanagh comes to her rescue. He will fix her impending family scandal for a price: he wants Faye as his mistress...

If you are receiving 4 books per month and would like to receive all 6, please call Customer Service at 1-800-873-8635.

YES! Please send me **The Hometown Hearts Collection** in Larger Print. This collection begins with 3 FREE books and 2 FREE gifts in the first shipment. Along with my 3 free books, I'll also get the next 4 books from the Hometown Hearts Collection, in LARGER PRINT, which I may either return and owe nothing, or keep for the low price of $4.99 U.S./ $5.89 CDN each plus $2.99 for shipping and handling per shipment*. If I decide to continue, about once a month for 8 months I will get 6 or 7 more books, but will only need to pay for 4. That means 2 or 3 books in every shipment will be FREE! If I decide to keep the entire collection, I'll have paid for only 32 books because 19 books are FREE! I understand that accepting the 3 free books and gifts places me under no obligation to buy anything. I can always return a shipment and cancel at any time. My free books and gifts are mine to keep no matter what I decide.

262 HCN 3432 462 HCN 3432

Name	(PLEASE PRINT)	
Address		Apt. #
City	State/Prov.	Zip/Postal Code

Signature (if under 18, a parent or guardian must sign)

Mail to the **Reader Service:**

IN U.S.A.: P.O. Box 1867, Buffalo, NY. 14240-1867
IN CANADA: P.O. Box 609, Fort Erie, Ontario L2A 5X3

Get 2 Free Books,

Plus 2 Free Gifts—

just for trying the Reader Service!

HARLEQUIN® Western Romance

Get 2 Free Books,
Plus 2 Free Gifts—
just for trying the Reader Service!

HARLEQUIN *Presents*

YES! Please send me 2 FREE Harlequin Presents® novels and my 2 FREE gifts (gifts are worth about $10 retail). After receiving them, if I don't wish to receive any more books, I can return the shipping statement marked "cancel." If I don't cancel, I will receive 6 brand-new novels every month and be billed just $4.55 each for the regular-print edition or $5.55 each for the larger-print edition in the U.S., or $5.49 each for the regular-print edition or $5.99 each for the larger-print edition in Canada. That's a saving of at least 11% off the cover price! It's quite a bargain! Shipping and handling is just 50¢ per book in the U.S. and 75¢ per book in Canada.* I understand that accepting the 2 free books and gifts places me under no obligation to buy anything. I can always return a shipment and cancel at any time. The free books and gifts are mine to keep no matter what I decide.

Please check one: ☐ Harlequin Presents® Regular-Print   ☐ Harlequin Presents® Larger-Print
                            (106/306 HDN GLWL)   (176/376 HDN GLWL)

Name _____ (PLEASE PRINT)

Address _____ Apt. #

City _____ State/Prov. _____ Zip/Postal Code

Signature (if under 18, a parent or guardian must sign)

Mail to the **Reader Service**:
IN U.S.A.: P.O. Box 1341, Buffalo, NY 14240-8531
IN CANADA: P.O. Box 603, Fort Erie, Ontario L2A 5X3

Want to try two free books from another series?
Call 1-800-873-8635 or visit www.ReaderService.com.

* Terms and prices subject to change without notice. Prices do not include applicable taxes. Sales tax applicable in N.Y. Canadian residents will be charged applicable taxes. Offer not valid in Quebec. This offer is limited to one order per household. Books received may not be as shown. Not valid for current subscribers to Harlequin Presents books. All orders subject to approval. Credit or debit balances in a customer's account(s) may be offset by any other outstanding balance owed by or to the customer. Please allow 4 to 6 weeks for delivery. Offer available while quantities last.

Your Privacy—The Reader Service is committed to protecting your privacy. Our Privacy Policy is available online at www.ReaderService.com or upon request from the Reader Service.

We make a portion of our mailing list available to reputable third parties that offer products we believe may interest you. If you prefer that we not exchange your name with third parties, or if you wish to clarify or modify your communication preferences, please visit us at www.ReaderService.com/consumerchoice or write to us at Reader Service Preference Service, P.O. Box 9062, Buffalo, NY 14240-9062. Include your complete name and address.

HP17R2